Jackknifing, Quin shoved damp strands of hair back from her face, every muscle taut.

Through some strange mental process she'd ended up in a ship's cabin with an injured stranger. She'd smelled salt and diesel fumes and blood—and she'd been acutely aware of *him*.

Her gaze swept the grove, as if she could see something—find something—tangible that would account for dreams that stepped out of nowhere and gripped her so tightly they seemed more real than the ground beneath her feet.

The memory of the last time she'd "dreamed" was abruptly vivid, and something in her mind connected and fused. Gooseflesh rose all along her back and arms, and prickled at her nape.

"Great," she muttered. The last thing she wanted to dwell on was the fact that she'd psychic-dreamed *twice*, and that, just to add to the general weirdness of it all, the same guy had starred each time.

FIONA BRAND

Touching
MIDNIGHT

MIRA

ISBN 0-7783-2152-5

TOUCHING MIDNIGHT

www.MIRABooks.com

Printed in U.S.A.

ACKNOWLEDGMENTS

Thank you to Claire Russell of the
Kerikeri Medical Centre for medical information,
both technical and anecdotal, for finding the perfect
drug to fit the crime—and supplying the spellings.
Any errors are, of course, my own.

PART I

Prologue

The interconnecting series of chambers lay buried deep beneath layer upon layer of rich soil and gritty rubble, protected and enclosed by massive blocks of granite—a complex outer sheathing in the form of a maze, which had been constructed with exquisite care to conceal the secret within.

Millennia had passed; civilizations had risen and fallen. The landscape itself had altered—resculpted by violent deluges of rain-rich frontal weather forced high over the Andes and the slow, ancient grinding of tectonic plates. But despite the powerful external stressors, the hidden chambers had remained locked beneath the ground, although with the passage of time the crumbling outer bones of the maze had been laid bare in places.

The western sector had sustained the most damage, situated as it was on the floor of a crescent-shaped valley that, with the erosion of softer limestone at its southern end, had become the natural conduit for the Agueda River. Over the years the Agueda had meandered and braided, its banks dissolving as it broadened, greedily eating away at the rich alluvial soil of the valley floor until it exposed amongst the chaotic tumble of river-smooth rocks the unmistakable edges of precision cut stone.

Destructive as the Agueda was, beneath the valley floor an infinitely more powerful force was at work. The damage was invisible but profound, as the hot inner sea of the Earth's mantle flexed and strained at cooler crustal layers, undermining the age-old rift that formed the cradle of the valley.

Tension built, rock compressed, softer materials began to liquefy, and the raucous community of parakeets perched on the thick canopy of trees that rimmed the valley went silent.

The first shock wave radiated from a point just fifteen miles away and only two miles beneath the Earth's surface, vibrating up through the still, silent chambers, disturbing deposits of rock dust ground as fine as talcum powder until they shimmered in glass-smooth pools of water formed by the slow leak of blocked aqueducts. The cleverly fitted granite blocks encasing the hidden chambers groaned beneath the subtle flexing, then shivered and crumbled, no match for the power that had thrust the Cordillera de Los Andes more than twenty thousand feet up into the atmosphere.

Long seconds passed in which decayed and misshapen blocks moved an infinitesimal degree—enough, finally, to undermine the technical and engineering brilliance that had produced a structure that had withstood century upon century of seismic shock waves.

Abruptly, on a densely forested slope, an entire wall collapsed and the ground itself ruptured, spewing rubble amidst the tangle of undergrowth and vines, and baring the northern gate of the maze.

Jewel-bright parakeets, tiny motmots and noisy jacamars exploded into the clear blue arc of the sky, squawking their displeasure, eyes sharp as they wheeled above the disturbance.

But, collateral damage aside, deep within the hillside, cushioned by layers of granite and soft, malleable dirt—the most primitive of shock absorbers—the inner chambers themselves remained, as always, protected…impervious.

One

The raucous scolding of parakeets pierced thirteen-year-old Lady Victoria Quinton Mallory's doze.

Her eyes flipped open. Birds circled above, noisy and agitated, and she became aware that both the ground and the interlacing leaves shading her from the afternoon sun were shivering.

A scarlet macaw landed on the thick, cylindrical branch of a rubber tree and added to the scolding, the sound as sharp and precise as Aunt Olivia's when she reminded Quin of everything she had to do—and most especially everything she *hadn't* done—which today had amounted to a list almost as long as Quin's arm.

She fixed the bird with a steely glare, not bothering to get up from her reclining position on two sun-warmed rocks that were handily positioned like an armchair. "Oh, be quiet! The quake's just a baby. Hardly even a two, I'll bet."

If a quake was a two on the Richter scale, no one even bothered to comment on it, if they noticed it at all. If it was a three or four, Aunt Hannah got that anxious look of hers and began fussing about the bone china. A five—which had happened once—and they had to get out in the open, and stay away from buildings and tall trees. If it was a six or a seven—which had never happened in Quin's memory—according to their gardener and handyman, Jose, you didn't do *nothing* but bend over and kiss your ass goodbye.

A chuckle burst from deep in her belly at the thought of Jose, who was short and thickset and close to seventy, even trying to complete that maneuver.

Experimentally, she said the words aloud, still grinning. Despite the fact that she was a teenager—practically an adult—she wasn't supposed to think "ass," let alone say it.

The macaw squawked again—this time the sound so uncannily like Olivia's that Quin jackknifed in reflex, her sneakered feet landing on soft grass, palms braced flat on lichen-encrusted rock. When it was clear that she was alone in the grove, she let out a breath. It wasn't that she was scared of Olivia—on the contrary, nothing much scared Quin at all—but she had a healthy respect for both her aunts, and there was an omniscient quality to Olivia's dark blue gaze that kept Quin on her toes.

Out of habit, she scanned the hillside, wondering if either of the aunts *was* near, even though it was unlikely they would trek this far to find her, but, as always, the grove was isolated and peaceful, shrouded as it was by tall, arching trees and enclosed by soft shadows. Where the canopy thinned in places, mellow sunlight shafted through to dapple the ground, warming the large rocks that lay scattered, as if a giant fist had hammered the ancient bones of the hill into asymmetrical rubble.

Letting out a breath, Quin relaxed back into her comfortable seat, rearranged her jeans-clad legs on their warm rest and flicked her long, dark plait to one side so it didn't bite into her spine.

Lids lowered against an errant beam of sunlight, she gazed out across the valley. Through a gap in the trees, she could see her home—the mission—where it nestled on the western slopes. Sunlight glinted off deep inset windows, turning the limed walls a pale honey. From this far away the cracks in the plaster and the sagging fence enclosing the small complex weren't evident, and she could pretend the building was much more than a simple dwelling with a medical clinic attached. Like maybe…a very small castle—still under construction, of course—or a school.

Not that a school was any more likely a scenario than the castle.

Olivia had explained why she couldn't go to a real school. It was because she was different.

Psychic.

How different that made her, Quin wasn't sure, because she didn't have a lot of people to compare herself with. There were Jose's five grandchildren, but they were all boys, so it was hard to judge, and the other children from the village who came to the mission for Aunt Hannah's weekly clinics never stayed long enough for her to learn much more than their names. In any case, there was no way on this earth she would admit to being any more different than her blue eyes and pale skin made her and risk being classed as weird.

A slight breeze rustled through the trees, carrying with it the mournful tone of a bell. Quin's stomach sank. The bell, lodged in the small tower above the chapel, had previously been used to call the Sisters Of Mercy to prayer, but the last time it had been rung for that purpose had been more than fifty years ago, when the order had abandoned the isolated outpost at *Valle del Sol* and withdrawn back to the main monastery in Lima. Since then the mission had passed through several hands and had been used variously as a private residence, a school, a boardinghouse and, under Olivia and Hannah's stewardship, a medical center.

Nowadays, when the bell tolled, it tolled almost exclusively for Quin, and it usually meant schoolwork.

The macaw screeched, the dissonant sound cutting

across the richer tones of the bell. Quin caught the flash of bright plumage as the bird hopped onto a lower branch, swung around and hung upside down, peering at her, eyes beady and intelligent. "Don't you start."

Olivia maintained that if Quin was going to be a savage, at least she would be an educated savage, and, with both aunts claiming doctorates from Oxford—Hannah's medical, Olivia's in anthropology and ancient history—there was no quarter given.

Not that Quin usually complained. She loved her lessons, and she loved books and history with passion—but most of all she loved Olivia's stories.

Olivia had *traveled;* her descriptions were so real Quin had practically felt the gritty, sandblasted rock of the Sphinx beneath her palms, smelled the dank mud of the Nile and felt it sliding between her toes.

She'd been brought up on history—devoured it at every mealtime and been lulled to sleep by it at night—tales that stretched from the ancient courts of the Incas to the pyramids at Giza. But, as much as Olivia gave her, her stories, the books that lined the mission's library and the albums of photographs had never quite been enough.

Quin didn't just want to read or hear about the pyramids, she wanted to *be* there—the desire a fierce hunger rooted deep in her bones. She wanted to see and explore and to touch—to bury her hands in soil that had been tilled by primitive civilizations and sift for fragments of the past. Most of all, she wanted to unravel the myriad puzzles that had been left engraved in stone and painted on walls, enduring through the ages.

Ancient languages and symbols fascinated her above all things and seemed to suit her quirky mind. She loved to dabble with context, to stare at inscriptions and glyphs, and pore over Olivia's books and notes, worrying at the puzzles like a terrier with a juicy bone. And sometimes, in the strange way of her mind, all the hairs at the back of her neck would stand on end and she would understand the meaning without having the first clue what the literal translation was.

A yawn rolled through Quin. She stretched and shifted position, inching her face away from the glare of the sun and easing muscles that still ached from stoking the mission's boiler and scrubbing out the dispensing room.

Gradually, the last subtle layers of tension dissipated and her lids drooped.

Quin was a fitful sleeper. Usually she got enough sleep at night, but if she missed a few hours she was in trouble, because she couldn't sleep at the mission during the day, no matter how hard she tried. She'd found that the more people there were around, the more unlikely it was she would sleep at all, as if the bombardment of so many different personalities in one place wound her so tight that she couldn't relax.

Lately, following an outbreak of influenza, the mission had become a hive of activity, with entire families from surrounding villages arriving for treatment, some of them electing to stay over rather than risk crossing the swing bridge that spanned the Agueda in the dark.

Here, in the grove, the "interference" caused by other human beings was absent, and, apart from the isolation, there was something more...a peaceful quality she couldn't explain and hadn't experienced anywhere else. Besides that, it was always warm, as if some hidden power source flowed up out of the ground, filtering through rocks and dirt and the thick leaf litter to permeate the air, floating and rippling, as elusive as the heat shimmer that hung over the hills in summer. When she allowed herself to drift, the shadows would go liquid, and seem to shift and move around her, and she would slide into a doze and maybe even snatch a few minutes of sleep.

Sometimes she saw people—light, insubstantial people—who came and went, silent and unobtrusive, as transparent as veils, but she didn't feel in the least threatened. She'd seen *them* all her life.

Another yawn shook through her. The warmth of the grove enfolded her, making her feel bonelessly content, as if she could melt into the sun-warmed granite, dissolve into the silence and doze for as long as she liked....

But she shouldn't; she had to move. The bell had rung, and Olivia would be getting worried—but her body felt leaden, her lids glued closed.

As she drifted deeper into sleep, a flash of gold followed by the glitter of a light blue jewel suspended like a droplet against a honey-tanned forehead momentarily startled her. For a disorienting moment she thought she was looking into a mirror as eyes uncannily like her own stared back—only the gaze was sharper, colder, the face definitely adult. Then the moment dissolved as blackness enfolded her, and she was pulled under, spiraling down like a swimmer caught in an undertow.

1200 B.C.
Temple of The Sun

Cuin, the Forty-third Cadis of the Sun God, and probably the last, stood patiently in her private quarters as her personal attendants helped her into one of her more elaborate day robes. Stiffened linen, heavily encrusted with thin gold platelets, iridescent sea pearls and a shimmering plethora of multihued gems, slid over her arms and settled on her shoulders, stealing all the warmth from her skin.

Chuli, Cuin's head physician, fastened the high collar of the gown with slender gold picks that glinted wickedly in the late afternoon sunlight.

"Ouch," Cuin muttered, as the stiff collar rubbed against the tender skin of her neck.

Chuli nodded her satisfaction at the result. The robe made Cuin look even taller. "Imposing."

"You mean choking."

Malia, Chuli's sister and Cuin's chief advisor ever since Cuin had become the Cadis—high priestess of the Sun God—at age thirteen, twitched the robe into place around her hips, grumbling when she found that a bauble had come loose. With a curt command that Cuin stay absolutely still, she ascended the small stool she'd brought so she could check that Cuin's headdress was correctly secured and straight.

"You've grown again," she muttered. "I'm going to have to get a taller stool."

A smile twitched at the corner of Cuin's mouth—the brief spurt of humor catching her by surprise. It had been a long time since any of them had had anything to smile about. "Either that, or you're getting shorter."

"Hmmph."

Chuli and Malia were both considered to be of a good height, but amongst the women of the temple, Cuin was uncommonly tall—topping the tallest of the priestesses by a good two hands' breadth. Even amongst her own race—the Cadians—which had dwindled almost into extinction, she was considered tall and remarkably different. With her fair skin and sky-blue eyes, she was a throwback to the old people—before their blood had intermingled with the local tribes and been all but lost.

Chuli coaxed at one of the collar fastenings with deft, nimble fingers, the tired skin of her brow creased in a frown. "Don't tell me you're putting on weight?"

"As well as growing taller?" Cuin snatched a glimpse of her narrow silhouette in a mirror of polished gold that was affixed to the wall, before Chuli demanded she lift her chin so the final, strangling pick could be inserted. "Chance would be a fine thing."

Like everyone else in the temple, she was in no danger of putting on weight. They were all hungry—their bellies practically scraping against their backbones—and tired of supplementing a diet of tasteless, weevil-infested dried fruit and manioc with more tasteless, weevil-infested dried fruit and manioc.

Malia made a clucking sound and adjusted the frontispiece of the headdress, so that the delicate teardrop sapphire sat dead center on Cuin's forehead. The light, scintillating blue of the stone was a close match to her eyes and a blunt reminder to the governor of Ar Province of exactly why she was the Cadis.

In a sea of dark eyes and dark skin, Cuin had stood out from birth, pallid and angular, narrow-featured and long-legged, as awkward and ungainly as a baby crane. She had been the only blue-eyed child born in more than ten generations—a throwback to the ancient race that had built the temple. Different or not, ugly or not, her eyes had saved her from being left to the crows and had mapped out her path from birth: they had marked her for the temple.

Malia made one last adjustment to the headdress, then climbed down from the stool. "All this fuss for that snake, Chumac."

"To keep Chumac in his place," Cuin corrected.

If that was possible.

The court had long been corrupt, and the present governor was the worst yet—sharp-eyed and ambitious, with his eye set on the failing king, Chataluk's, throne.

The corruption of the court had always been legendary, but through Chataluk's overlong reign it had reached gargantuan proportions, gradually seeping into the provinces and even into the temple itself.

In Cuin's opinion, the simplicity had been lost, diminished by too much pomp and ceremony, too many rituals—and far too much gold. The temple shouldn't be wealthy when the people starved. One of the first decrees she'd made when she'd taken office had been that the gold the temple possessed should be used to buy food from the richer northern provinces in times of famine, but lately, thanks to

Chumac's machinations, temple gold hadn't been a reliable coin for anything.

The governor had gradually cut them off from their sources of supply, threatening the merchants and farmers who usually kept the temple storehouses full to overflowing. When they were able to purchase food at all, it was at an inflated cost and almost only from merchants who dealt in contraband. In any man's language, it was a siege.

Chuli produced a glittering, jeweled knife, all humor gone from her expression. "You should wear this today."

Cuin eyed the blade with distaste and shook her head. Even for Chumac, she wouldn't wear *that* knife. It had been designed, and used, by a previous high priestess, who had given in to pressure from a new and powerful cult that had demanded the establishment of ritual sacrifice. "Death and blood are no part of this temple."

Although, if Chumac had his way, they would be.

Grimly, she signaled that the blade should be removed from her presence. "The only weapons I'll be fighting with today are words."

Useless, empty words, because, with her army depleted by Chumac's paymasters—despite the quantities of gold that lay in the storehouses—her only strength lay in the power and charisma of the temple. And Chumac had long lost all respect for that.

Lately, theirs was a cat-and-mouse game fought with strategy and wit, and Chumac was looking more and more like the cat that had got the cream.

Minutes later, she entered the formal reception room and mounted the dais steps, flanked by priest-esses and initiates and her temple guard, which these days amounted to only six men—two of whom she suspected were on the verge of abandoning their posts.

Chumac entered, short and muscular and girded in all his finery. He was followed by his usual reti-nue, which today included his war master, Hotec, as if he felt the need for extra support—or, more likely, indicated that he wanted to intimidate her.

If Chumac was smooth, Hotec was brutal. Abnor-mally tall, his shoulders as wide as a post, Hotec possessed a lust for death and killing that was evi-denced by the dried collection of human remains that hung from his belt. Lately it had even been ru-mored that he had committed the ultimate in atroci-ties by dining on his victims.

Cuin heard Chuli's faint exclamation, and her own gorge rose at the glimpse of something red and glis-tening flapping amongst the collection of bones and dried skin at Hotec's waist.

Stiffly, she averted her gaze from the grotesque dis-play. Now she knew why Hotec was part of Chumac's retinue. The insult was pointed—and unforgivable.

Chumac issued his list of demands through the

mouthpiece of his elaborately attired household priest, Nasek. The list, as usual, included a petition that she accept the governor's protection in these "dangerous times," and that, in exchange for his protection, she subjugate her temporal power to that of the secular—naturally, Chumac's.

"No." The word scraped harshly.

She'd been forced to give ground in the village, which supported the temple and the surrounding lands. With lack of manpower, she'd even conceded defeat in the outer perimeter of the temple, where security was difficult to maintain—but not within. *Never within.* To despoil the inner sanctity of the temple—the purity and intent of the teachings—went against every particle of her being. Chumac had his power, but she was the Cadis, and she wouldn't allow the temple to feed his hunger for Chataluk's throne.

Chumac's muddy gaze met hers, bold and overfamiliar, and in that split second wariness changed to raw fear. She was aware of an overweening confidence in the governor, a smugness that signaled secret knowledge and plans.

Abruptly she was certain she was no longer simply losing ground. Some time between this meeting and the last, something had happened: she had lost.

Her fingers tightened on the ornate gilded arms of her throne, the fine bones aching with the pressure. She held Chumac's gaze, keeping her own icy—calling on her flagging inner reserves, calling on the power of the Sun God to fortify her.

Instantly, she felt the change—the energy shifting within and around her—felt her spine straighten, her neck elongate. The quality of her stare altered as the fear drained away to be replaced with a cool, indomitable control. She felt the alteration in the air itself, the heat closing around her, as if the very atmosphere was charged with power.

Chumac recoiled as if—unseen as the phenomenon was—he was suddenly as sensitive to her altered state as she was. Hissing a word, he backed off a step, his fingers curling into a warding sign that signaled his allegiance to one of the new idolatrous cults. With a last, muttered profanity, he jerked his head at his men and strode from the room.

Hotec lingered, his dark gaze blank of the knowledge that had filled Chumac's, simmering instead with a malevolence that was too primitive to allow a woman any more power than he chose to give her. But, less sensitive or not, Hotec was no more able to stand the power that filled the room than Chumac had been.

With a guttural sound somewhere between a grunt and an oath, he turned on his heel, as if jerked by a leash, and followed his master.

Two

Long seconds passed while Cuin stared at the empty entrance to the reception room. Slowly, like water seeping from tightly cupped fingers, the power drained away, leaving her empty and diminished, as inadequate as the youngest novice in the temple. As the last whispers of power faded, a chill invaded her stomach, and her hand rose in automatic reflex, sketching a holy sign in negation of everything that Chumac stood for.

Malia touched her arm, and Cuin started, realizing she had been sitting frozen, staring at the empty entranceway for some time.

"What do we do now?"

Cuin willed her sluggish mind to think, willed warmth to seep back into her bones so she could move, but she felt curiously disengaged. Her stomach rolled, and she tensed, although she wasn't on the point of losing her noontime meal. *She hadn't had a noontime meal.* Which was why she was having difficulty focusing. Abruptly, the condition she'd allowed herself, allowed them all, to fall into shocked her. They weren't just hungry, they were starving to death—the decline slow and insidious—and she couldn't allow the situation to continue.

"We pack."

The temple had been here for millennia—an isolated remnant of a much more ancient past—surviving the descent into darkness long after everything else it was connected to had fallen. The order had managed to preserve fragments of the knowledge that once had been—holding fast to the ancient wisdom and the belief in the one, true God—but purity and common sense no longer fulfilled what the people wanted.

According to Chumac, they wanted a god for every season and a god for every reason—gods with teeth and claws, gods that fed from power and blood and fear.

The temple had survived through famines and uprisings, floods and earthquakes and the ever-evolving political climate, but it couldn't prevail without the support of the people it served.

If the message had been written in the sky, it couldn't have been clearer: the temple was finished, its time over.

Chumac wouldn't do anything as crude as attack them—yet. To openly attack the temple would negate what power they still had, and he needed the support of the temple behind his bid to take the throne when Chataluk finally passed.

But beyond that practical need, Chumac had no use for any of them. All he wanted was the shell—the illusion—and the sacred relics. He would replace her with his own puppet and put in place the rituals, and the gods, that best served his purpose.

The knowledge of impending disaster prickled coldly down her spine. She had thought they had more time.

Jaw set, Cuin rose to her feet, stiff with cold and light-headed from lack of food as she descended the dais and concentrated on reaching the ornate double doors.

Large and splendidly appointed as the reception room was, it was a mere anteroom in the outer portion of the temple. Outsiders were almost never allowed further into the temple complex than this, but if Chumac ever solved the puzzle of the maze and reached the inner chamber, he would find his greedy fist closing on a handful of nothing—and he would reach the inner chamber over her dead body.

In the meantime…there were people to save—knowledge and sacred artifacts to preserve.

The certainty of just how little time they had before Chumac moved against the temple made her heart pound and her throat clog with fear. She had a contingency plan; it was a desperate one, but she couldn't risk waiting any longer. She had to act now.

The warmth of the late-afternoon sun streaming through the tall apertures that lighted her private apartment barely registered for Cuin as Chuli and Malia shooed the other priestesses away and began the intricate process of removing her formal garments. Cuin held still with difficulty and studied the two women who had effectively become her family when she'd entered the temple. Age had whitened their hair, but it was malnutrition that had taken the spring out of their step, the sparkle from their eyes. The knot in her stomach tightened as she took note of the faint tremor in Malia's fingers, the gauntness of Chuli's face. Like everyone else, they'd lost weight, but unlike most of the priestesses, they didn't have the physical stamina and resources of youth. She was in danger of losing them both.

As soon as the headdress and the heavy, intricate robe were gone, Cuin dismissed the sisters, brushing aside their concern with a formal smile.

With fingers that shook with a mixture of weakness and pure, undiluted fear at what she had to do, she bound her hair in a simple plait, dressed in a plain robe, woven from a coarse mixture of vegetable fibers and alpaca, and laced on rope sandals. The bulky robe felt rough and prickly against her skin after the much finer weave of linen, and the sandals were, quite frankly, abrasive—the skin of her feet already reddening where the rope rubbed—but servant's clothing was necessary. With Chumac's soldiers filling the township, she couldn't walk abroad dressed in a high priestess's garments.

After draping a dull brown alpaca shawl over her head and shoulders to hide her face, Cuin briefly examined herself in the mirror. Satisfied, she summoned Malia.

Malia's eyes flared with shock. "You can't," she said flatly. "Let me go in your stead."

"No." Cuin led the way through the living apartments, took a lighted torch from the wall and opened the door into the maze. While they walked, she outlined exactly what she was going to do.

Malia's face grew pale. "This is madness. I thought we were going to get one of the guard to—"

"That won't work. I no longer know who's loyal and who's not, and if Chumac discovers my plan, we won't live to see another sunrise."

"He wouldn't dare—"

"These days, Chumac does what he wills."

Cuin halted in what was apparently a cul-de-sac and handed the torch to Malia. "Wait for me at the main gate, but be as inconspicuous as you can. I won't be able to return this way unless I've failed, and if I fail…"

Malia's gaze was bleak. They both knew that if

Cuin failed, most likely she wouldn't be back at all. Chumac wouldn't miss a chance to kill her, and then the weight of responsibility would fall on Malia's shoulders.

Cuin pressed firmly on a deeply incised glyph carved into the wall, then placed both palms on the block of granite and thrust the stone door open.

Dim light flooded the passageway, and a faint breeze stirred, making the torch in Malia's grasp flicker and smoke as Cuin stepped out into a dark tangle of shrubbery and vines, and instantly sank ankle-deep in mud.

Outside, it wasn't much lighter than it had been in the secret passageway, signaling that the sun had set.

Holding her robe around her knees to keep the hem from the mud, Cuin closed the door, which, from the outside, appeared to be a natural rock formation, then began fighting her way through the undergrowth until she finally emerged in the back yard of a cloth merchant. Draping the shawl over her head and shoulders, she ducked beneath sheets of dyed cloth flapping in the breeze, slipped past the stone hutch that housed the merchant's business and stepped into a narrow, cobbled avenue.

Hunching to reduce her distinctive height, she kept the shawl pulled firmly over her head as she walked past freshly lit torches.

When she entered the village proper, she relaxed

her hold on the coarse cloth enough that she could study the confusion of peasants returning from the fields shouldering baskets of produce, bare-footed children darting between buildings and vendors hawking food. On the few occasions that she had ventured out since Chumac had taken up residence in the valley, it had generally been in a palanquin— the curtains tightly drawn against the hard stares and taunts of Chumac's men. It had been months since she'd last risked leaving the temple; consequently, her face wasn't well known.

A delicious savory aroma wafted from one of the vendors' stands, where a woman bent over a brazier, roasting potatoes and manioc cakes. Cuin's mouth watered uncontrollably. It had been weeks since she'd had anything more than manioc gruel sweetened with a thin puree of dried fruit, and the thought of actually eating solid food was enough to make her feel faint.

Swallowing against the hollow burn in her stomach, and the temptation to offer the woman temple gold and risk her life for a roasted potato, Cuin turned on her heel and strode deeper into the village, taking care to keep her head bent against curious stares.

Rounding a corner, she stopped to orient herself in the deep shadow of a tree. The last time she'd walked freely around the village had been when she was a skinny child studying to enter the order—and even then, it had always been in the company of Malia and one of the temple guard. With her light blue eyes, she'd always been an object of intense curiosity—and a target, even as a child. Since then, the town had more than trebled in size, straddling the river and spreading out over the valley floor. Lately the population had swelled even further with the army Chumac was amassing, but, confusing as the changes and the crowded streets were, she could still remember where the tavern was located.

She heard the noise pounding from the drinking house before she saw it; seconds later the pungent reek of beer permeated the air. Light streamed from deep apertures cut into the thick walls of a large, sprawling building, picking out, amidst the milling confusion of men and women, the flash of a warrior's armband, a wrist glittering with jewelry and the satiny gleam of a long, shapely leg. Taking a deep breath, Cuin sidled up to the front door, studiously avoiding any physical contact.

Crudely designed though it was, the place was notorious, the tales that emanated from it legion, the men and women who frequented it not known for piety. Drawing the shawl even more tightly around her head, Cuin stepped into a cavernous room.

For the first time in her life—and hopefully the last—she was stepping inside a tavern and house of ill repute, looking for a man.

Three

The noise, the sheer assault on her senses, the thick stench of so many bodies packed together in one place, along with the rich odor of roasting meat, hit her like a blow, and for a moment she froze, physically unable to step any further into the primitive chaos, despite the fact that what she sought was here.

She needed a warrior who was skilled enough to face Chumac and Hotec in combat, a warrior who could lead men, and yet who was uncommitted to any lord—someone she could trust implicitly. Most of all, she needed a warrior she could command, because, ultimately, the lives of her novices and initiates and the safety of the sacred treasure would rest with him.

In the months she'd been gathering intelligence, she'd considered and rejected name after name until there was only one warrior left who, to her knowledge, hadn't yet given his allegiance to Chumac.

His name was Achaeus, and he was a foreigner—a mercenary who, from all accounts, had hacked his way down from some land to the north, aligning himself with various warlords as and when it suited him. His reputation was wild enough, the fear surrounding the strange armor and gleaming weapons that hung from his belt powerful enough, that it was rumored even Hotec gave him a wide berth.

According to her source, it was a fact that Achaeus spent his evenings here.

A meaty shoulder shoved her to one side as a knot of men squeezed in behind her. The protruding butt of a long, curved wooden club, secured across a broad back, caught her a glancing blow, and alarm jolted through her. Chumac's men.

Heart pounding, she inched aside, pressing herself flat against cold stone, trying to dissolve into the soot-blackened wall as they passed.

With the new arrivals, the sound level in the tavern rose. Hunching even lower, and holding the shawl wadded over her nose and mouth to filter the smoke and stench, Cuin took advantage of the temporary distraction and plunged deeper into the murk.

Long minutes of searching later, barely able to separate warrior from peasant in the tangle of inebriated bodies, she fetched up against a stone pillar and systematically began searching the gloom. The flash of metal reflecting the flames of one of the smoking braziers that were placed at intervals caught her eye. Abandoning her hunched posture, she rose up on her toes, craning to see. The flash came again as the warrior leaned forward, feeding wood into the fire. Too bright for copper, not bright enough for gold.

Adrenaline pumped, making her head spin. Seconds later, she shuffled past a group of men and women in varying states of undress, congregating around a table that was awash with ale. Keeping her gaze fixed on the packed dirt floor, Cuin counted paces as she headed for the next pillar. She was close enough to reach out and touch it when an elbow sent her stumbling against a hard chest. Her hand shot out and collided with a cup. Cold liquid soaked her sleeve, and a guttural roar vibrated in her ear. A large hand gripped the neck of her robe, knuckles digging into the soft skin beneath her chin. The fetid stench of rotted teeth and infected gums made her reel as the man leaned close; then a woman with loose, tangled hair, her robe gaping to bare the rounded globes of her breasts, intervened, eyes flashing as she knocked his hand away. There was a brief, sharp altercation. The woman glared at Cuin, spat a crude warning, then wound her arms around the man's neck and pressed her mouth to his.

Cuin backed away, gripping her shawl even more

tightly around her face as she cast around to get her bearings. Panic gripped her when she couldn't orient herself, couldn't see anything beyond an amorphous mass of bodies. Then a servant forged past, carrying a platter of steaming meat, and the bodies parted, and once more she caught the distinctive glint of metal. Setting her jaw, she continued her slow, clumsy shuffle toward the cold gleam—the shuffle no longer an act as she grimly concentrated on putting one foot in front of the other. It took an eon to reach the last pillar, and when she did, for long moments she simply leaned into the cool stone.

A roar from the far end of the tavern finally roused her. Reluctantly, she pushed herself away from the pillar and eyed the overlarge warrior sprawled on a bench, which had been positioned in the darkest corner of the alcove.

Even sitting down, he was taller than any warrior she'd yet seen, a muscular, dark lion of a man, his hair thick and long and coal-black, pulled back from his face in an archaic fashion to reveal high, taut cheekbones, a thin blade of a nose and a jaw that looked like it had been chiseled from granite.

He was relaxed, but even so, he looked dangerous. From the discreet distance she'd preserved, she could feel the fierceness that radiated from him, and her stomach tightened as if a cold fist had just closed around her innards. The fact that, for a crowded tavern, there was a lot of empty space around the warrior, as if even the hardened drinkers and harlots who frequented this place didn't dare get too close, added weight to her instinct to turn on her heel, walk back to the temple and forget her plan.

But forgetting her plan wasn't an option.

Keeping her gaze fixed on the light glinting off the strange, gray metal of his breastplate, Cuin started toward him.

As she reached the circle of warmth cast by the brazier, he lifted his head, and the warning flash in his dark eyes made her heart pound so hard she had difficulty catching her breath.

Loosening the wad of fabric that was pressed against her nose and mouth, she took a steadying breath. To her relief, the air at this end of the tavern seemed clearer. "I have a proposition for you." To her dismay, her voice came out as little more than a croak.

His gaze was dismissive. "Whatever you're selling, old woman, I don't want it."

"You haven't heard—"

"Leave."

Her teeth snapped together. "Or what?"

His gaze bored briefly into hers, as if he could see through the shawl that obscured her face, dark eyes so coldly dismissive she felt the chill invade her flesh. With an indolent movement, he went back to feeding wood into the fire, and the hope that had driven her from the safety of the temple on a quest that was all but futile sank close to extinction. She had found her warrior, she was certain of it, but the logic that had stopped her approaching Achaeus until she was desperate was now placed solidly in front of her. If he wouldn't ally himself with Chumac, why would he work for her?

For long moments Cuin lingered, too exhausted to heed the warning implicit in that last glance and move, her mind running feverishly over what she had that a mercenary who appeared to have no discernible price might possibly want. Chumac had gold aplenty, and the promise of advancement and glory in the bloodbath that would follow Chataluk's death. Aside from gold, she had nothing to offer but burdens.

Flames licked around the wood Achaeus had just thrown into the brazier and flared high, momentarily throwing his features into sharp relief—the spare cheekbones, the sleepy cast to his eyes, the barbaric metal breastplate that spanned his chest—and for a moment time itself seemed to stop. Blinking, she wondered if the fumes she'd breathed had made her drunk.

The design emblazoned on the strange, dull breastplate was a sun.

Warily, Cuin studied the insignia that proclaimed Achaeus's allegiance—not a bird or a mythic animal, or the fanged creature that Chumac and Hotec served—but *the sun,* and for the first time since Chumac had walked into her temple that afternoon, hope surged.

Gaze fixed on the elaborate sun motif, a close match to the motif carved into the doors of the temple, Cuin straightened to her full height—taller than almost any man she'd ever met. Achaeus thought she was a prostitute, selling her body to whoever had coin. If that was the only avenue to get him to listen, then she would use it. "I'm not old."

He didn't bother to lift his head. "And I don't have to pay for it."

Boldly stepping further into the light, she drew the shawl far enough aside that he could glimpse the lower part of her face. "I don't need money. I was proposing paying you."

His head finally lifted. His gaze fastened on her mouth, and a faint gleam of interest surfaced. "That's a new twist."

His hand snaked around her wrist and jerked her closer. His calloused thumb rubbed over her palm, the faint abrasion sending a raw shiver up her spine.

His gaze settled on her mouth again. "With that soft hand you're not the old woman you're pretending to be, and you're no more a prostitute or a servant than I am. Let's see who you really are."

He caught the corner of the shawl and yanked, baring her face. Abruptly, he was towering over her, fingers digging into her shoulders, black eyes locked with hers. He muttered something curt in a language she didn't understand as Cuin snatched at the tail end of the shawl, desperate to drag it over her head before one of Chumac's men noticed her. Her fingers snagged on wool, but in her haste she fumbled, and the garment slipped to the floor.

He muttered the curt demand again, his voice hoarsening; then the world spun as she found herself pressed back into the shadows of the alcove and pinned against the rough stone of the wall. With the cold metal of his armor biting into her breasts, his breath warm on her cheek, one muscled thigh pressed against hers, the fact that her face was naked and exposed suddenly became secondary.

Achaeus smelled like a wild animal—not heavily of body odors, but clean and faintly musky: of river water and wood smoke, and the sharp, resinous herbs that were used for bathing. The fact that he bathed should have been reassuring, but this close, he was even taller and more forbidding than she'd expected.

His gaze caught hers and held it. "Your eyes," he said slowly, biting out each word. "You look like you come from Ilium."

She blankly registered that his reaction to her eyes

hadn't been because he associated their unusual color with the temple. "I've never heard of—" She swallowed, and tested the strange, liquid sound of the name "—Ilium."

He continued to watch her, as if gauging the veracity of her words. Gradually the tension eased from his face, but he didn't release her. "Ilium fell. Her people are…scattered."

"I'm not from your city," she said carefully. "And you're right, I'm not a prostitute or a kitchen maid. I'm the Cadis."

She frowned as her assertion that she was the high priestess tumbled out, breathless and lacking her usual calm.

"You're lying." His tone was cold, neutral—but, most importantly to Cuin, untainted with the contempt that Chumac encouraged amongst his men.

She pointed to her eyes. "*These* make me the Cadis. But if you still don't believe, then follow me, and I'll prove who I am."

He studied her at length, as if contemplating some kind of minor insect species and deciding whether or not it was an annoyance. Amusement curved his mouth, and abruptly she became conscious of her disheveled state. Mud caked her sandaled feet and the hem of her robe, soot was smeared on her hands and shawl, and the reek of ale rose from a damp patch on her sleeve. Apart from the fact that she was filthy and unkempt, she was also dressed as a servant, a necessary disguise that now worked against her.

She sucked in a breath, frustrated that she'd forgotten the most important part of the negotiation. Reaching inside her robe, she pulled out a purse and extracted a bright gold piece, stamped with the temple seal.

"What in Hades do you think you're doing?"

His hand closed on hers, obliterating the gleam of the coin. Before she could object or catch her breath, she found herself jerked into an even darker corner of the room. His hand closed around her neck, keeping her pinned against the wall, head tilted at an acute angle so he could continue to stare down into her face with that cold, remote gaze. "If you're the Cadis, you can tell me in which direction Ilium lies, and whether or not my men and I will ever see it again."

Cuin was beginning to feel like a rag doll, her legs weak, her senses reeling from the assault of dealing with such a potent male. His grip wasn't tight enough to cut off her breath, but there was no way she could free herself. She closed her eyes briefly and reached for calm. She had wanted his attention, and now, for a reason strange beyond imagining, she finally had it. "I know not in which direction your fallen city lies. I'm not an oracle—I'm a healer."

With a biting curse, he slowly loosened his hold.

The roughness of his fingers against her skin sent an involuntary shiver through Cuin. Achaeus looked big enough and savage enough to take on half of Chumac's army single-handed, and, according to the information one of the servants had brought back from the markets, he was expert enough in combat to do it. He also commanded a small force of men, a number of them as strange and outlandish as Achaeus himself, and every one of them armed with weapons that cut through copper and wood like a hot knife through butter.

Excitement stirred in the pit of her belly, rose up and gripped her as thoroughly as the large hand that still manacled her neck to the wall. Achaeus was larger, fiercer and much more complicated than she'd ever imagined he would be, and it was all she could do to school herself to stillness as she tolerated his hold and stared boldly back.

If she could control him, she just might be able to outwit Chumac.

Four

Achaeus continued to study her, his gaze cold. "You're flashing temple coin, and you're soft enough to be an initiate, but there's no way you're the Cadis. Chumac has her locked up tight. She never leaves the temple grounds."

Cuin swallowed against the bitter gall of his words. She was aware that the temple's situation had deteriorated drastically, but she hadn't known their position was so publicly known. "The temple has a maze of passages. I used one of the secret tunnels to get here. If you'll just loose me—"

His grip tightened, chopping off the flow of words. He glared down into her eyes, as if he found them fascinating, and muttered again in that liquid, archaic language.

Cuin struggled to inhale and couldn't. Her fingers

curled around his big hand and wrenched, and the pressure on her windpipe eased. *"I don't speak your language."*

Abruptly she was free, leaning against the wall, glad for the support, since her legs had turned to water.

His gaze flashed in something close to an apology. "You look like you should."

Cuin lifted a hand to massage her throat and swallowed. The skin felt tender and sensitive where he'd gripped her. She hadn't enjoyed the experience, but beyond the insult of touching, he had done her no real physical harm.

Achaeus folded his arms across his chest. Flickering light from the brazier slanted across his face, making him look even bleaker, illuminating the swell of one muscled bicep and the dull sheen of the heavy blade hanging from his hip. "If you were a man," he stated mildly, "you'd be dead, but since you're a woman—and fair—I'm intrigued enough to listen to your proposition."

Cuin's heart thumped in her chest. It took long moments for her to realize that she had actually achieved, if not all, then at least a part of her goal. "Thank you."

With fingers that were stiff with cold and a little shaky, she stuffed the coin pouch back in her robe. She wouldn't make the mistake of offering him money again until they'd settled on terms. He obviously had his own brand of etiquette, and his own way of doing business. Until she had learned his ways, she wouldn't risk offending him. "We can talk at the temple."

He jerked his head, indicating a door off to the side of the tavern, and, pulse still pounding, she draped the shawl over her head and followed him into a narrow avenue that ran between the tavern kitchens and what looked like the tavern keeper's house.

The touch of his fingers as he took her arm was vaguely shocking, and for a moment she stiffened until she realized he was simply sheltering her from the bustle of foot traffic as they entered the main avenue.

"I take it we *are* going to the temple?"

She risked a glance at his face and looked quickly away when she saw him watching her with open curiosity—and something else she couldn't quite fathom. "Where else?"

Her tension gradually dissipated, to be replaced by a slow-building elation as he continued to stroll with her up the terraced gradations of the township that led to the temple gates. Walking with the barbarian was like keeping company with a very large, very unpredictable jaguar—the link between them fragile and likely to be shattered in an instant. If she did the wrong thing, said the wrong thing, she could lose him in a second, but with every step closer to the temple gates, the vice around her heart loosened.

Ridiculously, as they were halted at the gates and

asked to identify themselves, the thought uppermost in her mind wasn't the plight of the temple but the odd expression that had entered his eyes when he'd said she was fair.

Cuin slipped the shawl from her head and didn't miss the way Achaeus's gaze narrowed when the temple guard blinked and flushed, then bowed deeply as he backed away.

Malia, who was keeping watch in the lee of the guardhouse, stepped forward and wrapped a rich, soft robe around Cuin's shoulders, covering the coarseness of her disguise.

Achaeus backed off a step, his expression grim. "It seems I made a mistake—my apologies."

With a brief half bow, he turned on his heel, but Cuin caught his arm, halting him. "You promised you'd listen to my proposition."

"I promised nothing, and there's no longer any need for discussion. I know what you want."

He glanced at her slim, pale fingers gripping his forearm just above the curious metal gauntlet that protected his wrist, but Cuin refused to release her hold. He would have to prize her fingers off one by one if he wanted to be rid of her. She'd got him this far; she wouldn't lose him now.

She took a deep breath, gambling on the honor that had made him refuse her gold when most men would simply have taken it—and her—without agreeing to anything in return. "By my reckoning, there are twenty-nine women here—six of whom are in their dotage—twelve children, ranging from seven summers to thirteen, six temple guards…and myself."

The silence stretched taut, punctuated by the distant tinny notes of cymbals and horns, the cacophony of sound as a fight broke out in the tavern.

"I know what's at stake." He nodded toward the guardhouse and the two men stationed there. "If that's your first line of defense, you won't be safe for long."

If at all. With their wooden clubs and copper knives, the temple guard looked even more puny and ineffectual than usual. Compared with Achaeus, they were children playing at war. "We don't have a line of defense," she said bluntly. "All we have is the fact that Chumac wants the temple intact—for the time being. He's already bought most of the guard. All we have left are a few men."

"Half of whom are also taking Chumac's pay as well as yours."

Shock ran through her at the blunt confirmation of her own suspicions, but she didn't so much as blink. "That's why we need you. I'm trying to get everyone out."

His expression was unreadable. "Why did you come looking for me?"

She didn't miss the slight emphasis on the "you." "We needed someone who isn't in Chumac's pay," she said simply. "I couldn't entrust finding that person to anyone else."

"And you settled on a mercenary and a foreigner. Someone who has no attachment to your temple or your politics."

"What would you have done, given the same circumstances?"

"Nothing different." His gaze swept the massive edifice of the temple. "I don't understand you, or this place, but you've got guts—"

"So you'll take the job?"

"—and you're desperate."

"So—"

He was silent for a moment. Abruptly, his gaze settled on hers again. "Before I agree to anything, I want to see a full set of maps of the temple *and* the maze. And I want *you* to walk me through it all, and show me the secret ways and the door mechanisms. Before you say no, understand that that is the only part of this deal that isn't negotiable. If you want any of us to survive this, you can't keep anything secret from me." His gaze shifted to her mouth; then he shook his head. "I must be drunk—or sickening for something."

"But you'll do it. I can offer you all the gold you can haul, and help to carry it."

"Forget it." He stared out over the village, which flowed down the hill and sprawled across the other side of the river, at the armed encampment that grew daily, massing near the mouth of the valley and cutting off escape. "I've got no love for Chumac or any of his men—and no liking for this situation. That's payment enough."

"Nevertheless, you shall have your gold."

"If I get out of this with my skin, I'll be happy enough."

"There's just one thing." She eyed the hilt of his sword. "I can't allow you to take weapons into the temple itself."

Achaeus's teeth gleamed white in the darkness, and his chest shook as if she'd just recounted a particularly funny joke. "Let's get one thing straight. I don't go anywhere without my sword."

Achaeus's narrowed gaze swept the private courtyard that separated her rooms from the rest of the sleeping apartments, as if, even in the center of a structure that housed only women, he was suspicious. "Chumac's as mad as a snake and ambitious with it, and you've been a thorn in his side ever since he's governed this province. If he doesn't get what he wants before Chataluk dies, he'll bring this whole place down on your heads, and be damned about temporal power and sacred treasures."

"Why do you think I took the risk I did in finding you?"

His gaze clashed with hers as they walked in the

soft light of the corridors, his eyes a rich shade of dark brown, rather than black, as she'd first thought.

"That's the kind of risk you won't take again. Do you know how much Chumac is offering for your head?"

Achaeus mentioned a sum that made her head reel. That, and the fact that Chumac had gone far enough in his machinations to actually offer a bounty for her death, was startling enough that she ignored the command he'd just issued. For months now, precautions had been taken: her food was tasted; she didn't enter the outer part of the temple without an armed escort; and all public appearances had been cancelled.

Sweeping a heavy curtain aside, Achaeus stared at the novitiates' sleeping hall—at the small bodies curled beneath thick blankets. "I'll be satisfied if I can get these little ones out."

"Do you have any men you can trust?"

His mouth curled. "A few. Six, maybe seven, if I can haul Tule away from the woman he's just found, but with the situation as it stands, we won't be fighting, we'll be running." He let the heavy curtain drop back into place. "And if you're having second thoughts about hiring me, you've got to know that in this business there are only two types of warriors— dead ones, and live ones. I'm twenty and eight—relatively old for a mercenary, which should tell you something. I've done a lot of running."

"Hotec fears you, that's credential enough for

me." Cuin blinked as she led the way through the maze. Maybe it was a trick of the light—the late hour—but the entrance to the map room seemed to be getting further away, rather than closer, and as they strolled through pooling darkness intermittently broken by the flare of torchlight, the shadows pressed in more heavily. She frowned as the corridor shifted and tilted beneath her feet. Her hand shot out, searching for the support of the wall even as she recognized the illusion for what it was—another of the dizzy spells that lately had been becoming more and more frequent.

Warm fingers closed around her arm, holding her up when she would have fallen, and a curse she'd never before been privileged to hear scorched her ears.

"You're as thin as a child. When did you last eat?"

Cuin flinched at the flat tone of his voice, which indicated he was well used to command—and, she would wager, used to being obeyed without question. With an effort of will, she straightened and released herself from his grip. She needed to distance herself from him, to assert some semblance of authority, but she felt oddly light-headed, as if she were ready to float away. "At the sun feast."

"Two days ago." He muttered another curse, this one even more inventive, and Cuin was abruptly overwhelmed by the dark eyes surveying her, the fingers testing the thin muscle of her arm beneath her robe and finding it lacking, as if she were a roasting bird too scrawny for the table.

"We all ate at the feast," she said stiffly. "It's tradition."

"But other than that, you've been starving yourselves—probably on a roster system, so the children don't go hungry."

"Chumac's been systematically cutting off our lines of supply—"

"—gradually tightening the noose." Achaeus stared at the walls of the maze, his distaste clear. "This place isn't a temple, it's a prison."

Cuin didn't argue, because that was exactly what the temple had become and the reason they had to leave. Wrenching as it was, in the end they would only be leaving a building—a physical location. Providing the ancient wisdom was preserved, and the healing precepts kept intact, the essence of the temple itself would survive.

Achaeus jerked his head, indicating that they should continue on to the map room, his expression grim. "Don't worry about Chumac, and don't worry about the children—I'll get them out. Just organize the provisioning: enough food, water and warm clothing for everyone, and not much more than that. We'll be moving fast. We can't afford to take anything we can't carry on our backs."

As Cuin moved forward, she stumbled, her coordination abruptly gone, and with a soft oath, Achaeus swung her into his arms as if she weighed no more than a sack of feathers. Cuin's cheeks flushed at the unconscionable intimacy of his hold, the thud of his heart so close to her ear, but she couldn't argue. If he didn't carry her, she would have to crawl. "There are scrolls and relics we *have* to remove. They can't be left for—"

"I told you not to worry about Chumac."

Arrested, she studied the taut line of his jaw. "What are you going to do?"

His gaze flashed to hers, and a chill tightened her spine at the purpose there.

"I'm going to kill him myself."

Setting her down by the door, he supported her with an arm around her waist while he studied the glyph. "Show me how to open this."

"Touch the glyph there, then push…here."

The door to the map chamber swung open. Achaeus's gaze pierced the torch-lit expanse of the room. "Where are the maps?"

She pointed to the intricate mosaic underfoot. "The floor." She smiled faintly at the humor and sheer practicality of a race that had long since faded into obscurity. "The ancients put everything on the floor. That way it wouldn't be lost, and even a child could read it."

* * *

Cuin gave the order for the thin stone tablets containing the ancient teachings of the order, the records of the temple since its inception, to be packed along with every sacred article but one. That one, according to temple law, could only be handled by her.

Achaeus's lieutenant, Kade, a thin, hawkish man with a body like whipcord and no discernible sense of humor, had organized the evacuation into groups— each to be led by one of Achaeus's men. They would be traveling on foot, so as to leave as little trace of their passing as possible, and holing up during the day in a cave in the hills. From then on, they would continue to travel only at night, to avoid detection. Cuin and Achaeus would be the last to leave.

Cuin paused at the large double doors of the inner chamber, placed her palms flat on the ornate gold sun and pushed. The heavy doors glided open. The maze had been designed to confuse and protect, but the inner chamber itself, which was of much earlier origin than the maze, didn't have any locks; it had been created for all.

Upon opening, other mechanisms activated, and sunlight flooded the room, pouring like liquid gold through a complex system of skylights and mirrors.

The light and energy of the inner chamber shimmered and poured around and through Cuin as she stepped into the room, making her go both hot and cold at once, and dissolving the tension that held her jaw clenched tight.

Complicated as the engineering and construction of parts of the temple complex were, the design of the inner chamber was deceptively simple. The smooth, sloping walls of the pyramid joined at the apex, and a large dais sat squarely in the middle of the room. There were no furnishings or decoration other than the exquisite gold frescoes that emblazoned the walls and the mosaic that covered the floor. On occasion furniture was brought in for certain celebrations and rituals, but for the most part the room was complete in itself—a chamber of light, designed to both hold and to give out light.

Achaeus strode through the doors, his gaze cool, as if, temple or not, he didn't trust one smooth-fitting stone of this room any more than he did any of those in the outer courtyards.

As alien as it was for a warrior to enter the inner chamber, as forbidden as it was to bring weapons into this room, Cuin didn't feel any sense of wrongness at his presence—just as she no longer felt any unease with his presence by her side. In an odd way, his male vitality dovetailed perfectly with the chamber. She'd always thought of this as the province of females, but it was a plain fact that it had been designed and built by men, for men. Out of sheer practicality, the order had eventually become all female, because the brutally hard struggle for existence in these hills and valleys demanded that every physically able male put his hand to manual labor and, when necessary, take up arms for battle.

Cuin knelt to one side of the dais and pressed the center of the sun motif carved into the smooth gold surface. A portion of the dais slid open, and she extracted the last of the stone tablets that Chuli would distribute amongst the priestesses to carry, wrapped in with their clothing bundles.

When the tablets were stacked neatly to one side, she nodded, and Achaeus motioned two warriors forward, watching with an eagle eye as they carefully wrapped each tablet in soft, felted wool and left the room.

Cuin's gaze rested on the last, and most important, relic, where it lay nestled in a box carved from lapis lazuli and sumptuously padded with the finest linen.

The gold gleamed pure and bright, the curve of the ring broad, the clasp softened with age so that it seemed to have melted against the crystalline purity of the diamond it held.

The diamond itself was large and ancient, possibly more ancient than the gold it was presently set in. It was said to have once belonged to one of the sun men, the godlike beings who had walked the earth at the very beginning of time, before the golden age had crumbled into darkness.

She would take the ring, but not yet. Until they

were ready to leave, she wouldn't risk carrying the Sun Stone on her person. If there was one holy treasure Chumac coveted, this was it. Sliding the compartment closed, she rose to her feet and left the room, Achaeus at her side, like a very large, very protective jaguar.

Everything was set, the plan already in motion. Achaeus's men had begun collapsing parts of the temple and the maze, creating a crude barricade of rubble, leaving only key areas they needed to traverse untouched. The children were packed and ready to be escorted away at sunrise, in approximately five hours—the timing of their departure planned to coincide with a diversion that Achaeus had planned.

Five

The diversion was a dawn raid on Chumac's camp.

Chumac was dead, his guard decimated. Only Hotec and Chumac's clever priest, Nasek, had escaped, sliding away as the fighting had escalated. By the time Achaeus and his men reached the temple, still dripping from the river crossing, it was clear that Chumac's army was in disarray.

"The head of that particular serpent's been removed," Achaeus said, as he finished wedging the last intact door to the maze closed. He caught Cuin's gaze on his sheathed sword. "They don't like the edge on our iron."

"And they like us even less." Tule tore a strip of cloth from the bottom of his tunic, strapped it around a slash on his sinewy forearm and used his teeth to tighten the knot. "The serpent's head may be gone, but the body's still writhing. Hotec's busy gathering a force."

Achaeus's gaze was grim. "Under Nasek's command. Priest he may be, but he's been running Chumac's affairs ever since he became governor. He won't accept defeat easily."

Assim, a lean dark warrior, almost as tall as Achaeus, tested the door. When it wouldn't shift, he turned his coal-black gaze on Achaeus. "Leave," he said shortly. "We can take care of this."

Tule grinned. "Then I've got business in town."

Achaeus's fingers closed around Cuin's arm in what had become a familiar hold. "The only business you have is making sure Hotec's kept busy until we're free and clear, then you save your own skins. I'll see you both at sundown."

A shiver swept Cuin's spine at the curt series of commands. Beneath the terse words lay a bedrock of brotherhood and care. Achaeus and his men were bound by years of battle and loss. If Tule and Assim didn't show by sundown, he would go looking for them.

Taking up a torch, Achaeus led the way into the maze, but before they had traversed more than a few twists and turns, he halted, placed the torch in one of the brackets that were placed at intervals and shrugged out of the satchel that was strung across his back. "Breakfast," he said in explanation. "You're going to eat."

"I've already eaten." Her stomach still felt full from the feast Achaeus and his men had supplied the previous evening—the first fresh food they'd had for weeks—but even so, her mouth watered as he produced the perfect green globe of a melon, followed by a bright cluster of guavas.

"I watched you eat—it wasn't enough." With expert movements, he sliced the melon and split the guavas open. "Don't worry," he murmured as he spitted a slice of melon and passed it to her. "This knife doesn't get used in battle."

Cuin bit into the melon, savoring the fresh, sweet flavor. "Where did the fruit come from?" And, more to the point, how had he had time to find food at all? At dawn everything was locked down tight, the only movement that of farmers making their way to the fields and the sleepy change of sentries.

He passed her a guava. "Chumac's food store." His expression was hard. "He no longer needs it."

Cuin eyed the juicy flesh of the guava, then doggedly began forcing it down. Just one summer ago, her conscience wouldn't have allowed her to eat food taken from a dead man, but lately, she'd had a course in practicality. Chumac had stolen from the people— men, women and *children*—growing progressively richer and more powerful while many had starved. As much as her mind and stomach wanted to reject the fruit, Achaeus was right; it was a fact that her body needed the fuel.

When the last of the fruit was gone, Achaeus shouldered his satchel and reached into a leather pouch that was fastened to his weapons belt. "And this is for you."

Lean brown fingers uncurled and poured cloth so fine it flowed like liquid—a red flame in the darkness, bright as the feathers of one of the more exotic parakeets. Wonderingly, she caught at the long length of ribbon as it threatened to run through her fingers like water. The cloth warmed instantly to her touch, yet was so light she could hardly feel it. Her throat closed as she stared at the brilliant, floating fabric. She had received many tributes and gifts over the years, but they had always been for the temple, never for her.

The fabric was rare and bound to be costly, but if it came from Chumac, she couldn't accept this gift, no matter how well meant. Reluctantly, she shook her head.

His gaze gleamed with amusement, and, with a start she realized he knew exactly what she was thinking. "It didn't come from Chumac. It's silk from Cathay. I bought it from a Syrian trader who used to operate out of Ilium. Turn around."

The soft demand was as subtly shocking as the ribbon filling her hands like a fiery, weightless flower. Achaeus didn't threaten her on any physical level, but he made her helpless in a completely different way, turning her body into a strange mechanism that no longer obeyed the commands of her mind—making her feel emotions she'd only been aware of in others, never herself. Any form of carnality was forbidden for her—forbidden for all the priestesses—that was the reality of the temple. Occasionally a member of the order suffered, her vows strained to the breaking point by her desire for marriage and children, but that turmoil had never touched Cuin. Until now.

She'd poked and probed at the reasons why she should feel this way for this man, *now,* and ended up with more questions than answers. Perhaps the bald reality that Hotec wanted nothing so much as to spit her on his sword had affected her judgement? Whatever the reason, for the first time in her life she longed to anchor herself in a man's touch and taste for herself what it was that had made almost every woman in the village a mother, and the longing was edged with a hunger she was having difficulty suppressing. It was a stark fact that while she was the Cadis, she was used to having whatever she desired—and now she wanted the only thing that was truly forbidden to her: a man.

The breath frozen in her lungs, Cuin turned, giving Achaeus access to the thick dark plait that fell to her hips. His fingers, normally so dexterous with weapons and tools, were unusually clumsy as he wove the ribbon into her hair and, as long seconds passed, she became increasingly aware of Achaeus and the suffocating intimacy of what she was allowing.

Years had passed since Ilium had fallen, and yet, with all that he had lost and discarded, Achaeus had chosen to carry the ribbon with him. She may have been cloistered in a temple for most of her life, but she understood the way it was between a man and a woman. The silk was delicate and fine and utterly feminine—meant for a woman's hair. And not just any woman; it was a courting gift.

As she turned to face Achaeus, his palms framed her face, holding her captive. "Look at me. I won't hurt you."

"Most men wouldn't dare touch me." But the words carried no sting. Achaeus had touched her within seconds of their first meeting, and he had continued to touch her.

"I'm not most men." His hands tangled in her hair and cupped her nape. "And I've got nothing to lose."

Briefly, the rawness of everything he had lost was reflected in the depths of his eyes: family, friends, his home—a woman. Then his mouth touched hers and clung, unexpectedly soft and warm, surprising her beyond measure.

As his mouth lifted, Cuin went up on her toes, au-

tomatically following the source of warmth and softness as he slowly lifted his head. She lifted her lids
slowly. "So that's a kiss."

The faint wariness that lurked in his gaze, faded.
"No, this is a kiss."

His mouth touched hers again, and this time her lips
gave way under firm, coaxing pressure as his tongue
slid into her mouth. Shock momentarily paralyzed her.
He tasted like melons and guava, sweet and tart, and
inimitably male. His arms closed around her as the kiss
deepened, and, once again, she lifted up on her toes,
drawn deeper into his warmth as she curled her arms
around his neck and fitted her body against his. The
metal of his armor was cool against her breasts, and
the hard shape of his male flesh pressed into the soft
curve of her belly, making her stomach flip queerly
and an odd, shivering heat start in the pit of her belly.

Now she could see what all the fuss and anxiety were
about. Now she could see why this was forbidden.

The aching, shivering sensation grew, but as
Achaeus lifted his head, she became aware that the
shaking was emanating from outside her body.

The vibration turned into the grinding roar of an
earthquake as the ground surged and bucked.
Achaeus caught her to him as they fell in an awkward
sprawl, cushioning her landing with his body, and the
section of the maze they'd walked through just minutes ago collapsed, the detonation deafening. Dust

spewed in a choking wave, and with a muttered oath, Achaeus rolled, taking her with him so that they were wedged against a wall. For long minutes he held her pinned beneath him as the ground continued to surge, and dust and fragments of stone showered down.

When the movement finally stopped, Achaeus pulled Cuin to her feet and gathered up the torch, which had been dislodged from its holder. He opened the flaps on the satchel and slipped out a metal canister that contained the maps he'd drawn of the maze. He selected the level they were on and spread the rough parchment out on the floor.

Frowning, he examined the complex drawing and pinpointed their position. "The stonemasons who built this place knew what they were doing—I've never seen stone fitted so cleanly—but if this part has caved in, the chances are the whole structure could collapse. Show me the safest route out."

Coughing as dust swirled and settled, coating everything in gray, and still shaken from the unprecedented power of the earthquake, Cuin crouched beside Achaeus and studied the honeycomb of tunnels. "When we leave the inner chamber, this is the route we should take."

"We're not going to the inner chamber—there's no time."

Her jaw set. "I can't leave until I've got the Sun Stone."

"No." His glance was unequivocal. "The risk is too great."

Grimly, she stood her ground. "I'm the Cadis. I have a responsibility—"

"The temple is finished. I don't care if the gateway to paradise itself lies here—we're leaving." His expression was bleak. "The only responsibility you have is to twenty-nine women, twelve children and yourself. You'll have your work cut out just surviving—and in this land, it won't be long before every one of those women, old or not, has a husband."

Cuin flinched. The brutal succinctness of Achaeus's logic was as sharp as a lash, and the notion that she could strike out on her own and collect the jewel herself died. Cloistered and protected for years, she wasn't capable of the feat of endurance and strategy required to escape the valley alone. She *needed* Achaeus. Better that the jewel was buried with the temple than that it fell into pagan hands.

The temple is finished. It won't be long before every one of those women, old or not, has a husband.

Achaeus hadn't included her in the statement, but it was sweeping enough to hammer the reality home. In leaving the temple, they were leaving everything that was familiar and safe, and stepping into the unknown.

A raw shudder swept her. The adjustment was huge. *A husband.*

Yet the shock of her changed status wasn't so great that she couldn't accept it. Months of persecution and fear had done their work, slowly grinding away almost every part of the old life, turning their refuge into a prison and turning them into fugitives— yet, like amputees, they'd resisted change, clinging to the severed limb of the old until finally it had been forced from them.

Chest squeezed tight, eyes burning, Cuin stared at the wall of rubble dimly visible at the edge of the circle of torchlight until her vision blurred and swam. The total destruction of the path they'd just walked somehow seemed symbolic; there was no going back, only forward.

There was no longer a temple, and she was no longer the Cadis; she was simply…Cuin.

Brushing dust-laden strands of hair back from a face that was unaccountably damp, she forced her attention back to the map and blinked until her vision cleared. Achaeus hadn't asked her to find the fastest way out but the safest. That made sense, given that the structure was built from so many disparate parts. She had to think…*think*—she could walk these passages blindfolded, she knew them so well.

Her finger traced a route that passed achingly close to the main chamber and the Sun Stone, but she firmly closed the door on the idea that she could make a detour. With Hotec on their heels, along with the threat of more shock waves and cave-ins, it was suicidal to remain in the maze any longer than they had to. "Even though it might seem a contradiction in terms, the oldest structure will be the safest."

Frowning, Achaeus studied the quadrant she'd pointed out, then jerked his head in assent. "The workmanship there *is* different—the construction more complex—and the stone's as hard as adamantine. As for the rest of this place…" He rerolled the map, returned it to the canister, then slid the canister back into his pack. "If Hotec manages to gain entrance, he's welcome to it. The whole lot's ready to crack like a rotten egg."

They were almost at the West gate when the aftershock hit, the jolt not as violent as the first, but prolonged.

Achaeus pulled her tight against him, one large hand pressing her head into the curve of his shoulder and neck. She could feel his warmth, smell that familiar spicy blend of herbs and clean male skin—the resinous scent that always emanated from his hair—feel the thud of his heart, the faint, regular vibration comforting as the world shook itself to pieces around them.

With a jolt of surprise, she realized that when she was with Achaeus, even when they were at loggerheads, she was *happy,* the joy permeating even the darkest moments. She would happily die in his arms.

The grinding roar increased. Pain scored her back, her head—a heavy weight forced her down, down— as if the whole world had up-ended and was caving in. Then everything went black....

Six

A sharp sound jolted Quin out of sleep. She became aware of a stiff breeze cutting through the trees that sheltered the grove, and an ache at the base of her spine, as if she'd been lying on the rock for far too long.

A hard grip on her shoulder jerked her fully awake. She blinked into a glaring white light, and for a split second she swam in confusion, certain she was still in the underground tunnel staring into the guttering flame of the torch while the walls crumbled....

"About time. Girl, you frightened the living daylights out of me."

A sense of inevitability grounded Quin with a thump when she recognized Aunt Olivia crouched over her, a frown on her face.

Olivia's hand closed around hers, warm and calloused from endless hours spent tending the vegetable garden and orchard, and Quin scrambled to her feet, limbs stiff and awkward, and found herself pulled into a hard hug.

When Olivia released her, Quin's apology died on her lips. Even without the light of the torch, she could make out the worry etched into Olivia's face, and she was stricken with remorse.

She'd expected it to be daylight when she opened her eyes, but the sun had long since set. The faint rim of color still showing above the distant hills told her that it must be after nine—not quite full dark, but close.

She'd expected to catnap for a few minutes, and instead she had slept for more than five hours. A quick glance at her watch confirmed the time.

Five hours.

She flinched, her mind reeling, for a moment deaf to Olivia's scolding. It felt as if she'd been in the dream no more than a few minutes.

As Olivia began easing out of the rucksack that was strapped to her shoulders, Quin gripped her arm, halting the movement, and was abruptly reminded of how she'd felt when she'd been very small and had crawled into bed with Olivia whenever she'd had a nightmare. This hadn't been a bad dream, exactly. That was the problem; she didn't know what it had been.

Tersely, she related what she could remember of the dream, although parts of it had already slipped into oblivion. She could remember the woman's name, because it had been the same as her own, but when she reached for it, the name of the warrior eluded her.

Olivia's faded blue gaze sharpened as she listened. "Who was he? Did you recognize him?"

Quin's face went utterly blank as if she were looking inward to some secret place.

Olivia had long since ceased to question the strangeness of her great-niece. For a start, she knew that whatever odd genes Quin had inherited had originated from Olivia's own side of the family.

The Chambers' family skeleton was, by now, well documented. They had a long history of both men and women who had exhibited abilities beyond the norm, and those same abilities had relegated a good many of them to mental institutions. The rogue genes had skipped a generation, leaving Olivia and her two sisters, Hannah and Grace, living "normal" lives, only to reappear, seemingly stronger than ever, in Grace's youngest daughter, Rebecca, and then in Rebecca's child, Quin.

Quin shook her head. "He was *Ingles*," she said, using the Spanish word for European. "Very tall, with black hair."

Ingles. Olivia didn't like the detail; it pushed Quin's dream too close to the realm of psychic phenomena. There weren't many Europeans around *del*

Sol or the nearest village, Laguedo. Apart from old Avery Stanton, a doctor from the coastal settlement of Vacaro, who visited occasionally, the only Europeans Quin had ever seen were members of the medical teams who came to do vaccinations or, more rarely, mining companies' employees checking for mineral deposits. Not one of those men fit Quinn's description of the man in her dream.

Olivia eyed Quin sharply, frowning at her bare, sun-browned arms. Now that the sun was down, the temperature was chilly, courtesy of an icy westerly wind blowing off the Andes. "How do you know he was a European? If he had black hair, he could have been Latin or Indian."

"He could have been Latin," she allowed. "Definitely not Quechua or Mestizo." Her shoulders lifted in a brief shrug. "I don't know what made me think he was European. It was just an impression."

Olivia allowed herself to feel a cautious relief. She hoped that what Quin had experienced *had* been a dream and not a vision of some kind. God knows the girl had had a tough enough time of it as it was. She'd lived here since birth and run wild with the local children. Already the villagers knew she was different. Olivia did her best to keep the girl isolated from them, but Quin was her own worst enemy. She disappeared at the drop of a hat, flitting off into the jungle and mooning around the hills.

Quin's light blue gaze pierced Olivia's in the gloom, and Olivia's skin went goosy beneath the thick insulation of her sheepskin jacket. Sometimes the girl's gaze was ancient in her thin face, giving Olivia the ridiculous impression that the child was older than both her and Hannah's ages combined.

"I think he's coming here."

The flat certainty in Quin's voice made the small hairs at Olivia's nape lift. *Over her dead body.* "What on earth makes you think that?"

"I don't know, I just—" Quin shivered as if someone had just walked over her grave, and her gaze slid away, abruptly a child's again. "I just have this feeling, that's all."

A feeling.

With an effort of will, Olivia reined in the pent-up fear and frustration that had eaten at her when Quin had failed to turn up at sunset. The last thing any of them needed—and most particularly Quin—was for her to start giving credence to "feelings" and visions. "For a start, my girl, he doesn't exist. You had an unsettling dream—end of story. Don't go looking for complications."

"I have to help him," Quin said flatly, completely ignoring Olivia's statement. "Why else would I have dreamed like that?"

Impatience surged through Olivia, momentarily eclipsing the cacophony of aches and pains from stiffening muscles and brittle bones that made her feel every one of her sixty-one years. As much as she loved Quin and tried to understand the difficulties posed by her extra abilities, sometimes she wanted to shake all the nonsense out of her. "Help *who*, exactly? It was a dream. Forget about it."

"What if I can't?"

Despite the vulnerability inherent in the question, Quin's jaw was stubbornly squared, and Olivia heard what she was really saying. *What if I don't want to?*

Grimly, Olivia eased out of the light rucksack she'd brought with her, dumped it on the ground, rummaged inside, and handed Quin a jacket and a torch. The psychic stuff might rattle her cage, but *this* she could cope with. "Try harder."

For a moment she thought Quin was going to argue. She was as strong-minded, as tough, as any of the local boys—a demanding, complex being, neither child nor adult. It was a certain bet that she would be hell on wheels when she was fully grown. Lately, controlling all that pent up energy and intellect had had both her and Hannah tearing their hair out, but God help her, the girl was bright and, so far—touch wood—exhibited none of the mental fragility that had almost seen Quin's mother—Rebecca—forcibly committed. Despite the fact that Quin had inherited "the Chambers Curse," this time it seemed that the varied and tortured talents that had haunted Olivia's

family as far back as the Norman invasion had finally
metamorphosed into something useful. Quin could
heal.

In her strange way, she healed everyone. Olivia
hadn't credited it at first, until she'd been stricken
with one of her periodic bouts of malaria and Quin
had touched her with hands that had poured golden
warmth. She'd been up and about within twenty-four
hours, when normally she would have been confined
to her room, too weak to do anything useful, for days.

Hannah had benefited, too. The arthritis that had
been slowly stiffening her joints, and which would
have stopped her performing even the most basic of
surgeries, had miraculously eased.

As Quin shrugged into the jacket and zipped it,
Olivia played the torch around the grove, spotlight-
ing the giant rocks, now cast in a deep well of gloom,
and the claustrophobic tangle of vines and undergrowth that crawled over everything, absorbing light
even on the sunniest days. Her spine tightened as the
play of shadow revealed what daylight had previously hidden amongst the untidy scrabble of boulders
and stones—the straight edge of a stone that had
been hand-cut and dressed.

For a split second her heart stopped in her chest
and she forgot to breathe. The cut edge pulled at her,
making her mouth water and her fingers itch to touch
stone that had been worked by a people who had

lived hundreds, no, *thousands,* of years ago—the lure close to irresistible. A large block this far up the hill meant it was likely there was a structure buried right here, beneath their feet, or perhaps further up the slope—since the block could conceivably have slid down the hill. And if there was a structure on the hillside, then it was also highly probable that the site continued on down to the valley floor, because that was just plain good sense. Whoever had built here would have needed the water and, besides, the river would have provided transportation.

Abruptly, she swung the torch away and turned her back on the mystery of Incan stone in a valley this far east of the Inca Trail. If her logic was correct, the site would be large, and they couldn't afford the publicity that even a small find would attract. When she and Hannah had removed Quin's mother from John Mallory's custody—and from England—they had acted against a court decree. To compound their crime, Rebecca had been pregnant. They had effectively stolen Lord Mallory's wife and his heir. In saving Rebecca from incarceration in a mental institution, they had become fugitives, but it had been worth it. Rebecca hadn't lived beyond childbirth, but Quin had thrived. Olivia was certain that if Mallory had had a hand in Quin's upbringing, he would have crushed her. *"Don't come here again."*

Her voice was harsher than she'd intended, and for

the space of a heartbeat, Quin's gaze fixed on hers, openly curious.

"What did you just see?"

Not for the first time, Olivia wondered if the girl could actually read minds; then she dismissed the fanciful notion and busied herself refastening the flap of the pack. "Nothing, except that this place is even creepier by night. I don't know what you see in it."

Quin's grin flashed white. She pointed at the opening in the trees, which framed the mission where it nestled, lights glowing, in the distance. "What do you think?"

The view was clear and unimpeded, and encompassed the river crossings and the track up the hill. As a lookout, it couldn't be better.

Olivia let out a breath and straightened, relieved that Quin had allowed herself to be distracted. She obviously hadn't seen the cut stone. If she had, she would have recognized it immediately and pestered the living daylights out of Olivia until she'd confirmed her "find."

Quin had never visited any archaeological sites, but she'd seen enough pictures and diagrams—and she had an uncanny knack for identifying and dating artifacts that others brought to the mission. Tomorrow, if Olivia could slip away unnoticed, she would come back and bury the stone. The girl was fascinated enough with this place as it was. If she knew there was a ruin here, they wouldn't be able to keep her away *or* keep her quiet.

Quin flicked on her torch and reached for the rucksack, easing it on with the supple grace of youth. Since she was already two inches taller than Olivia, and physically stronger, Olivia didn't argue.

Quin adjusted the shoulder straps until the fit was snug. "By the way, how did you find me?"

Olivia turned up the collar of her jacket as they began picking their way down the hill, her expression wry as she followed in her great-niece's wake. Somehow the girl had derailed the monumental telling off Olivia had planned to deliver and was now attempting to take charge. "Did you really think we didn't know about this place?"

As the last light disappeared from the horizon, the glow from the narrow mission windows looked small and insubstantial against the vaulting darkness. Warm and welcoming though the lights were, Olivia's stomach tightened with worry of a different kind.

Thirteen years ago they'd had money, and it had bought them this bolt-hole, but the years had eaten away at their nest egg, until now they were practically as poor as the local people who came to the mission for help.

The community at Laguedo was comprised mostly of the elderly and the young, because the able-bodied men and women had migrated to the cities or, worse, melted into the hills to join up with communist guerrilla groups or the local drug cartel. The mission stumbled on, short of funds, short of food and medical supplies, but mostly, woefully short of labor, and out here *everything* required physical effort.

The road system was almost nonexistent, consisting of narrow tracks that were dangerous at best and often impassable in winter. In addition, the swing bridge that spanned the Agueda River, providing the only road into and out of the valley, was a constant deterrent to using the aging Bedford truck they'd bought with the property. The bridge had been built by the mission over sixty years ago, and had originally been intended for use by pedestrians and carts only. Every time Jose inched the old truck over the bridge, Olivia held her breath, waiting for ancient beams and steel hawsers to finally give up the ghost.

Isolation aside, there was no piped water supply or sewage system. An ancient generator supplied them with heat and lighting—most of the time—and the hot water system was supplemented by a coal-fired boiler. Every six months a run to the coast kept them supplied in dry goods for most of the year, if they were careful, but stringent budgeting didn't count for much when a disaster like an earthquake or a flood sent people flocking to them for shelter and medical attention. The Peruvian government provided compensation, but it was usually much later, and not nearly enough to cover their outlay.

Over the years, she and Hannah had taken up the financial slack with their own funds, but now their resources were close to exhausted. At their current rate of expenditure, within two years they would be broke—unable to afford to pay wages and unable to buy medical supplies. Without funds, they would have to close their doors, which would break both Hannah's heart and her own. The impoverished local people *needed* the medical center.

To survive, they needed cash. They could stumble on if she made a trip to England to liquidate assets, but the risk that if they did so they would lose Quin was so high that neither she nor Hannah was willing to consider that option unless they were forced to it. Almost equally as hazardous was the option of selling their property and chattels through a legal firm in Lima, but if they did that, they could attract Quin's father—Lord Mallory—to Peru.

Even if they got their hands on more money, it wouldn't be enough—they still needed an able-bodied workforce and, in this desolate part of the country, that was an almost insurmountable problem. Trying to hold young men in the valley was like trying to hold water in a colander. And trying to find a replacement for Jose, who not only did the heavy gardening work but kept the buildings and the Bedford in reasonable repair, had so far proved impossible. It was only a matter of time before he retired, and on the day he left, their viability would disintegrate. To Olivia, the equation was simple. Without the support of a man who was physically strong and had enough knowledge of mechanics to keep the truck and their generator running, they couldn't survive here.

They could lay their hands on more money if they were pushed, but the issue of funding aside, what they really needed was a miracle.

Seven

Five years later
The Tasman Sea, thirty miles off the eastern coast
of Australia, latitude thirty degrees south.

Michael Linden nudged the cabin door open with his foot, sighted down the short barrel of a SIG Sauer, and coldly surveyed the man lying bound and gagged in the cramped forward cabin of the *Mariane.*

Jake Lombard was the eldest of the Lombard brothers. He was also reportedly the toughest, and Linden hadn't wanted to touch him, but Harper hadn't allowed him the option of choosing a softer target. The crazy son of a bitch had wanted to inflict maximum damage on the Lombard family, and taking down the heir apparent was the ultimate hit.

As logical as Harper's strategy was, it didn't

solve Linden's problem. He'd been left hanging out to dry with a target who was rumored to be even more of a cold-blooded killer than he was himself.

His gaze was wary as he inventoried his prisoner. Lombard had been shot in the thigh, but Linden didn't trust a gunshot wound to control a man who had a reputation for being ice-cold and ruthless.

Linden didn't mind "cold" as an adjective. He expected anyone with any kind of grip on reality to have discarded the fuzzy illusions that most of the human race were burdened with—it was the "ruthless" part that worried him. That one descriptive word, supplied by a psychopath like Egan Harper, put Lombard in the category of target that Linden usually went out of his way to avoid. In his opinion, pitting himself against someone who had the potential to take him out was a major flaw in any execution contract.

But, speculation or not, Linden was also aware of the hype that surrounded the wealthy Lombard family of hoteliers. Money and media attention were notorious for building marketable fantasies. Whether Lombard's reputation was deserved, or the product of a few overactive imaginations and a nice little publicity campaign to scare off business competitors, didn't matter. When it came down to it, Linden could only rely on what he'd observed, and so far, that involved two salient facts. Lombard had watched his girlfriend die without flinching, and he was tough enough that he hadn't whined about his own wound.

Linden nudged the door wider and studied the pulse at Lombard's throat. The fact that he was forced to remain in such close proximity to his target while he waited for the execution order made him, quite frankly, nervous. He didn't like to be this close— ever—and damned if he would do it again.

But Harper wanted Lombard kept alive, at least for another few hours, in case there was a hitch with the money.

Linden's mouth curved cynically. Of course there would be a hitch with the money. In his view, Harper was mentally deficient if he thought he was actually going to collect. He seemed to have forgotten the truism that people who had the balls to make the kind of money the Lombard family had, generally knew how to hang on to it.

Crouching down in the cramped quarters of the cabin, Linden shoved the barrel of the SIG into the soft flesh just below Lombard's jaw, gritting his teeth at the rhythmic, oily heave of the launch. He could already feel himself turning green. The sea had gotten progressively lumpier through the day, and at the moment his time limit below deck was approximately thirty seconds before his stomach tried to turn itself inside out.

Suspicious when there was no response from the

apparently sleeping man, Linden jabbed the gun into Lombard's throat again, noting that he was pale and sweating, and a flush rimmed his cheekbones. This time Lombard's eyelids flickered, but he remained slack, his breathing slow and shallow.

Oh yeah, he was a sick puppy. "Not so tough, after all."

Linden estimated that Lombard could last another two or three days without medical care, but he'd lost a lot of blood, and infection had set in. Even if he was hospitalized at this point, he would still be a stretcher case for a month.

Satisfied that his prisoner was finally out of commission, Linden felt beneath the semiconscious man to check the knots on the rope, then inspected the bloody mess that was Lombard's thigh. As he bent closer, his nostrils filled with the thick, sweet scent of blood, and nausea rolled through him in a hot, greasy wave.

"Shit."

Clenching his jaw, he straightened, stumbling against the wall as he backed out of the stuffy cabin and kicked the door closed.

Jake's lids flipped open, all his attention focused on the narrow hallway outside the cabin door and the sound of Linden's receding footsteps.

It was time to get to work. Linden checked on him at approximately hourly intervals. Factoring in a few minutes as a margin of error, he estimated he had a window of forty-five minutes, max. Ideally, he should wait until dark before making a move, but that was hours away, and he couldn't take the risk of waiting that long.

Most hostages didn't live past the first twenty-four hours. According to his calculations, at least thirty-five hours had passed since he and his fiancée, Rafaella, had been taken captive while leaving a restaurant in downtown Sydney—long enough for any deal that Harper had floated to evaporate. His family would have stalled for time while they threw their resources into finding him, but Jake was pragmatic about his chances. Harper was too well organized; this time he'd assembled a team of professionals.

Jake had even heard of Michael Linden. He'd sniped in 'Nam in the sixties, then disappeared for a while before resurfacing as a mercenary. When he'd gotten tired of being ripped off and jerked around by multinationals trying to "reshape" economies in third-world countries, he'd put himself on the open market as a professional hit man.

Linden had been cool and very slick. He'd held them in a warehouse until he'd received a phone call; then he had calmly raised his arm and fired two shots. Grief and icy rage knotted his stomach. Rafaella had died instantly, but Linden had been careful not to kill

Jake. Within an hour of the kidnapping, they had put to sea; shortly before dawn, Linden had disposed of Rafaella's body over the side.

Gritting his teeth, Jake flexed frozen shoulder and arm muscles, and slowly forced his wrists apart, ignoring the burning pain where the rope sawed into raw flesh.

The rope they'd used to bind him had originally been tight enough to cut off his circulation, but it had been wet for a day and a half now—soaked with the seep of blood from his thigh and wrists.

He hadn't been able to undo the knots, but he'd loosened the hemp enough with constant flexing that he would finally be able to make the stretch required to force his hands under and around his buttocks, then jackknife his legs and feet through the loop made by his arms. Once he could remove the gag from his mouth and actually see what he was doing with the rope, he would be able to work the knots with his teeth.

Craning his head, he fastened his teeth on the edge of the sleeping bag he was lying on, clenching on fiber-filled nylon as he wrenched his shoulders and arms down and simultaneously curled his body into a tight ball, groaning as fiery pain exploded through his thigh as he forced his wrists down his back and finally managed to hook them beneath his buttocks.

Sucking in a breath, he gathered his strength for

the next effort. The series of movements required to complete the maneuver of sliding his hands beneath his feet made his head pound and hot lights explode in front of his eyes. Warmth spread across his leg, and distantly he realized he'd torn open both the entry and exit wounds in his thigh again. For some time he floated hazily, his head buzzing, body slack, his awareness oddly skewed, as if his mind had temporarily disengaged itself from his body—but he hadn't passed out; he was still conscious, still functioning.

The next step was to restore some sort of circulation to his fingers, because he would need a measure of dexterity when it came time to attack the knots at his ankles. He wanted to get moving, find a weapon, formulate a strategy for escaping, but he had to do things in the right order. Missing a step could be fatal. And he hadn't waited this long to mess up his only chance at survival.

Once the gag was off, he attacked the knots with his teeth. Minutes later his hands were free, and he noticed with a blank sense of surprise that the bastards had left him his watch.

That was a mistake. Linden might be good with a gun, but he wasn't good with people. Jake had seen that character trait in snipers before—they could kiss their weapon good-night, but they didn't understand what mattered to people, or the basics of breaking down a prisoner.

Allowing him to keep his watch was a fundamental mistake, because it gave him information, and information was power. He could mentally orient himself much more quickly, because he could monitor time and keep an accurate log of the routine of his captors—and he could run a schedule.

The time was two-forty-five in the afternoon, which meant it had been *forty* hours since he'd been kidnapped, not the thirty-five he'd estimated.

Grimly, he worked the knots at his ankles, then tore his pants leg where the bullet had punched holes front and back and used the fabric to bind the wound, pulling the broad strip of cloth tight in an effort to immobilize the muscles.

He had been lucky; the bullet hadn't shattered bone or nicked an artery. If the artery had been cut, he would have bled out inside half an hour. But, luck aside, the wound could still kill him. The initial paralyzing shock of the round punching through his thigh had worn off, but the combined effects of blood loss, dehydration and soft tissue damage had kicked in with a vengeance. It had become infected, and the poison was spreading through his system, draining his energy and clouding his mind. His inability to accurately judge time indicated that his physical condition was worse than he'd thought. His perception had become impaired, and with every hour that passed, he would become weaker and punchier.

Bracing one hand against the wall, he hauled himself upright and tested his ability to stand. If he couldn't stand, he couldn't walk; if he couldn't walk, he would die.

The bandage was firm enough that he could bear his own weight—just. He would be able to walk, as long as he avoided putting too much pressure on the leg.

Moving awkwardly, Jake began searching the cabin for a weapon or anything else that might boost his chances of survival. Despite being tiny, the small forward bunkroom provided access to some of the largest storage areas on the launch, just beneath the bow. The first locker contained boxes of wet suits and soft-soled neoprene boots, the second was stacked with buoyancy compensators—the inflatable, sleeveless jackets divers used to control descent and ascent. The final locker contained life jackets, several bottles of sunscreen and a variety of pairs of sunglasses. There were no hard objects of any kind, unless he counted the metal valves attached to the tubes hanging off the BCs. Any hardware like diving knives and spear guns would be stored along with the snorkeling gear and oxygen tanks somewhere on deck, which put them effectively out of Jake's reach. To have any chance at all, he needed to be armed *before* he ventured outside. Linden was never without a sidearm, and he had to assume that the other man on the launch, Horton, was armed, as well.

The life jackets were a good option, and so were the wet suits. If Jake went into the water in his weakened state, he was going to have difficulty staying afloat, and the chances were he could be in the water for hours waiting for rescue.

Pulling out the first box of wet suits, he began checking them for size.

As much as he wanted to kill both Harper and Horton, his best option was stealth. He didn't know if the launch had a runabout, but most vessels this size had some kind of secondary craft with them. If there was a runabout tied behind the boat, he might have a chance, but if it was an inflatable lashed to the bow, he would be in trouble. Manhandling an inflatable into the water would take time and make too much noise.

Warm as it was, if he ended up swimming, his main problem was going to be hypothermia. Neoprene didn't keep the water out, but it did keep in body warmth, and it had the added advantage of being buoyant. Wearing a wet suit, his whole body would float.

He selected the largest, thickest grade of suit he could find and stripped off his shoes and pants, opting to leave his shirt on to provide another layer of warmth. Clenching his jaw, he eased the overalls on, wincing as the tight neoprene slid over his bandaged thigh. He fastened the Velcro flaps at his shoulders, then thrust his arms through the jacket, zipped it and tested the suit for suppleness. Limited as he was with his leg movement, he had to make sure that his upper body was unrestrained. When he was satisfied that he could move unimpeded, he selected a pair of neoprene boots.

A sharp clattering made him freeze in the motion of pulling on the second boot. The faint sounds came from the galley. Given the fact that it was early afternoon, Horton was either making a late lunch or getting a drink, in which case he wouldn't come near Jake, because Linden was the only one who checked on him. Horton was the amateur—in charge of piloting the boat and assigned all the menial tasks.

A full minute after hearing the faint sounds of Horton leaving the galley and climbing the ladder back up to the flying bridge where he habitually sat, Jake opened the cabin door.

The rich aroma of coffee hit him as soon as he stepped out into the cramped corridor, making his mouth draw tight and his stomach clench. He was so dehydrated, he was hardly producing any saliva, and the knowledge of just how close he was to complete incapacitation knotted his belly. He had to rehydrate as quickly as possible, and a jolt of caffeine wouldn't hurt, either.

But before he allowed himself to either eat or

drink, he examined the drawers and selected a short-handled knife with a pointed blade. After sliding the knife into the sleeve of the wet suit, he grabbed the half-full coffeepot from its rest and the carton of milk that was sitting on the bench. Swiftly he removed and discarded the lid of the coffeepot, tipped the contents of the sugar bowl into the coffee, then eased back into the cabin nearest to the galley and closed the door. With hands that shook, he emptied the carton of milk into the coffeepot, swirled the now lukewarm mixture around to dissolve the sugar, then drank with long, steady gulps, not waiting to taste the liquid, simply filling his belly as quickly as he could.

Heat formed in the pit of his stomach as his system grabbed the calories and the sugar acted quickly to steady him.

His next foray out into the main cabin netted a portable emergency radio, which operated on a VHF ship-to-ship band.

It wasn't as good as the EPIRB which had been attached to the wall, but right now the emergency positioning beacon was out of the question. It was too awkward to carry when he was going into a combat situation, and he couldn't afford to activate it unless Linden and Horton were incapacitated, because the light and sound effects would instantly alert them to the fact that he had escaped.

He switched the portable radio on, set the beacon

to transmit on the ship-to-ship frequency, and zipped it inside the front of his wet suit. It wasn't the perfect solution but, until he had control of the launch, it was the best he could do.

Since leaving Sydney Harbor, they'd been on the move constantly. Linden was moored now, which meant he'd found a reef, but the chances were he'd steered clear of going too far north toward Great Barrier Reef, because he wouldn't want to be disturbed by tourist traffic. Jake's best guess was that they were situated somewhere between Sydney and Brisbane, far enough out that they wouldn't be disturbed, in a relative dead zone as far as seacraft went, except for shipping. If they were anywhere near the shipping lanes, chances were a ship would pick up the beacon if it came close enough, which was the problem. The VHF radio was meant for emergency use only, the range no more than a few kilometers. If he had to rely on it, he was probably screwed.

There was also the sobering fact that ships had been known to ignore beacons. And even if a vessel did pick up the signal, locating his exact position would be like finding a needle in a haystack.

He did a quick search of the cabins and came up empty. If Linden had any extra weaponry with him, he was keeping it topside, or on his person. Checking his watch and noting that his forty-five minutes were almost up, Jake briefly returned to the forward cabin, slipped on a life jacket and moved back out into the main cabin to wait.

Eight

The faint vibration of footsteps warned Jake that one of the men was coming below deck. Seconds later, Horton stepped into the galley. Uncoiling from a semicrouched position, Jake locked one hand around Horton's throat, choking off sound as he drove up with the knife. Horton's forward movement impaled him further, but at the crucial moment, Jake's leg crumpled, and he lost his tight grip on Horton's throat.

A gurgling moan escaped, low-pitched and irregular enough that Linden wouldn't mistake it for the cry of the gulls wheeling above the boat. Sucking in a breath, Jake shoved Horton into the doorjamb, no longer concerned with muffling sound, and pressed hard on his carotid. Within seconds Horton's eyes glazed over and he went limp, but it was seconds too long, as Jake heard the telltale creak overhead as Linden moved toward the ladder.

Withdrawing the knife, Jake allowed Horton to drop to the deck and searched him for a firearm. When he came up blank, he unhooked the fire extinguisher from its wall bracket. All he could do was keep his forward momentum. If he retreated back into one of the cabins, he would be trapped; Linden would simply bide his time and pick him off. Using the thin ply wall of the galley as cover, Jake gauged the moment when Linden's balance and line of sight would be most compromised—the split second his feet hit the pitching deck—then lunged through the opening and depressed the lever on the fire extinguisher.

Powdery white chemical sprayed into Linden's face. He reeled, slamming into the railing, and the gun discharged with a flat crack. Paneling splintered as Jake ducked and crabbed sideways in automatic reflex, lurching as one foot caught on Horton's outstretched arm, forcing him to transfer all of his weight to his injured leg. Hot pain exploded up his side, and the knife slipped from his fingers as he grabbed the railing to steady himself.

Jake's head jerked up as Linden recovered his balance and ripped off coated dark glasses. His face was covered in white powder, but where the sunglasses had been there was a strip of tanned flesh. His vision was virtually unimpeded as he swung the handgun up. Adrenaline pumped. With a grunt, Jake pivoted on his good leg and threw the extinguisher, knocking Linden off balance once more and sending the gun spinning over the side.

For an endless moment the gun hung above the waves, sun glinting off metal; then it dropped into the sea with a faint plop, taking Jake's options with it. He was injured and unarmed, and his leg kept failing him. He had no idea how well armed Linden was, but, given that he was a professional, Jake had to assume the man had a backup gun. If he were doing the job himself, he would have both an ankle gun and a knife.

Gripping the railing, he pivoted, twisting his body to protect his injured leg. As he half stumbled, half fell into the sea, a lukewarm trace of black humor penetrated the cold rage that had driven him from the moment Linden had put a gun to his head. Next time, he wouldn't leave home without an automatic weapon and a supply of C4.

Drawing his backup gun, Linden gripped the railing and scanned the sea, cursing beneath his breath at his stinging eyes and the sun glaring off the choppy expanse of blue. He checked the other side of the launch and came up empty again.

A faint splashing sound at the rear of the boat had him spinning. For tense seconds he couldn't discern what was wrong; then he realized that the runabout, which normally trailed several meters back from the launch, was more distant than it should be. Lombard must have untied the rope at the bow of the small boat in an attempt to steal it.

Linden stepped over Horton, who was still twitching, and examined the wet weather steering station inside—a duplicate of the one on the bridge—and hit the ignition. Shoving the launch in reverse, he opened the throttle, uncaring that the anchor was down. There would be slack in the rope, and chances were that the anchor would naturally unhook rather than hold, allowing him to back right up to the runabout.

Water splashed over the stern, and diesel fumes filled the cabin, as the launch churned backward. When the runabout loomed closer, Linden cut the throttle and flicked the gear lever into neutral, leaving the engines on idle. The launch continued its wallowing backward momentum as he gripped the handgun and walked to the stern, grimly keeping his balance as he checked over both sides of the railing in case Lombard tried to pull anything else.

Gaze cold and alert, Linden secured the runabout, registering the small lurch that signaled that the anchor, which had pulled free when he'd started backing the boat, had once again drifted to the bottom, caught and taken hold. Almost instantly, the heaving motion caused by the ocean swells pushing against the side of the boat started, and Linden braced himself, keeping his gaze on the runabout as it swung around nose-first into the current along with the launch.

Lombard was too badly hurt to get back on the *Mariane* unless he used the backboard at the stern, and Linden had that covered.

Long minutes passed while Linden watched the runabout and the blue-green water at the stern.

The abrupt dip of a large sea bird momentarily distracted him. Automatically, his gaze swept the area the bird was hovering over, then fixed on a flash of yellow.

Snarling in disbelief, he hauled himself up the narrow ladder and onto the flying bridge. He grabbed a long dark case stored beneath one of the bench seats, set it on the cushion, released the catches and flipped the lid. Methodically, he extracted the stock and barrel of a Remington rifle. With slick movements, he locked the two pieces together, slid the bolt into place, attached the telescopic sight, then slotted two cartridges into the chamber. The scope was zeroed for six hundred meters—more than enough. The Remington wasn't the kind of state-of-the art, precision tool he used for long-range work—damned if he was going to bring any of his good gear onto a boat—but it was perfect for the unstable sea conditions.

Fitting the stock to his shoulder, Linden searched

the sea and finally spotted Lombard, several degrees south of where he'd calculated he should be, which meant that either the launch had continued to swing in the current, throwing off his estimate, or the canny bastard had changed direction.

Despite the fact that Lombard was hampered by the life jacket, he was swimming strongly and was already more than two hundred and fifty meters from the *Mariane*.

With calm, steady movements, Linden activated the image intensifier and reacquired Lombard with the scope. The bright yellow of the life jacket made him an easy target, but the sway of the flying bridge, worse now in a stiffening afternoon breeze, kept spoiling Linden's aim and, quite frankly, made him sick.

Sucking in a deep breath, he forced himself to ignore the sour taste in the back of his throat and the continual disruption to his balance. As he exhaled, he unclenched his jaw and counted, using the discipline of more than three decades of sniping to steady his aim.

Slowly, tension flowed out of him. He drew another breath, held it, then exhaled, until he finally reached the place in the breath cycle when the fine tremor set up by muscular tension dissipated.

He squeezed the trigger once, twice. The first shot was wide—punching into a shoulder; the second caught Lombard in the head, jerking him sideways.

Linden continued to observe, patiently waiting out the swells to check that Lombard didn't move. After several minutes, he lowered the rifle, satisfied.

As he dismantled the gun to clean it, Linden's gaze caught on Horton's out-flung hand, which was just visible from his position on the flying deck. The twitching had finally stopped.

Of everything that had gone wrong with this job, Horton's death pissed him off the most.

As far as Linden had been able to ascertain, Horton's only area of expertise had been driving the boat. That had been damn useful while he'd been alive, because Linden hated boats. He had enough knowledge to get by, but that was it. With Horton gone, he was left with the problem of getting back to land and disposing of a launch that had become the kind of crime scene that would have any forensic expert rubbing his hands with glee.

When he'd finished cleaning and dismantling the weapon, Linden began loading the runabout with his equipment, food and water, and enough spare fuel that he wouldn't have a problem reaching land. Using a compass to take a bearing, he ascertained his approximate position, then lifted the floor panels at the rear of the launch and pulled the bung. Immediately, water fountained into the boat.

The launch took an hour to go down, because he'd forgotten to open all the doors to the cabins and the trapped air kept the *Mariane* afloat, but Linden waited it out. When the charter vessel finally disappeared beneath an eruption of bubbles, he tossed the rope that secured the runabout to the launch, and which he'd used as an impromptu anchor, into the sea, powered up the motor and headed for land.

Nine

The container vessel Volodya, *sailing out of Sydney. Crew, 19. Call sign VDSR3.*

The radio operator clicked the hand piece of the spare VHF set he was repairing, swore beneath his breath and rummaged for the screwdriver. Seconds later, he examined the exposed circuitry, systematically tracing the connections to see which one had failed this time. Absently, he reached for his coffee, grimacing when he found it had gone cold and a thick skin had formed on top.

Setting the mug down amidst the chaotic tumble of tools and colored wiring, he picked up the soldering iron and delicately melted both ends of the broken connection, coaxing them together to complete the circuit. He had fixed this set a hundred times, and no doubt he would fix it again, but on the long haul from Sydney to Vacaro, an isolated settlement on the Peruvian coast, performing minor repair work of any kind was a welcome distraction.

As he reassembled the radio, his finely tuned ear gradually became aware of a consistent, low-level noise. At first he thought it was static, perhaps caused by the handset of the radio on the bridge being put down carelessly, so that the channel had been left open. A quick telephone call to the bridge confirmed that the radio was presently not in use, and that the handset was hooked correctly in place.

Frowning, the radio operator turned the volume up and sat back to listen, all his attention centered on what he now discerned to be a faint electronic pulse. The signal was weak and fragmented, and occasionally it disappeared altogether, but no one who'd worked in shipping could miss its meaning.

"Shit," he muttered, and scrabbled for the phone, knocking the coffee over. The sound was a mayday.

Anatoli Baklanov, captain of the *Volodya,* listened to the signal, his expression impassive. Shipping law and simple decency demanded he give the order to turn the ship and render aid to whoever was in trouble, but lately, for Anatoli, the subject of laws and contracts, rules and regulations, had become a gray world. He was no longer certain where the line between right and wrong was drawn—or where he and his crew stood in relation to it.

In the shipping world, they were small fry. Mainly operating as a cargo service in the Pacific Basin, but with a recent change of ownership, the company had also expanded into the container trade, inching in where they could to compete with the larger companies plying between North America, Australasia and Japan.

On this trip, they had had several new destinations added to their usual route, lengthening their circuit by a good three weeks. Some of the ports on the manifest made Anatoli's stomach hollow and his gut burn. He had his suspicions about the new owner and some of the cargo they had taken aboard, but his concerns had all been met with blank looks and smooth answers. The bottom line had been that if he no longer found his job satisfactory, he was welcome to leave.

In Anatoli's view, that was all very well—he could find another job—but his crew was another matter. The *Volodya* carried nineteen men, and, of those, a core of fourteen had been with him for more than a decade. Six of the fourteen had served under his command in the navy. If he went, most of the crew would walk with him, and that posed difficulties. In the cutthroat world of shipping, the likelihood that they would all find new berths was slim.

The radio operator sat back in his chair, the knowledge of their dilemma clear in his gaze. "We can't just leave him."

Anatoli continued to listen to the weakening signal—now almost gone. His responsibility toward his men weighed heavily. He had come to the realization that they had all made a terrible mistake in accepting employment with the *Volodya*'s new owner. In signing the new contracts, he was now certain, they had allowed Varinski to turn them all into criminals.

With a last feeble pulse of static, the radio went silent, and for the first time in more than twenty years, Anatoli lost his temper.

Varinski might have made them criminals on paper, but he would be damned if he would abandon his humanity.

Curtly, he gave the command and hoped they weren't too late. They were presently traveling well under full speed at twelve knots, but even so, it would take time to turn the ship.

An hour later, the inert form of what appeared to be a diver was winched on board. The ship's doctor, Pyotr Chapaev, a medical student who had dropped out of the program in his fourth year and who also doubled as a kitchen hand, was uncertain for the first few minutes whether the man was dead or alive.

Anatoli watched over the procedure as Pyotr sliced the wet suit away and searched for a pulse. He didn't want to feel relief that a man had died, but it was a fact that his death would simplify the situation for him and his crew.

Squatting down, he touched the unconscious man's wrist. Even though he knew the diver had probably been in the water for hours and was likely hypothermic, the icy feel of his skin was unsettling. He studied the man's chest and could detect no movement.

Chapaev primed a needle and searched for a vein.

Anatoli frowned as Chapaev inserted the needle. "Give it up, Pyotr, he's dead."

Pyotr barely registered the captain's command as he injected the adrenaline. The tenets that he'd lived by when he'd been training to be the most brilliant doctor in Petrograd—before his wife and child had disappeared and his life had turned to shit—crowded out everything but the vital needs of his patient. Tipping the diver's head back, he sent oxygen into the man's lungs in short bursts. As he placed both hands over the diver's chest and began to pump, he spared the captain a quick, impatient glance. "He's not dead until he's warm and dead. His core temperature is twenty-nine degrees centigrade. If he's still not breathing when he reaches thirty-two, you can have him…." His mouth quirked in what he'd always been told was a ghoulish grin. "Until then, *he's mine.*"

Broodingly, Anatoli moved out of the way as the blankets and hot water bottles Chapaev had demanded arrived, and the first officer and the engineer, both of whom had medical training, moved in to assist.

Not for the first time since he'd given the order to turn the ship, Anatoli questioned his sanity.

The fact that they had found the man at all had been little less than a miracle, because it had taken them fully thirty minutes to relocate the signal after they'd turned the ship. When the transmission was strong enough that they should have been practically on top of the lost craft, the *Volodya*'s engines had been disengaged.

Without visual confirmation of any wreckage, and with the beacon still operating, they'd had to assume that what they had was no longer a boat in trouble but a man overboard. In a last-ditch effort, a tender had been lowered into the water by crane, and even that decision had hung on a knife's edge, because the sun had been setting. If the conditions hadn't been abnormally calm, and many of his crew ex-navy and trained in search-and-rescue work, it was unlikely they would have carried on with the search.

The first officer's head jerked up. "I've got a pulse."

Pyotr's own heart hammered as he monitored the pulse. It was thready, but regular. "He's not breathing on his own yet—we could still lose him." But optimism leaped through his veins. Sometimes the very cold that killed also preserved life, putting the body into a state that was close to suspended animation. That was what he had banked on, but it was always a wild card. If there was one thing he'd learned at medical school it was that human life was a crazy, crazy thing. Sometimes people died for almost no reason at all, and other times people quite simply refused to die. He'd seen it with an old woman who had lost both her legs and half of her bowel in a bomb blast, again with a young child who had shrunk and withered with leukemia until he was little more than a skeleton before he had gone into remission. Now, unbelievably, he was seeing that phenomenon again.

With a grin, Pyotr watched as his patient stabilized further—his heart settling into a rock-steady beat. Whoever the stranger was, whatever drove him, Pyotr wouldn't want to be in the shoes of whoever had pumped two bullets into him, then tried to vaporize his head with the third.

Two hours later, Anatoli once again surveyed their unconscious passenger. Chapaev had removed a bullet from the man's shoulder, installed a drain to both shoulder and thigh, and cleaned and bandaged his head wound. Now he was in the process of hooking the patient up to a saline drip to minimize shock and dehydration.

Their comatose diver was alive but, breathing, he posed a problem.

So far, luck, if that was what it could be called, had been on their side. There was no damaged craft or outraged owner to contend with, and only one survivor, who was in no position to demand more than the captain was prepared to give.

The fact that he had obviously been detained and shot made what Anatoli had to do clear-cut. They had rescued a man who was probably involved in illicit dealings—a drug dealer or a criminal. They had given him every chance at life, but Anatoli wouldn't put back into port for him; the risk was too great.

Under no circumstances would he draw unnecessary attention to his ship and the cargo they were carrying by taking an unconscious man suffering from gunshot wounds into Sydney Harbor. Customs and the local police would go over his ship with a fine-tooth comb, and when they found what Anatoli suspected was in the hold, they would all go to prison.

He had examined every angle, and they were in the clear. Without the broadcast of an EPIRB, which would have been picked up and recorded by Australian ground receivers in the COSPAS/SARSAT satellite system, there would be no record that a search and rescue had even taken place, and he had refrained from noting any details in the *Volodya*'s log. If the man died, which was still more than likely, they would bury him at sea. In the end, it would be no different than if they'd taken a slightly more southerly path and missed his beacon altogether.

If he lived, he and the crew would have to work out a course of action that would deflect undue attention away from the *Volodya.* None of it sat right with Anatoli, but he had no other choice. He was the captain; the mistake in signing with Varinski had been his. He was walking a narrow enough tightrope as it was without the complication of this foreigner. His first priority, as always, had to be his men.

Ten

Valle del Sol, Peru

Quin pushed through a thick wall of greenery and stepped into the grove she'd spent so much time in as a kid, her mud-encrusted boots making short work of the tangled network of weeds and vines that threatened to drown half the hillside.

Adjusting to the dappled light, she looked around curiously. It had been years—five years, to be exact—since the "dream," since Olivia had read her the riot act and put this place off limits, and the neglect showed. Most of the large rocks were now submerged beneath weeds, and the gap in the trees that had been so useful as a lookout had long since grown over.

Making a beeline for her rock, Quin dropped her rucksack and settled her long frame into her usual reclining position, letting the sun-warmed granite ease muscles that ached from hours spent putting in the main potato crop of the season. It was hard, back-breaking work, but it was work that couldn't be post-poned. If she didn't plant, they didn't eat.

A yawn started deep in her belly and expanded into her chest, leaving her wrung out and exhausted and, lately—crazy as it seemed—feeling old. Her eigh-teenth birthday—the age when she'd expected to en-roll in college—had come and gone, and her prospects hadn't changed; she was still mired in Valle del Sol.

She'd long since given up on the idea of obtain-ing a degree—there was barely enough money to pay for essentials, let alone the luxury of an extended education—but even so, letting go of that particular dream had *hurt*.

Her mouth kicked at one corner. Oh, yeah, great going, Quin. A pity party.

She'd come here to take a break from the heat and dust and, she grimaced, *solanum tuberosum*—pota-toes. A degree aside, what she really needed was a tractor.

The breath eased from her lungs as the subtle, soothing warmth of the grove enfolded her. She stared at the mesmerizing shimmer of leaves floating above, lime green and liquid gold, swimming in the hazy heat of the afternoon. As she sank into a doze, a vague presentiment niggled at her. The last time she'd fallen asleep here, something had happened.

Shifting her shoulders to fit more comfortably into the curve of the rock, Quin dismissed the thought with sleepy logic. The dream, such as it was, had happened five years ago, when she was a kid. Nothing had ever come from it, and nothing had changed. It was a fact that Valle del Sol was rock-solid boring. No strange men, no collapsing tunnels.

Another yawn almost took her under, and she felt herself begin to drift—the velvet blackness soothing after the heat of the sun….

A man lay still and silent on a bunk that was too narrow to comfortably accommodate either his length or his muscular frame. A bloodstained bandage was wound around his head—white against close-cropped black hair and tanned skin. Another bandage strapped his torso and shoulder, the gauze disappearing beneath the sheet that was pulled to his waist.

His chest moved, the shallow rise and fall almost imperceptible, his breath a raspy whisper in the dim room.

A door swung open. A brawny, fair-headed man entered carrying a plastic cup, and Quin shrank back into a corner, taking refuge in the dense shadows. The underlying throbbing she'd barely noticed registered now, louder because the door to the room was open. With a start, she realized that the sound was a ship's engine.

The blond man spoke in a guttural language. The low register of his voice jerked Quin's attention back to the tableau playing out in front of her as he lifted the injured man's head, muttering beneath his breath at the effort it took. He tilted the cup and coaxed water between the man's lips, spilling some, and massaged the man's throat to help him swallow. When the cup was empty, he eased the man down flat, shook his head and uttered another short phrase.

Quin didn't understand the actual words, but this time she understood the sense of what was said.

"Why haven't you died?"

Still shaking his head, the blond man stepped out of the room and closed the door behind him.

Minutes passed in which the stranger lying on the bunk neither moved nor acknowledged Quin's presence as she remained crouched in the corner. Finally, feeling as wary as a small hunted animal, she forced herself to examine every inch of the cabin.

Apart from the injured man, it contained one other bunk, and a large metal locker set against one wall. A bulb was screwed into a fitting in the ceiling, and the walls, floor and ceiling were all painted a uniform gray. A small salt-encrusted porthole just above the man's bed allowed natural light to filter into the room, but the murky beam of daylight barely succeeded in penetrating the gloom.

Acutely aware that the blond man could walk in any

second and find her, Quin straightened, thankful that the room was so dark as she started across the room. Apprehensive or not, she knew why she was here.

Every muscle in her body poised for an all-out brawl, or flight, she stopped just inches from the bunk, which she could now see was steel-framed and bolted to the floor, but the man's eyelids didn't so much as twitch. She also noticed for the first time a bag of clear fluid suspended from a hook on the wall, the tube snaking down to a shunt in his wrist.

The fact that he was ill enough to need an IV should have reassured her, but this close, and despite the fact that he was unconscious, the man was formidable, his shoulders and chest broad, his arms well muscled. Even lying down, it was clear he was well over six feet tall—one of the few men she'd met who would tower over her own five feet ten.

Her gaze skimmed tensely over the square line of his jaw. Apart from the bandage, the only thing that marred his face was a thin scar, which sliced from one straight, dark brow into his hairline, but the scar didn't detract. Crazily enough, it only made him seem more attractive—and more dangerous. It was a face that both fascinated and compelled, a face that sent an icy shiver of recognition down her spine.

Seconds ticked by as she continued to study the man, her spine tingling, her mind grasping at the uncanny fragment of knowledge, and still he didn't stir.

Finally, dismissing the weird moment as just that, Quin forced herself to get on with what she had to do. If the patient woke up, he woke up. Despite the muscles, she would lay odds on her chances against him. Head wounds were a real bitch. She'd had one once, courtesy of the slippery rocks that rimmed the Agueda. The first day out of bed, she'd walked into a wall.

Running her eye over the bandaged wounds, she noted the fresh seepage of blood at his shoulder. When the blond man had lifted him to tip water into his mouth, the wound had probably broken open.

Her gaze flicked to his closed lids. Emboldened by his unconscious state, she touched the pulse point at his wrist. At the contact, her solar plexus contracted with a short, sharp shock, as if the simple touch had released some kind of electrical charge, and she had to control the urge to snatch her fingers back. She was suddenly vividly aware that he was male with a capital *M,* his masculinity underlined by the absence of a shirt and the faint scent of sweat rising off his skin.

Clamping her jaw, she ignored the unsettling jolt and placed both palms over his forehead.

Instinctively, she knew that this was the wound that needed the most healing—this was the one that would kill him.

She was unsurprised to feel the familiar gentle warmth start, first enveloping her head, then flowing down her back and into her chest—so warm it felt as if her whole chest glowed—then on down her arms, until it poured from her palms.

The warmth steadied her and filled her with confidence. Quin didn't know where the heat came from, exactly, although she had a fair idea, and she knew it was good. Ever since she could remember, she'd instinctively put her palms on any part of her that had hurt, and the heat had flowed and magically eased the pain. In her child's mind, logic had demanded that if she could soothe her own hurts away, then her ability had to work on any of the animals that were sick or injured.

One day, Maria, Jose's wife and the cook, had seen her "fixing" one of the cats that haunted the back door of the kitchen waiting for tidbits. She'd requested that Quin try putting her hands on her head, because she had a headache. When the heat had stopped, Maria had made the sign of the cross, blessed her and dragged her in to see Father Ignatius, who was sitting down to lunch in the front parlor with the aunts, claiming loudly that Quin had "The Gift."

Father Ignatius had looked into her eyes with his thoughtful black gaze, held her hands for a while, and after consultation with the aunts, said he didn't see anything wrong with Quin helping the pets, so long as Olivia and Hannah kept an eye on her, but helping people wasn't such a good idea.

Olivia had been sharp with Maria and told her to

keep quiet about her disappearing headache, but somehow the rumor had spread, and, as she'd gotten older, Quin had found herself occasionally called into the clinic to "help." Hannah and Father Ignatius didn't make a big deal about it, and they'd refused to label what Quin did as healing for fear they would be inundated with people looking for miracle cures, but there was no denying the effect of that gentle heat, or the fact that they all knew something out of the ordinary was happening.

As Quin continued to hold her palms over his forehead, the man lying motionless on the bed didn't wake or move, but his breathing seemed to smooth out and deepen. The healing was having a soothing effect all around. Her own pulse rate had slowed, and her muscles had loosened, relaxed by the lulling warmth. Her lids drooped slightly as her mind began to drift; then, abruptly, as if some internal switch had been thrown, she became aware of the man himself as vividly as if one of those big hands had snaked out, gripped her by the scruff of the neck and wrenched her up onto her toes.

Adrenaline pumped, needle sharp, her whole body electrified by the shock of the connection. For a split second Quin was certain he was awake, dark eyes fastened on hers, but a quick glance told her the man was still unconscious, although at some level he was fully aware of her.

Flinching from the intrusion, she tried to shake off the touch of his mind. She was used to picking up on the way people felt, sometimes even their actual thoughts, as naturally as most people picked up on the nuances of conversation, but never with this clarity—and she had never experienced anyone making any kind of mental contact with her.

Somehow this man could access her mind, despite the fact that he was unconscious—or maybe because of it—and she didn't like the sensation one little bit.

With an effort of will, she forced herself to relax in the hope that with the absence of tension, the intrusion would fade, but the second she let down her barriers, impressions came at her in a torrent.

Confusion. Grim determination. A towering anger. Something had happened—something had been taken from him—and the knowledge fueled his already powerful desire to live, although to call the emotions that drove him "knowledge" was incorrect. He had no knowledge, just instinct. Like an embattled swimmer in a dream, a part of the man had remained doggedly sentient, fighting the downward pull of the coma and the release of death. He wanted to live—the desire raw and edged, as powerful as a vice closing over her heart—and he wanted *her* to help him.

For long seconds, Quin was caught in the grip of his need, the pure, hot focus on survival. When the healing flow finally slackened, she remained frozen, barely registering that her hands had gone cold and that the soft warmth had seeped from her body.

Moving stiffly, as if she'd just woken from a deep sleep, and acting on the sure knowledge that when the healing in one place was finished, it was finished, and there was nothing she could do to make it keep going, Quin moved her palms to his shoulder. Once more she steeled herself against the assault of the man's mind, but this time the connection was gentler, as if the fierce emotions had exhausted him, and he was simply content that she was there.

When the heat finally stopped, Quin straightened, swaying slightly on her feet. The muscles in her shoulders and the small of her back ached, and the cabin had grown progressively gloomier, as if the murky afternoon was darkening into night. She studied the rest of the man's body, which was covered by a sheet. He needed more healing—she knew it as inexplicably as she knew she was there to heal him—but, as exhausted as she felt, she wasn't brain-dead enough to lift that sheet. Since he wasn't wearing a shirt, chances were her patient wasn't wearing anything else, either.

She decided to try holding her hands a few inches away from the man's skin and moving slowly down his body. When she reached his right thigh, the flow of warmth started again.

Even through the layers of the sheet and the thick padding of the bandage, she could feel the heat that poured from this wound, which could only mean one thing: it was infected.

The warmth flowing from her palms increased. Her head and her back, her arms, the whole upper part of her body, became not just warm, but so hot that she broke out in a sweat, and, in the curious way of dreamers, Quin abruptly became aware that she *was* dreaming.

For a disorienting moment she was aware of herself in two places at the same time—the faintly surreal setting of the ship's cabin and the warm haven of the grove; then the powerful pull of the dream sucked her back in.

The heat flowing through her intensified, making her feel light-headed and a little dizzy, both hot and cold at once; then, as abruptly as it had begun, the flow stopped, and the room began to dim and recede. The rough texture of the cotton sheet beneath her palms faded, the man's features blurred, and fierceness gripped her. It hadn't been enough. *He needed more.*

Quin clutched at one tanned, long-fingered hand where it lay limply on the cotton sheet, but where, bare seconds ago, he'd been as solid as she, now her hand passed through him as if he had no more substance than a hologram. It was then that she noticed that the mind link was gone. Dream or reality, exhausted or not, he needed her, and she didn't want to leave, but as powerfully as she'd been pulled into the dream, she found herself expelled and floating in formless darkness.

Her eyes flipped open, then just as quickly blinked shut against the brassy glare of the sun as it sank below the western rim of the valley.

Jackknifing, she shoved damp strands of hair back from her face, every muscle taut. Through some strange process she'd ended up in a ship's cabin with an injured stranger. She'd smelled salt and diesel fumes and blood. She had felt the floor beneath her feet vibrate with the rhythm of the ship's engines, and she'd been acutely aware of *him*.

Her gaze swept the grove, as if she could see something—find something—tangible that would account for dreams that stepped out of nowhere and gripped her so tightly they seemed more real than the ground beneath her feet. And, as hard as she tried to relegate the dream images into something approximating normality, one fact kept undermining her efforts. Now that evening was approaching, the ambient air temperature was cool. Dressed in jeans and a tank top, she should have been shivering, but she was as cosily warm as if she were wrapped in a light, invisible blanket. She'd experienced that kind of warmth before—many times—although never to this degree, and it only happened when the healing flowed.

Regardless of how much she tried to categorize

what had happened as just a strange and vivid dream, there was no way she could ignore that part of it. The healing, at least, had been real.

As she snagged the strap of her rucksack, the memory of the last time she'd "dreamed" was abruptly vivid, and something in her mind connected and fused. The tantalizing knowledge that had eluded her during the dream surfaced, and this time it stayed. Gooseflesh rose all along her back and arms, and prickled at her nape. Now she knew why the man had been so familiar, and she wondered that she could ever *not* have recognized him.

As she pushed free of the rapidly darkening grove, the plummeting temperature finally penetrated, and she gave a raw shiver.

"Great," she muttered, as she slipped and slid her way down the rough slope in the gathering dark. The last thing she wanted to dwell on was the fact that she'd psychic-dreamed *twice,* and that, just to add to the general weirdness of it all, the same guy had starred each time.

Eleven

Quin swung out of the truck, narrowing her eyes at the cloud of dust that enveloped her and bracing herself against the cool, blustery wind blowing in off the sea—an astringent counterpart to the heat of the midday sun.

The docks at Vacaro were bustling. A container ship was anchored close in, and another was headed out to sea, leaving churned water and a stream of diesel fumes in its wake—growing smaller by the second.

She found Diego, the agent who dealt with the mission's order, just outside the rabbit warren he labeled his office, busy tying down the tarp on his small truck.

"About time." He jerked his head toward a pallet. "It's all over there. Yours is the last one." He handed her the clipboard that held their consignment note. "What took you so long?"

Quin signaled for Luis, the youngest of Jose's five

sons, who was presently working for the mission, to back the old flatbed up to their pallet of goods. She grimaced as black diesel fumes burst from the exhaust. "The Bedford broke down and it took a while to get it going. Same old story."

Diego fished in his pocket, handed her a pen and gestured at the paperwork.

She frowned. "What's the hurry? Shouldn't we check the goods off first?"

His dark eyes shifted restlessly along the docks. "I have to go. If there's a discrepancy, let me know and I'll follow it up."

"How do I know you'll follow it up?"

He paused long enough in tying down his load to shoot her a reproving glance. "I've been doing your order for ten years. Have you ever known me not to chase up a discrepancy?"

Quin eyed Diego as he moved around the truck, his blunt profile, the wisps of salt-and-pepper hair plastered over his balding head, the signature braces stretched around a belly that, these days, was broader than his shoulders. Usually he was painfully slow and meticulous, and she was left kicking her heels, waiting, while he double-checked that every last sack of flour and box of tinned goods had been accounted for—which was precisely why the aunts had dealt with him for ten years. When it came to business, Olivia and Hannah didn't take any prisoners.

Scribbling her signature on the packing note, she peeled off her copy, and handed the clipboard and pen back to Diego. "I still don't understand the hurry."

Diego tossed the clipboard and the pen through the side window of the truck. Quin frowned at the further uncharacteristic display. Some people were rabbits and some were tortoises: Diego was definitely a tortoise. Compared to his usual methodical demeanor, this was close to a manic state.

"Some strange things have been happening around here. This morning a sick *Ingles* got off-loaded by the *Volodya*. Manny thinks they really brought in a body, which would account for them leaving so fast."

At the word *Ingles*, every nerve ending in Quin's body jumped to attention. The dream she'd had just days ago was still fresh and sharp in her mind; *any* mention of an *Ingles* would have compelled her attention, and a sick stranger being off-loaded from a ship was too strong a coincidence to ignore.

Luis jumped down from the cab and joined them. "What *Ingles?*"

Diego shrugged. "No one's been to look. Everyone's too busy guarding their supplies." He swung behind the wheel of his truck, slammed the door and turned the key in the ignition. "Apparently Ramirez is in town. I'm not staying to find out."

Quin put her hand on the window and leaned

down, preventing Diego from leaving. "Why would the *Volodya* leave a man here?"

Diego eyed her fingers with barely concealed impatience. "Who knows? Maybe he stowed away and got kicked off? Maybe he's got some infectious disease? Whatever...the Russians dumped him and left fast. They didn't even stay to go drinking at Manny's, and that's unusual." A grin lightened his expression. "Manny's still crying into his beer."

Quin's grip on the window tightened. "How do you know the *Ingles* is sick?"

Diego jerked his head in the direction of the end warehouse. "He got off-loaded down at number five on a stretcher at first light. I haven't seen him walking around, so he must be bad, but I don't think he's dead. They wouldn't have bothered bringing a body ashore. They would have buried him at sea."

Sweat trickled down the groove of Quin's spine as she worked, sticking her shirt to her skin as she lifted a sack of flour onto the bed of the truck.

Luis hefted a box of canned goods, his brow thunderous. "What do you want to see this *Ingles* for?"

Flour puffed into her face as she dropped a second sack onto the deck. "I just want to."

Luis snorted. "That's crazy. If he's sick, you could catch something."

She grinned. "Not me, Luis. Us."

"Oh no, *I'm* not going. When we're finished loading up, I'm driving this truck out of town. Didn't you hear Diego? Ramirez is skulking around somewhere. You can stay if you want."

He dropped the box into place on the truck and turned a steely glare on her. "Not that I'll allow you to stay."

Quin grabbed another sack, suppressing a grunt as she straightened with the load. The fact that Ramirez, a notorious outlaw, could possibly be in town was disconcerting, but no one had actually seen him. So far, it was just a rumor. "You can't tell me what to do."

"I'm bigger than you."

"Fatter, maybe. I'm an inch taller."

He flexed his bicep. "See that. No fat, baby, just sheer muscle."

Quin rolled her eyes. "Whatever. I'm still taller."

"Just like a woman. What's that little inch got to do with anything?"

Quin suppressed a smirk. "Are you telling me size doesn't matter? Not much," she cut in, before Luis's male outrage could swell out of control, "except that you're the one who's got the problem with it."

He let out a muffled snort, hefted another box of canned goods and dropped it on top of the first. "It's probably those shoes you wear."

Quin set the sack down on the bed of the truck.

"They're sneakers, not high heels, and, if you recall, I've been taller than you since I was twelve."

Luis muttered beneath his breath. "No wonder Olivia wanted you out of the place. You'd drive a saint crazy. What's wrong with you, girl? This sick guy can wait for Lopez."

"Don't call me 'girl.' And no, he can't," she said shortly. "You know how slow Lopez is. His practice is so huge, he could be days away."

Luis stopped in the act of lifting two sacks of grain, his eyebrows raised goadingly as he unsubtly demonstrated that although he was an inch shorter, he was a lot stronger. "Don't tell me. You've got one of those *feelings?*"

"What if I have?"

Luis heaved both sacks onto the back of the truck. "Then that's just too bad. I have to balance your 'feeling' against the possibility of running into Ramirez. There's only one reason for him to be here just when all the supply ships arrive." He vaulted onto the flatbed and began arranging the supplies so they were packed tight enough not to move in transit. "Those old ladies back at the mission can't afford to lose this shipment."

"I need to check on him, Luis, that's all."

His gaze was flat and cold. "No. And that's final."

Quin didn't bother with a comeback, because she knew that Luis was right and she was wrong. Ramirez was a dangerous criminal. There was no way they should go near an empty warehouse if there was any likelihood he was in the area. Besides, Luis was in charge on this trip, and she'd promised the aunts that she would listen to him—so long as he made sense.

She picked up the packing note, ticked off the last items and tried to forget that a sick stranger had been dropped by the *Volodya,* but the fact that a *Russian* ship had dropped the man kept intruding into her mind.

In the dream, the sailor who'd tended to the injured man had spoken in a foreign language. It hadn't been Spanish or English, both of which she spoke fluently—or French or Italian, for that matter. The aunts had taught her enough of both languages that she understand their basic phonetics. The language in her dream had been more abrupt, the consonants hard.

It was entirely possible that the language had been Russian.

Twelve

Luis parked the truck on the expanse of bare dirt outside warehouse number five. It was clear from the number of tire tracks cut into the powdery surface that recently there'd been bustling activity, but now the building appeared to be deserted.

One of the large sliding doors had been left partially open, giving a narrow view into the shadowy interior.

Luis studied the opening, his expression tight. "I don't like it. One minute, and then we're leaving."

Quin pushed the truck door open, her whole being focused on the warehouse. "A minute's all I'll need."

She would know in the first second.

Less than a week had passed since the dream, and the image of the stranger lying sprawled on the ship's bunk was etched on to her memory.

Reaching behind the passenger seat, she retrieved the medical case that was always stored there and swung out of the truck. Dust swirled as she strode toward the opening, stinging her eyes as she lifted a hand to shield her gaze from the sun.

The five warehouses were all as alike as peas in a pod, each with a set of offices to one side. Logic dictated they would have put him there, out of the way of the goods and heavy machinery the *Volodya* would have off-loaded.

The sharp sound as Luis slammed his door, his curse as he paused to lock the vehicle, cut through the pressurized whine of surf and wind. "Quin, wait. Let me—"

Luis's hand landed on her arm as she stepped inside the warehouse. Impatiently, she shook him off.

"Shit." His hand locked around her arm, dragging her to a halt.

Her gaze jerked to the raw flash of panic in Luis's eyes—a split second later, she saw Ramirez.

Adrenaline pumped, a hot flash that made her stomach knot and her heart pound.

Quin caught a flickering movement out of the corner of her eye as two men slid through the shadows to position themselves behind her and Luis, cutting off their escape, and her throat locked. Well, that answered that question. Ramirez wasn't just going to let them walk away.

Her gaze skimmed the interior of the building. She counted eight men. With the two she knew were behind her, that brought the total to ten. She and Luis were almost ridiculously outnumbered.

Ramirez detached himself from the wall, moving with lithe grace—a dark, well-muscled Mestizo, part Spanish, part Indian, abnormally tall, with biceps bulging from the cutoff arms of his shirt.

More shadowy figures flowed down a narrow set of stairs that led to a mezzanine floor situated to one side of the building, and Quin's stomach plunged again. Four more that she hadn't seen, bringing the total of Ramirez's gang to fourteen. Too late to wish she'd listened to Luis. Walking into the semidark of the warehouse after the glare of the midday sun had been flat-out dumb; they'd both been blinded.

Ramirez came to a halt just meters away, his open shirt flapping slightly, revealing dark, defined muscles and the hilt of a knife glinting at his waist.

"Luis," she said tightly, and he stepped forward, shifting the open shirt that hung from his shoulders enough that the handgun he'd shoved into the waistband of his jeans became visible.

The Browning had seen better days. It had a gouge in the handgrip that made it uncomfortable to hold for any length of time, a magazine that jammed and a kick like a mule, but it was a nine-millimeter, and its firepower was impressive. Luis had worked for a whole year to buy it from his older brother, who was currently running with the local band of the Shining Path, and he handled the weapon with the same kind of reverent respect he would have given to a religious relic. He'd let Quin shoot the Browning just twice. Both times he'd snatched it from her grasp when she'd complained that the gouge was scratching her palm.

Ramirez's gaze fixed on the handgun, and the tension ratcheted so tight that Quin could feel it like an actual pressure against her skin.

She never thought she would be so glad that Luis carried such a lethal piece of equipment.

A lazy command echoed through the warehouse, whispering off corrugated iron walls. There was a rustling movement, the metallic snap as magazines were shoved home and rounds chambered. Dull light glinted off metal as a motley assortment of arms was trained on them.

Ramirez lifted his arm from his side to reveal that he held a sawed-off shotgun, which previously had been concealed against his thigh. With a slick motion, he brought the gun to bear, and for an endless moment Quin found herself looking down the twin barrels.

With an effort of will, she dragged her gaze from the weapon, every part of her negating what was happening. Since she'd been old enough to comprehend language, she'd been taught about the sanctity of life. If Ramirez was going to shoot, he would shoot; she wasn't going to give him the added satisfaction of watching him pull the trigger.

A soft laugh added another layer to the tension. "Not going to play, huh?" He muttered an eclectic mix of insults in Spanish and Quechua for the entertainment of his men.

Peripherally, Quin was aware of the barrel swinging down, and oxygen flooded her lungs, making her head spin.

Ramirez's gaze sought hers. Despite her reluctance to look into the eyes of a man who had a well-documented history of brutality, and who could kill for no perceptible reason other than that she and Luis had walked into a building he had staked a claim on, she found herself staring back.

He indicated her medical bag with its Red Cross insignia on the side. "I know you. You're from the mission."

There was no point denying it. Two years ago Ramirez had melted out of the jungle that flowed in the southern end of the valley and brought one of his men to the medical center. Quin had been helping Hannah that day and had ended up strapping the man's broken arm after Hannah had straightened the bone and splinted it.

He jerked his head, as if he'd just come to a decision. "I need medical attention. I ~~was~~ waiting for Lopez, but somehow, I don't think he's coming."

Placing his gun on the floor, he shrugged out of his shirt, the movement quick and graceful and punctuated by an angry grunt. He turned and jerked a finger at a swelling in his back.

Quin eyed a boil the size of a tennis ball that was swelling to an ugly point just below his left shoulder blade and felt her insides go queasy. Apart from Lopez, Quin was the closest thing there was to a doctor for almost a hundred miles on this rough, almost deserted piece of coastline, but that didn't mean she had a calling. "I'm not a doctor. You should wait for Lopez."

There was an uneasy ripple of laughter, the muttered Spanish equivalent of, "As if."

"Lopez has probably already called the military. If I wait much longer, the only 'attention' I'll get is a body bag."

"Anyone can lance a boil. Why don't you get one of your men to do it?"

Ramirez slid the knife out of the waistband of his pants. The blade glinted in the narrow slice of sunlight that beamed in the door. "And which one would you choose to put the knife in my back?" He indicated the medical bag. "You can do it. And *you*." He pinned Luis with a flat glare and jerked his head to the right. "Over there. In the corner, where I can see you."

Ramirez muttered a curt order, and a small table and a chair were produced from one of the offices. He gestured her toward the table and crossed his arms over his chest as she set the medical case down and flipped the lid.

His breath washed over her face as he leaned forward to examine the scalpel she'd selected, and she tried hard not to dwell on the fact that apart from the boil on his back, Ramirez also needed dental surgery.

"I want you to stitch it," he said in a low voice. "I don't want a scar."

Quin clenched her jaw and tried not to breathe. "I can't stitch it. Not unless you want a repeat performance. The wound has to drain. Once all the poison's out, it'll granulate."

"Granulate?" His eyes narrowed. "What in hell's *granulate?*"

She pulled on a set of latex gloves, and reached for a bottle of disinfectant and a plastic bag of cotton swabs. "It's a fancy word for a scab, okay? Now sit down and keep still."

Gaze still slitted, Ramirez set the knife on the concrete floor alongside the gun—both within inches of his booted feet—then straddled the chair, presenting his back. He was still for approximately half a second, then craned around to watch, black eyes suspicious. "Is it going to hurt?"

Quin repressed the slightly hysterical desire to

laugh. For a man who was reputed to be the next best thing to a drug lord, Ramirez's fear was absurd. "No, it's not going to hurt. Much. You've left it so long, you've probably killed the nerves. You're lucky you didn't end up with an ulcer—or septicemia."

Quin uncapped the disinfectant and soaked a swab. She hovered over the boil, reluctant to start. Despite the fact that she hadn't yet touched him, Ramirez flinched.

Quin jerked back, almost dropping the swab.

"Hurry it up," he snarled, "before I decide I'm crazy for allowing a *woman* to put a knife in my back."

"Then stay still," she snapped.

Ramirez swore beneath his breath, then planted his forearms on the back of the chair and leaned forward so that the skin over the boil stretched tight.

Taking a deep breath, Quin cleaned the area, picked up the scalpel and set a hand on his bare shoulder to steady him in case he flinched again. The last thing she needed was to stab herself in the hand with the scalpel—or, worse, stab Ramirez in the wrong place.

Automatically, as her palm settled against taut muscle, she began to heal. The warm flow reached her palm, flowed into Ramirez, and abruptly, she hesitated. She had never thought about who the healing went to before. Always it had been for people in need, but most of those people had been what she would term "good." They had usually come to the mission for help and weren't running from the law with a shotgun in one hand and a knife in the other. If she'd taken the time to make a conscious choice, she wouldn't have healed Ramirez in that way, but it seemed that the healing energy didn't discriminate.

Taking another breath, she allowed the flow to continue and turned her attention to the swelling distorting Ramirez's back. She had watched Hannah lance boils, but never one this big. The trick was to stretch the skin, then slice once, deep enough that the wound would drain properly, but if she sliced Ramirez too deeply, chances were he would turn around and shoot her. If she sliced him too shallowly, she wouldn't get all the infection out, and he would come looking for her. Either way, the equation didn't work in her favor.

Gripping the scalpel and schooling herself not to squeeze her eyes closed at the crucial moment, she plunged it into the shiny tip of the boil. Liquid splattered the back of her hand, and Ramirez swore, jerking away from the pain. The muscles of his back spasmed, ejecting more pus and blood along with a glutinous lump, which oozed over the lip of the wound and slid down his back like a large, greenish slug.

Gritting her teeth to control her instant gag reflex, Quin set the scalpel down and reached for the swabs she'd set out. The back of her hand might be coated, but thanks to the latex gloves, nothing had actually touched her skin.

Minutes later, she applied a loose dressing over the still weeping cut, peeled off the gloves and handed Ramirez a bag that contained spare dressings. "Change the dressing every day. The wound will seep, but that's what it's supposed to do." She dug into a pocket of the case and brought out a precious foil pack of flucloxacillin. Take two of these a day, and that should fix it."

Ramirez took the dressings and the antibiotics, then gingerly shrugged into his shirt.

Quin's gaze darted to Luis, where he was still standing sandwiched between two of Ramirez's men, watching her like a hawk.

At a sharp head jerk from Ramirez, the two men stepped away from Luis, and he warily made his way toward her.

Quin quickly repacked the medical kit, disposing of the gloves and soiled swabs by shoving them in a plastic bag, bile burning in the back of her throat at the gooey mess.

"Hey," Ramirez said, his gaze catching hers, the goading gleam absent. "Thanks." He watched as she packed the case, and she had the odd impression that he was at a loss as to what to say next.

His palm settled on the case as she snapped it closed, preventing her from lifting it off the table. His dark gaze bored into hers. "What did you do?" he demanded. "With your hands?"

One of the men muttered a crude aside. There was a rough shout of laughter from further back in the ranks, but Ramirez didn't smile.

Quin kept her expression impassive. She was surprised Ramirez had been aware of the healing. Some people felt it, some didn't. Ramirez didn't strike her as the sensitive type. "I just lanced the boil."

One of the men told Ramirez to let her go, and she recognized the man whose broken arm she'd strapped two years ago. Another gestured sharply toward the door, his urgency to leave unmistakable.

Ramirez swore beneath his breath and finally stepped back.

The second he released his hold on the bag, Quin straightened, gripping the case, more than happy to step closer to Luis.

For a fractured moment Ramirez continued to stare at her, and she sensed that, despite his curiosity over the healing and the danger *he* was in, he was reluctant to give up his power play.

Adrenaline surged as the tension increased. She could feel him teetering on the edge of a decision. Grimly, she waited him out, sensing that to move first was to lose.

Taking a deep breath, she stared Ramirez in the eye. "You know, you should still see Lopez…just in case."

Ramirez gave a snort of laughter. "You know what, *cara,* I like you."

A shudder went down her spine. Ramirez liking her was the last thing she wanted.

He tossed the antibiotics in his hand, still grinning as he swaggered toward the door. "Better go see your next patient, doc. Although you might have trouble fixing that one."

As the last member of Ramirez's motley gang melted out of the warehouse, Luis ground out an oath and took a step forward.

Quin caught at his arm, dragging him back. "What do you think you're *doing?*"

He glared at her, face pale, jaw taut. "They might rip off the truck."

"And if they do, how are you going to stop them? I see they took your gun. Not that it would be much good even if you still had it."

He shrugged her hand off. "You thought it was pretty good earlier on."

"That was a mistake." A potentially lethal one. "I'm sorry, Luis, I could have gotten you killed."

"Yeah, well, with that gang, just breathing could have gotten us both killed." He stared out at the car park, which was now bare of everything but their truck, dust whipping off the ground in sheets. "The sadistic son of a bitch."

Quin gripped the back of the chair Ramirez had

used, reaction setting in. Now that he and his men really had gone, she felt as if she'd been run over by a train. Her legs were wobbly, and her hands were shaking.

Bad as the encounter had been, they had been lucky—incredibly lucky. If Ramirez and his men hadn't been worried that Lopez, or any other of the townspeople, had called in the military, he might have continued with his cat-and-mouse game. She and Luis could have been killed—or worse.

Luis touched her shoulder. "Let's get out of here."

Quin's fingers tightened on her medical bag as her gaze skimmed the shadows and settled on a row of doors. "Wait. Just a minute."

She hadn't gone through that debacle with Ramirez just to walk away without at least looking at the hurt stranger. Ramirez had said she would have trouble fixing him, which meant he *was* here—and still alive.

Luis shook his head as if even the words she'd spoken were incomprehensible. "A minute?" he repeated harshly. "You want a minute? You've got thirty seconds, then we're leaving. If I have to drag you out of here, I will."

Thirteen

Tension gripped Quin as she checked first one door, then another, and finally stepped into a dim, airless room.

She blinked, for a moment transported back in time to a small, dark cabin with a porthole letting in light, and then reality reasserted itself. There was no porthole, just a grimy window cracked at one corner. This room was altogether larger and dirtier—the floor thick with dust—and there were no metal lockers or bunks, just two scuffed wooden desks that had been pushed together to form a crude bed for the patient.

Her heart pounded as she stepped further into the room and studied what little she could see of him. He was wrapped in a blue tarpaulin—a corpse shrouded for burial, except for one small detail: his head was visible.

A white bandage was wound around his forehead, and a thick growth of dark beard obscured the lower part of his face. For a moment she was convinced it *wasn't* him, and something in her plummeted; then she noticed the saline drip attached to his arm.

All the small hairs at her nape lifted as she walked toward him, gaze glued to the shallow rise and fall of his chest. Common sense told her it couldn't be the same man she'd dreamt about—*twice*—but, so far, every detail was the same except for the beard. But then, a week had passed since she'd dreamed of healing him, in which case the beard made absolute sense. Unless one of the crew members on board the *Volodya* had taken the time and trouble to shave him, of course his beard would have grown.

Disorientation gripped her as she peeled off the tarpaulin and the layer of blankets beneath to reveal a bandage swathing one shoulder and part of his chest. She peeled the blankets below his hips. Beneath a pair of plain drawstring track pants, the thick pad of a bandage wrapping his thigh was plainly visible. The medical details aside, it was the small scar on the man's temple that set the seal on what was happening. The detail was too perfect to be denied. She had seen that scar, and she had seen *him* before—twice. But craziness or coincidence aside, the fact that the saline bag was empty underlined that the how and why of his existence didn't matter; whoever he was, he needed help, and he needed it now.

Dimly, she became aware of Luis beside her.

"Hold this." As she handed him the medical bag, memories of long summer evenings spent listening to Father Ignatius, his voice ancient and cracked as he wove mesmerizing tales of miracles and redemption, surfaced. Sick as the stranger was, conventional medicine would have to wait.

Closing her eyes briefly, she whispered a prayer, then placed her hands on the stranger's chest. Heat arced, the flow so fierce it made her head spin. For long moments the heat continued to flood through her into the almost lifeless husk lying in the shadows of the dusty office; then, as abruptly as it had begun, the healing stopped.

Outwardly, there was nothing to indicate that anything out of the ordinary had happened, but she felt the strange inner knowledge she'd come to trust settle inside her. *He wouldn't die now. He had stabilized.*

A small touch on her shoulder had her turning.

Luis's jaw was tight. "It's time."

"We can't leave him."

"And we can't take him with us. He doesn't have any passport or papers. I've checked."

Quin frowned, her focus still firmly centered on the sick stranger. The legalities, for the moment, were all but incomprehensible to her. "We're taking him.

We'll worry about a passport later. We can put him in the back of the truck."

Luis eyes slitted. "He's rat bait. He'll be stinking by the time we hit the pass."

Quin's temper flashed. "If I have to, I'll drag him myself. You can watch, or help." Methodically she removed the shunt in the man's wrist, slid her hands beneath his shoulders, hooked her arms under him and pulled upward.

"Don't do that!" Luis snapped, exasperated. "You're too skinny. You'll break your spine."

Gritting her teeth, Quin managed to lift the man's shoulders and head, but it felt as if she was hauling on a sack of wet cement. Lean as he was, he was still too heavy for her to shift. She eased him flat. "Then you'll have two cripples on your hands."

"No, I won't," Luis said coldly. "I'll have one. You."

Quin held his gaze. "Help me."

For long seconds he didn't move, and for a moment she thought she'd pushed too far and lost his support. Luis was hot-blooded and excitable, his existence almost as precarious as one of Ramirez's outlaws, but always before he'd been loyal; it was a shock to think he might desert her now.

He let out a breath. "What is it about this guy? Anyone would think he was *special,* when he's just some sad gringo who happened to get himself in a fight. I oughta walk—"

"But you won't." She grinned, relief and something perilously close to joy bubbling up inside her. "Get his feet."

His brows jerked together. "*You* get his feet. I'll take his shoulders."

She moved quickly to obey.

"Mother of God," he murmured as he took the stranger's weight, "he weighs a ton. The crocs are gonna be happy. Dinnertime coming right up."

Quin gripped the man beneath his knees, trying to secure her hold on the slippery tarpaulin. "The crocs won't get him." The words came out more vehemently than she'd meant, and Luis spared her a curious glance.

She didn't know how she knew, but she was certain the stranger would live. He was still unconscious, but Quin didn't care. He was going to live, and she felt almost giddily happy.

She didn't know what she would do with him when he did wake up. He could be a murderer, a drug runner—a terrorist. From what she'd seen, two of the wounds, at least, looked like bullet wounds. After being abandoned by a shipload of hardened sailors, who usually looked after their own, the chance that he was a good man was so slim as to be almost nonexistent, but Quin couldn't *not* help him.

Luis grunted and swore as they eased the stranger free of the desk.

They didn't get him more than a few feet before Luis gave the order to set him down on the floor. "This isn't going to work. We'll have to drag him. The tarpaulin will slide on the concrete. He's got enough blankets around him to act as a cushion."

Quin studied the door to the dusty office, which opened directly onto the warehouse. "Back the truck in. That way, we only need to move him a few meters."

"There's no way I'm backing the truck into the warehouse. We shouldn't have come here in the first place. We drag him, or we leave him."

Quin looked at the set of Luis's jaw and decided he wouldn't budge, but she wasn't happy.

"Okay then, we drag him." It would be a smoother way to shift him, and, given his head wound, they couldn't afford any unnecessary jolts.

Minutes later, they emerged through the warehouse door into the glare of full sunlight. The sea breeze had turned into a stiff wind, whipping at the waves and creating a fine, hazy mist that obscured the distant, jagged line of the mountains.

It took long minutes to rearrange the load on the back of the truck to make room for their passenger, and create a makeshift bed out of blankets and clothes. As they worked, Luis cursed nonstop, looking over his shoulder every few seconds to check that Ramirez and his gang weren't sneaking up on them, or, almost as bad, if Lopez and the *militar* had arrived and caught them red-handed trying to assist an illegal immigrant.

The next hurdle was lifting the unconscious man onto the bed of the truck without hurting him. They found that while lifting the stranger off the desk and lowering him to the floor of the warehouse office had been difficult, trying to elevate him was impossible. In the end, they resorted to stacking boxes of tinned goods to form a crude set of steps.

Hooking his hands beneath the stranger's shoulders, Luis once again took the brunt of the man's weight as they negotiated the stacked boxes.

Once their patient was settled, they began repacking the supplies around him, wedging him in tightly, only leaving space for Quin to sit so she could support his head. Head wounds were tricky things, and she had no way of knowing how serious this one was. Without cushioned support, the bumpy ride would likely finish him off.

Quin wedged the medical bag next to where she would be sitting, climbed over the supplies and watched as Luis picked up the end of the rope that was used to tie the tarp down. "You were right. Eventually we're going to need a passport for him."

Luis's expression was incredulous. "Huh! I'm finally right. Now I suppose you expect me to come up with a passport?"

"Not you, but you must know *someone*."

He dropped the rope and jabbed his chest. "Why must *I* know someone? You think I'm a criminal or something?"

"You knew Ramirez."

"So did you."

Quin wasn't about to be fobbed off. "I've only seen him. You *know* him."

His jaw clamped. "I do now."

"Well, all right then. But, you've got contacts."

"I might know someone, who might know someone else who could help you, but…"

"It's going to cost, I know—"

"Yes, it's going to cost, and I don't even know if it can be done."

"Then I'll ask someone else."

"*Cristo.* You would. Look, I'll make some inquiries, but I don't know…"

"Try."

He stared at her in frustration, then jerked his head, indicating that she should take her seat. "I don't know why you're going to all this trouble for a stranger. You should turn him in. It's not as if you can afford to support him. Last time I heard, the mission was flat broke."

Quin clambered to the rear of the truck, careful not to bump their passenger. "Then you heard wrong."

Her jaw tightened grimly. She was lying through

her teeth, and Luis knew it. They *were* broke—for the moment—and she didn't know what to do about it. They had barely been able to pay for their supplies, and she could only chop so much wood and grow so many vegetables in a day. The mission was large and sprawling, with draughty, high-ceilinged rooms that were hard to heat in winter. The mechanics of their daily existence aside, the buildings themselves were crumbling; the plaster cracked and decaying, the roof tiles gradually disintegrating. The process was slow but inevitable, which didn't change the fact that it would break Hannah's and Olivia's hearts to give up the mission. "The mission doesn't turn away people who need help. He's a good man."

Luis jerked the rope through an eyelet in the tarp. "From where I'm standing, all I can see is that he's a man."

"Whether he's male or female hasn't got a thing to do with it."

"Say it often enough, you might start believing it."

"It's not like that." Although when she looked at him she did feel something, but it was confused—a raw pull….

"Yeah, right. Besides, he's old enough to be your father." He rolled his eyes, this time with a trace of humor. "And you're the virgin from hell."

"Bet on it."

Luis's expression was chagrined. Occasionally

he'd made a move, but Quin had always been quick to discourage him. Luis had been in and out of relationships since he was fourteen, but Quin had never wanted anything to do with the kind of serial monogamy he practiced. The way she saw it, the occasional gleam in his eye had gotten to be a habit, an obligatory part of his easy charm.

With a sharp motion, Luis pulled on the rope, snapping the final corner of the tarp into place and plunging her into darkness. Suppressing a grin, Quin eased into a cross-legged position, her spine pressed flat against the large wooden toolbox that butted up against the battered steel of the cab.

She heard Luis mutter another curse; then the vehicle rocked on its rusted springs as he swung behind the wheel and slammed the door.

The Bedford's engine rumbled to life, setting up an instant vibration that shook the length of the vehicle, and a corresponding shiver coursed the length of her spine at the strangeness of everything that had happened.

She had given medical attention to the most-wanted outlaw in the country, then picked up an illegal immigrant who was suffering from gunshot wounds.

Despite Luis's reluctance, there was no way she could have taken the neater, simpler option of walking away from the stranger and informing the authorities. He had been lying in that warehouse for the best part of a day, and Quin would lay odds that if she left him, Lopez wouldn't risk coming near him for fear of running into Ramirez. There was the added complication that, if he had survived at all, with no papers, he would very likely end up in jail.

She felt odd and unsettled and fiercely proprietorial. In a strange way she couldn't begin to fathom, she had been linked to this stranger for years, and now that she'd found him, had him practically delivered to her doorstep, she wasn't backing away from the responsibility.

Pulling a sack of flour from the stacked supplies, she arranged it so that her back was more comfortably supported. The road up through the mountains was narrow and bumpy—in some places little more than a goat track. She was going to be black and blue before they got to the other side. And when they got to Valle del Sol…

Gingerly, she eased the stranger's bandaged head onto her lap, cradling him against the small jolt as Luis hit the first pothole.

When they got to Valle del Sol, Olivia and Hannah would hit the roof.

Fourteen

Hannah's surgery had originally been one of the two accommodation blocks built by The Sisters Of Mercy. The small uniform rooms had since been converted into a large, airy waiting room, a surgery, and two small private rooms with beds for those patients who needed to stay over. The unconscious stranger was presently in one of those rooms.

Luis appeared at the open door, his jacket collar pulled up around his neck to ward off the night chill. His gaze touched meaningfully on Quin's. "I don't like leaving you ladies alone with him. In case you hadn't noticed, he's big."

Hannah didn't bother looking up from the sheaf of notes she'd made in her neat, slanting hand. "I don't think you have to worry."

Luis looked at her skeptically. "Why? What's wrong with him? He can't walk?"

She pointed to the right side of his face. "See how the muscles drag down slightly? He's had a cerebral bleed. His entire right side is paralyzed." She lifted the unconscious man's lids and flicked on a small penlight. The right pupil contracted, the left didn't respond. "He's also got a cranial nerve injury affecting his left eye. When the bullet hit, it put a hairline fracture in his skull and traumatized the orbit. The paralysis aside, he'll have trouble with his vision—maybe even blindness in that eye—and if he isn't speech impaired, I'll eat my stethoscope."

A small shock went through Quin. She had helped Hannah remove the bandages and apply fresh ones. She'd seen the ugly entry and exit wounds in his thigh and shoulder, and the graze on the side of his head. Her mystery man had been shot three times. She had known that at the very least he was suffering from a severe concussion.

Hannah set her pen down. "It might not be as bad as it sounds. He's survived this long, and as the clot in his brain reabsorbs, the various dysfunctions will drop away. With therapy, he can make at least a partial recovery—but it'll take months, maybe even years."

Luis lifted his shoulders. "Guess he's safe enough, then."

Hannah shot him a reproving glance. "For the moment." Leaning forward, she picked up first one hand, then the other, and examined the calluses there. "Hmmm…that's unusual. He's ambidextrous. Perhaps that'll help."

Quin studied the odd calluses on the edge of each palm. "How?"

"The left side of the brain controls speech, and that's where the bleed has occurred, but if he's ambidextrous, that means his brain works differently from that of most people. He would have developed pathways and functions on the right hemisphere that will still be intact." She lifted her shoulders in a shrug. "It's a slim chance, but at least it's a chance."

She indicated the plastic bag that had held the saline solution and the tubing that went with it. "Do you have any idea who did the initial care?"

Quin's gaze was wary. Compared to Olivia, Hannah appeared to be laid-back, even relaxed, but that impression was deceptive. Hannah might move at her own pace through the day, methodically attacking one task at a time, but she always achieved an immense amount of work. In her own quiet way she was as intimidating as Olivia. "Apart from the *Volodya*'s medic, no."

Hannah studied the small ECG monitor she'd hooked the patient up to, checked the time on her wristwatch and made a further note. "Whoever did the work on his shoulder wasn't a surgeon. It's not textbook, but it'll do. At least he'll have the use of that arm if he recovers."

If.

Hannah moved to the foot of the bed and lifted the blankets, exposing his feet. "It would be interesting to know exactly what happened on the *Volodya*. Aside from the bullet wounds, he's got lacerations on his wrists and ankles that are consistent with being tied up." Shaking her head, she let the blanket drop.

Luis sent Quin a hard look, and jerked his head at the door, silently asking her to go with him. "Maybe he was a stowaway."

Olivia appeared in the doorway, her gaze sharp. "Stowaways don't usually have bullet wounds. The only thing that makes sense is that they dropped him in Vacaro. The place is practically deserted." She stared at the new arrival in the clinic, her expression impassive. "I've checked with Diego. Sounds like the only people who know anything about him are the crew of the *Volodya*, and if they dumped him and left in a hurry, they're not going to admit to a thing. If we want the facts, we'll have to wait for him to wake up."

Hannah smothered a yawn as she adjusted the bottle of IV fluid feeding into the man's wrist. "Don't hold your breath. If he regains consciousness, I doubt he'll be able to tell anyone anything in a hurry."

* * *

Quin followed Luis out into the night, shivering as the cool, moisture-laden air penetrated her flannel shirt. "Are you going to get the passport?"

Luis lifted his shoulders, the gesture dismissive. "What's the point? He still might die."

"The point is, Diego will suspect we picked him up, and he's likely to say something to someone. It might take a while, but when the police start investigating, they'll eventually decide to look us up. It's even possible that one of Ramirez's men might talk about what happened. The one thing we can count on is that word will get around that we went to that warehouse."

Luis's gaze snapped to hers. "And now Olivia and Hannah are involved. This is turning into an even bigger mess than I thought it would be. How do I arrange for a passport when we don't even have a name?"

Quin reached into her pocket. Silver glinted beneath the porch light as she turned a watch over in her palm. "I've got some initials. J.T.L."

Luis made a dismissive sound. "Let's hope he didn't steal the watch before he got shot."

Quin's head snapped up. "He's not a thief."

"And he's not a murderer or a drug runner, even though Mr. Popularity has three bullet holes in him." Luis shoved his hands on his hips. "Okay, genius, what do we call him? Juan, Joachim, *Jorge?*"

Quin slipped the watch back into her pocket. "I've decided to keep it simple and just call him by his first initial, Jay. Jay Lomax."

"*You've* decided? What about Olivia and Hannah?"

Quin dropped her voice to a whisper. "*Keep your voice down.* Olivia knows he hasn't got any ID. I told her I'd see about getting it from Vacaro."

"Olivia's not stupid. When she finds out he's an illegal alien, she'll go crazy."

"Don't worry," Quin said with more confidence than she felt, because she suspected that Olivia already knew exactly how desperate their patient's situation was. "She won't."

"Then you're the crazy one. Just as long as you don't implicate me. This is totally your show."

"That's right—it is. How much money will you need to buy a passport?"

"I don't know. I never bought one before." He poked her arm, his expression half playful, half serious. "I'm curious about how you're going to come up with this money. What have you got to sell? You already owe me for the gun." He rubbed her arm suggestively.

Quin slapped his hand away. "Not that," she said coldly. "And Ramirez is the one who owes you for the gun, not me."

His jaw locked into a hard line, "*Ramirez*... When I catch up with whoever's got the Browning, I'll—"

"What? Take out the whole gang just to try and retrieve that old wreck of a gun?" The memory of staring down the twin barrels of the sawed-off shotgun sent a cold shudder up her spine. That was something else she hadn't told Olivia. She glared at Luis. "Don't even think about going near Ramirez again."

Luis shivered, as if the chill night air had finally seeped through his jacket. "Don't worry, I'm not stupid, but one day…"

"*No.* Drop it. That kind of thing can be… I don't know…" She shook her head, unwilling to talk about Ramirez, or even think about him. "Think about him too much, and maybe you'll turn around one day and he'll be there."

Luis shoved his hands deep in his jacket pockets and stepped off the veranda. "Now you're scaring me. You sound like some creepy old witch."

"Using common sense doesn't make me a witch." She watched his retreating back. "And by the way, Luis, touch me like that again and I'll slice off your finger."

"Ouch!" He clutched at his back as if she'd just stuck him with a knife and craned around as he walked. "No wonder you can't get a man. Your tongue's as sharp as Hannah's scalpel."

Fifteen

Quin woke, lids flipping open, mind oddly clear, as if she hadn't been sleeping deeply but floating somewhere on the edge of consciousness.

It was two o'clock in the morning, and the moon was full and bright, light spilling around the edges of the thick drapes, but it wasn't the light that had woken her. The sound came again, a raspy little creak, as if someone had just forced the latch of a door or a window in the kitchen, which was directly below her room. Seconds later, the raspy little sound was followed by a familiar creak. Someone had just walked on the third floorboard out from the kitchen table.

Sliding out of bed, she moved silently across her bedroom and out into the hall. She considered rousing Olivia and Hannah, then dismissed the idea. While neither of the aunts was exactly frail, they didn't possess either her height or strength; instead, she stopped at Jay's door.

After four months, the man she'd named Jay Lomax was nowhere close to fully recovered from the brain injury, but physically, he was remarkably able, and had regained the use of his right arm and leg. Part of the reason for his rapid recovery had been the superb physical condition he'd been in before he'd been shot; the rest had been the result of focus. He'd worked every muscle grouping in his body he could, given the restriction of his healing wounds. He'd pushed himself to the limit, and had seemed to know almost as much about the way his body worked and medical matters as Hannah.

Once he'd been able to stand unaided, frustrated by his continued confinement, he'd taken to limping about the compound with the aid of a staff he'd whittled from a tree branch. From there he'd progressed to walking circuits of the orchard, until his muscles and coordination had improved to the point that he could not only walk, but run.

Hesitantly, Quin pushed Jay's door open, but her tension at invading his privacy faded almost immediately. Moonlight flooded across the floor, more than enough of it for her to see that the bed and the room were empty.

Minutes later, she reached the bottom of the stairs and flattened herself against the wall. A movement to her left snapped her head around. Simultaneously, a large hand clamped over her mouth and nose, cutting off her breath, and an arm snaked around her waist, hauling her back into an alcove. For frantic seconds she fought back, until she felt the uncanny touch of a mind. *Jay.* His hand loosened, allowing her enough leeway that she could take a breath, then once again locked tight over her mouth and nostrils.

Long seconds passed as he continued to hold her, and disbelief and fury combined as she reached out with her mind and connected with…nothing. For a wild moment she wondered if she'd imagined that brief connection; then she realized that the blankness was Jay's doing. He didn't want the communication.

Her head spun, and her chest burned with the need to breathe, and the warnings that Luis had given her played through her mind. Jay had been dumped and left for dead with three gunshot wounds—the chance that he wasn't a killer himself was practically nonexistent. She swallowed, becoming frantic, and he allowed her a small amount of air just as two dark figures walked silently by.

The hand still clamped over her mouth and nose relaxed, allowing her to breathe; then, as abruptly as he'd grabbed her, Jay let her go. He put a finger to his lips, reinforcing the need for silence, but Quin didn't need the sign language. They had intruders in the house—even she could understand that one.

Why didn't you let me breathe?

She didn't realize she'd spoken with her mind until the answer came the same way.

Because you could have made a noise.

With a gesture telling her to stay put, Jay disappeared in the direction the two figures had gone, and for dizzying moments Quin stayed in the alcove, waiting for the pounding in her chest to subside. If she'd ever needed proof that Jay had lost none of his mental faculties, she'd just had it. He might have lost all memory of his past, and he still had difficulty with speech, but no part of his intellect had been impaired. His mind had been coldly controlled, the message curt and clear. She had come downstairs to do what she could about the break-in, but she'd been too late: Jay already had the situation under control.

When she was calm, Quin peered down the corridor. When she saw that it was clear, she followed in Jay's wake, picking up a heavy brass candlestick from a side table on the way. She could understand why Jay had grabbed her and shoved her against the wall—in her white nightdress she stood out like a beacon, while he was dressed in dark pants and a dark T-shirt, and was much less visible. If she'd continued walking along the corridor, the two men who had broken into the house would have seen her. She even understood why he'd had to clamp his hand over her mouth, because she would have made a startled noise, then demanded to know what was going on, but the way he'd pinched her nostrils, stopping her breath and only allowing her to breathe when she absolutely had to, had been nothing short of ruthless.

Hugging the wall, she inched along the hallway, bare feet silent on the boards. A cool draft drifted around her ankles as she tested the weight of the candlestick in her hand. The metal felt cold and hard and satisfyingly heavy.

The faint tinkling of broken glass halted her in her tracks. For long seconds she listened, ears straining; then she began her slow progress again, inching forward until she reached the entrance to the library.

Holding her nightgown so that none of the cloth would swing forward and become visible, she peered into the room.

Moonlight flowed in through the tall mullioned windows, bleaching the floorboards silver and outlining the two intruders, one squatting by a glassed cabinet that housed Olivia's antiquities, the other moving around the large walnut desk that resided in one corner of the room.

The man searching the desk opened a drawer, rummaging quickly, the narrow beam of light from a penlight glowing. He worked his way down one set of drawers, then switched to the other side of the desk. As he bent to slide the last drawer open, a shadow detached itself from the wall and merged

with that of the intruder. Moments later, Jay lowered
the intruder soundlessly to the floor and switched off
the torch. He stayed crouching over the man, a hand
at his throat, as if measuring his pulse, then moved
across the room and chopped down with his hand
once, the movement measured and precise. The second intruder slumped to the ground.

Moments later a golden glow suffused the room
as Jay flicked on a lamp and the extent of the damage was revealed. Glass littered the floor, along with
papers from the desk and books from the shelves,
where the intruders had randomly pulled whole sec-
tions down, searching for a hidden wall safe.

Jay didn't look surprised when he saw her in the
doorway. As she moved into the room and set the
candlestick down on the desk, she had the odd notion that he'd known she was there all along.

Quin studied the smooth way Jay was moving, the
utter efficiency in everything he did as he searched
the man lying sprawled by the cabinet. He extracted
something shiny from the man's rucksack and
straightened, a knife in his hand.

For months now she'd seen him as an invalid, but
that impression had just been corrected. "You can't remember your name, your family, or where you came
from. You don't even know how old you are…." Her
gaze locked on the reddish contusion on the side of the
sprawled man's neck. "But you can remember *that*."

And a whole lot more. The words played through Jay's mind, edged and clear and instantly available, but when they hit the unruly tangle of his tongue, all that came out was a grunt.

His jaw clenched in frustration. He knew phonetics, and he understood English, Spanish and a smattering of the Quechua that was spoken here, but his mouth and tongue—his vocal cords—had forgotten that most basic of functions: how to make the sounds his mind directed them to make.

Unclenching his teeth, he tried again, letting out a breath and forcing his muscles to relax. This time he managed a sound, but it was more like a "d" than the "r" he was trying for.

He studied the knife, felt the awkward weight of it with his fingers. The wooden grip was worn smooth from years of use—a kitchen tool, not a finely balanced weapon for close-quarters combat. With lightning reflexes only slightly blunted by his months of incapacitation, he flipped the knife, gripped it by the blade and threw it. The tip of the blade pierced the chunk of wood perched on top of the pile in the log basket. Despite the fact that the knife was a little on the light side and the handle over-large, he had hit the log dead center.

Suppressing his frustration, he found a pen and a notepad, and wrote the word he couldn't say—rope—ripped off the sheet and handed it to Quin.

Quin's face was pale as she absorbed what he wanted, her pupils dilated—a classic sign of shock. As tough as she was, she wasn't used to physical violence, and he'd been hard on her, but if he hadn't kept her silent, the two men would have been difficult to contain, and he couldn't protect the three women in the house, all in different rooms, at the same time.

As she left the room, he checked on the man behind the desk. He was still unconscious. Like his friend, his reflexes had been nonexistent, his muscle tone poor—easy pickings.

The chilling assessment came easily, a new facet of him that slid into place as neatly as a well-oiled part in a machine.

When he'd woken with the sure knowledge that someone was breaking into the house, the burst of adrenaline had altered his mind. Like a door opening on a cold river, the expanse of knowledge that had flooded him had been profound, and this time the door hadn't slammed closed. For the first time since he'd regained consciousness, he hadn't had to struggle to think, to concentrate. His mind and body had shifted into another mode. He had sorted and discarded techniques with none of the cloudiness and headaches that usually accompanied trying to remember. The knowledge had simply been there, as if danger had been the key to unlocking it.

Quin reappeared with a coil of thin nylon rope. Seconds later, Olivia and Hannah stepped into the room.

Olivia took in the scene with one sweeping glance. "I thought I heard glass breaking."

When both men were secured, Hannah briefly examined them, then stood, pushing soft gray hair back from her forehead. "What on earth did they think they could steal? We haven't got anything worth taking except a few pieces of furniture, and they'd have the devil's own job dragging those out of the valley."

Olivia went down in a crouch and began emptying the contents of one man's pack. "Artifacts. They probably searched all the outbuildings, and when they didn't find anything, decided to try their luck in the house."

Quin knelt beside Olivia and helped her retrieve their few antiquities, which had been wrapped in pieces of rag. Each piece was familiar: a torc from Wales, a scarab from Egypt, an ancient glass vessel from Greece.

Her fingers closed around a fragment of stone she hadn't seen before. Curiously, she examined the symbol, the depth to which the stone was cut and the precision with which the work had been done, automatically trying to grasp the likely time period. There was no question that the symbol was Incan—a warning—and so ancient that her spine tightened and her belly clenched.

As she stared at the incised curves, knowledge flickered, abruptly disorienting, as elusive and slippery as the eel-like serpent carved into the stone; then her mind fastened on exactly what Olivia had said. The thieves had been searching for artifacts. She studied the chunk of stone. And this was a *new* artifact.

To her knowledge, Olivia hadn't had a new artifact in all the years they'd been at Valle del Sol. She'd turned her back on the archaeological world out of necessity. Other than teaching Quin, she had stubbornly avoided anything at all to do with the subject. She didn't follow what was happening in the field, and she didn't participate in digs. As far as Quin knew, no one from the aunts' past had any clue as to their current whereabouts, and Olivia took particular care to keep it that way.

The artifact was Incan, and Quin was almost certain it hadn't been sent to Olivia by an old associate. The only logical conclusion was that she had found it locally. "Why would anyone hunt for artifacts here?"

Olivia didn't try to dissemble. "There's a temple site here, and it's extensive. Every time we have a flood, the river throws up a piece of carved rock or a shard of pottery. I usually go out and check, and hide anything I find, but it looks like someone else found something and decided to look for more."

She didn't add that, if these two men had come,

more would follow. Unearthing an archaeological site was akin to igniting gold fever; there was no sense involved, just greed.

Olivia studied the unconscious man lying next to the shattered glass of her cabinet, the papers from her desk scattered on the floor.

The break-in was a shock, but she had half expected something like this to happen. With every flood it had become more and more difficult to contain the secret, and the last flood had been a doozy, wiping out the lower fields for weeks and replotting the course of the river. But the blow of discovery aside, the fact that the Incan site was now common knowledge was just a detail. On a scale of disasters, it didn't rate with the simple fact that they were broke.

She bent and picked up a letter she'd received only that morning. According to the Peruvian government, the grant they'd applied for had just dissolved into a handful of nothing. The money wouldn't have done much more than keep them in diesel and some basic medical supplies—enough that they could have limped through another winter—but even so, the loss stung. The roof was leaking, and, according to Luis, the Bedford needed a new gearbox. If anything else went wrong, they would go under.

The disappointment of the collapsed funding on top of the break-in was abruptly too much. For the first time in years, Olivia lost her temper, anger flaring so hotly it warmed the chill out of her bones. Once her temper had been legendary, but, as the years had slipped by, she'd forgotten what it felt like to be not just angry, but spitting mad.

She was tired of trying to squeeze money out of a funding system that had about as much substance as fresh air, and she was tired of hiding from Quin's father, John Mallory.

She wasn't poor—both she and Hannah had resources they could call upon—and now they had no choice.

It would be a risk going back to England, but there was too much at stake not to take the risk. She had toyed with the idea for the last few months but had pulled back from making a decision, because it was entirely possible there was still a warrant out for her arrest. She might not make it through passport control at Heathrow, let alone manage to sell her townhouse.

Ignoring Hannah's worried gaze, Olivia picked her way through the chaos of books and papers, reached up and pulled an atlas from one of the rich, mahogany bookshelves. "I'm going to England. And you, young lady, are going to school."

Quin froze in the act of sweeping shards of glass onto the hearth shovel. She picked up a jagged piece that had snagged between polished boards and added it to the pile. "We can't afford that."

"We can now." Olivia cleared a space on the desk,

set the book down, opened it to a page she had already marked and stabbed a finger at a location.

"I've picked out a university that attracts major funding for its archaeological program, and I've checked on the head of department. I might have been out of the loop for a while, but I still know who's who in that world. Theodore Hawthorne may be getting on in years, but he's a first-class archaeologist."

Quin's stomach lurched at the opportunity Olivia was handing her. Since she'd been a child, she had dreamed about following in Olivia's footsteps.

Mouth dry, she stared at the map—the jumble of the room and the unconscious men lying bound on the floor dissolving. "The United States?"

"Oxford would have been my first choice," Olivia said crisply. "But that's too closely connected to the Mallory family. You're of age, so it shouldn't matter, but humor me on this. I don't trust your father an inch."

Olivia reached into a drawer, drew out a thick brown envelope and handed it to Quin.

Inside the envelope, Quin found a dark blue prospectus and a sheaf of loose papers containing course dates and information on student accommodation. Heart pounding, she flipped through the pages, her throat closing at the trouble that Olivia had gone to. She studied the cutoff date for enrolment, and her stomach plunged. "Even if you could get me in, it's too late to enroll."

"I've already spoken to Theo. There's a place for you if you want it." Another risk Olivia had had to take, this one almost as bad as running the gauntlet of Heathrow would be. The academic world was small and peppered with gossips. Theo had promised to be discreet, but Olivia had no illusions that the fact that Quin was her niece—*and* the missing Mallory baby—would remain a secret for long.

Quin stared blankly at the atlas. Washington, New York, Boston. The names were exotic, enticing, woven with possibilities. She pulled her gaze from the map and closed the prospectus, her mind working furiously. She wanted to go, and now, incredibly, it seemed that she could, but now that the opportunity was staring her in the face—the dream so close she could almost touch it...

She shook her head. "I can't."

Olivia and Hannah were both in their midsixties, and while they both frequently stated that they were as tough as old boots, Quin knew the reality. She had done increasing amounts of the heavy work around the mission for years, and now that Jose had retired, unless they managed to hire a casual, like Luis, she was the handyman and gardener. "Who would look after you when I'm gone? Who would chop wood and keep the garden going?"

"I will."

Both Olivia's and Quin's heads snapped around at the unexpected clarity of Jay's voice.

He rose fluidly from his crouched position beside one of the bound figures, the stiffness in his right side no longer apparent, and Quin was abruptly aware that somehow, in the space of a few minutes, *everything* had changed. Valle del Sol was opening up to *huaqueros*—looters; she was going to college; and Jay was no longer an invalid, but a very large, very in-control male.

Olivia's gaze was sharp, measuring, and for long moments silence reigned, the ticking of the antique carriage clock on the mantel the only sound. "I can't pay much."

Jay's head jerked in brief assent. The familiar silence of his reply—bypassing the need to struggle with words—should have been reassuring, but now it went with a sharp, cool look that was utterly devoid of frustration.

Quin could sense the difference in him—see it physically in the way he held himself. Despite the uncanny link that existed between them, there had always been a yawning gap, and it had just grown even wider.

Without thinking, she reached out with her mind and found...blankness. Jay had firmly closed the door on the strangeness of the mind link. The invalid she'd healed had ceased to be, buried beneath a new, mysterious layer, and she had to wonder who *this* Jay was.

One thing was certain, he didn't need her anymore. He didn't need anyone. He was now completely independent, capable of leaving the mission if he wished.

Ambivalence filled her—a stomach-churning mixture of fear and elation. Everything had changed, and now she was heading into the unknown. By her reckoning she would be gone for five years minimum, more probably eight or nine, if she opted to go for a doctorate.

After spending most of her life yearning to leave the valley, she had to wonder if she would ever see it again.

PART 2

Sixteen

A full moon crested the eastern rim of the hills and spilled light into the crescent-shaped chalice of the valley, glowing coldly on the limed walls of the mission and reflecting off the surface of the Agueda.

A shimmer broke the placid calm, blurring the smooth, glassy perfection, but for long seconds the silence continued to reign, until an owl hooted and took flight, ghosting above the water's edge. Seconds later, the owl plunged, its talons closing on a tiny field mouse, disturbed and thrown off guard by the strange, shivering ripples that had turned the mirror-like surface of the Agueda into rough silk.

"Miguel!" Pedro called, directing his flashlight

into the narrow underground aperture Miguel had uncovered just a week ago. "It's time. We need to go."

"*Idiota!* Get that light out of my face. There's something here…." Miguel scraped at the dirt, wriggled forward in the tight wormhole he'd dug and extended his hand. "I can't quite reach it…."

"I don't like it." Pedro's voice faded as if he'd retreated to the opening of the tunnel. "Juana said not to come. It's not a good night."

"What do you mean, *not a good night?*" Miguel gained another inch, bending his body at an impossible angle to ease between giant blocks of stone that had fallen and wedged at right angles, leaving just enough space for him to reach into the one small pocket they hadn't yet been able to investigate. "And don't give me any more crap about the 'Sun Stone' or the 'Eye of the Sun God,'" he muttered, his patience stretched to the limit by Pedro's babbling and a legend that had already taken a month of his life for no visible pay. "If there's a jewel that big in this pile of shit, I'll marry that ugly sister of yours. And if there's even a fragment of gold or copper or some lousy old broken pot, I don't care if it's protected or cursed, or grows nine legs and runs in circles. I'm selling it."

"If Lomax sees the light—"

"He won't, because you draped a tarp over the entrance." Miguel sucked in a breath filled with the dank, thick reek of mud and the sharp scent of his own sweat. There was something there—a shape, maybe even a glint of metal. He played his light over the dirt face, minutely studying every grain, every smear. "Holy Mother."

"What is it? What can you see?"

Miguel surged forward, wriggling in the claustrophobic space. He felt the muscles in his back stretch, the vertebrae creak, as he drove upwards with his trowel, scraping all the skin off his knuckles as he swept dirt from the irregularly shaped stone standing square in his path. Dirt showered his face, stung his eyes, and a pale worm wriggled frantically away from the beam of the flashlight as he stared at the precise join he'd just uncovered.

Miguel didn't know much about archaeology or architecture—he could barely read or write, come to that—but he knew a keystone when he saw one, and this was the mother of all keystones.

Dirt showered his face again, this time peppering his mouth and nostrils. "Hey, Pedro, you sonovabitch," he snarled. "Stop walking around up there. You're supposed to be helping me." A paroxysm of coughing cut short a list of expletives. "Now I've got a mouthful of dirt."

And worms. He spat. He hated worms.

Pedro's voice was unexpectedly close. "Whoever's up there, it isn't me."

Pedro stepped back from Miguel's feet, lifted his lantern and craned around, studying the shrouded entrance to the tunnel, looking for some sign of movement. The tarpaulin was still draped in place, blocking out the moonlight and closing them into this damp, stinking little pit.

He hadn't heard a thing but Miguel swearing and cursing for the past hour, but that didn't mean there wasn't someone up there.

Cold clenched at his spine, and his belly turned to water at the possibilities. "Maybe it *is* Lomax." Miguel was scathing, but Pedro had a healthy respect for him. He'd spent a year in the army before he'd thrown that life away to hook up with Miguel, supposedly to earn big money in the mines, and he *knew* the kind of man Jay Lomax was. It was something in the eyes, a way of moving…. "He's like a cat, that one. If he does sleep, it's with one eye open."

Miguel rolled his eyes, spat more mud and swore. "Shut up about Lomax." He scraped at the stone, ignoring the throbbing pain in his back, the stinging across his knuckles. The edge of the trowel caught on something hard, and he wriggled forward another half inch and trained the weakening beam of light on whatever it was that had made that hard, metallic sound, praying that it hadn't been granite.

Light caught on the hot gleam of gold. Adrenaline pumped, almost stopping his heart.

Miguel had heard it said that whatever was here was forbidden, that this place had the curse of the serpent on it, but for all he cared, the devil himself could be in residence here and he wouldn't be deterred. He had no time for the old superstitions. Gold was gold—and, in the artifact trade, ancient gold would earn him a suitcase full of American dollars.

He reached forward, the ache in his back excruciating as he scraped dirt from the shiny surface—gently, gently, he didn't want to damage the goods.

The bold outline of an eye appeared.

A second dose of adrenaline shot through Miguel's veins. His head bounced back in instant reflex and smacked against stone, and the flashlight slipped from his fingers, the feeble beam almost extinguished in the mud.

He sucked in a breath, calming the rapid beat of his heart and ignoring the hot throbbing at the back of his skull. "Holy mother of God."

For a brief instant, with the flashlight flickering across it, the eye had appeared to move—but it must have been a trick of the light. He was getting as bad as Pedro and that crazy woman he was sleeping with. "Pass me another bucket."

Reluctantly, he inched backward far enough that he could pass Pedro the bucket he'd filled with dirt. It was a frustrating business, and slow, but short of bringing in mechanical equipment and exposing their presence, this was the only way they could dig.

Pedro handed him an empty bucket. "What's up there? What have you found?"

"Something that'll change that old witch Juana's predictions." Miguel spat more mud. There was mud everywhere—they were both coated in it—but this time it would pay off. "Gold, *stupido!*" He didn't bother to keep the glee from his voice as he struggled back into the slippery hole, for the first time in his life glad that he was small and lean, instead of tall and thick and stupid, like Pedro. For once his lack of stature had paid off. He would have to share the proceeds of the gold; there was no wriggling out of that—Pedro was connected, a distant cousin of Ramirez—but even so, a half share would make him rich.

Miguel ignored Pedro's incessant questions as he continued to excavate, his gaze fastened on the growing expanse of smooth metal that gleamed like liquid heat in the darkness, reflecting the failing beam of light so that the dim, filthy hole seemed almost as bright as day.

It was beautiful—*beautiful.* He could see the eye now, and what looked like a hand. Strange symbols, not like any of the Incan or Mayan ones he'd seen. Still, what did he know?

He grinned as he worked, carefully scraping at the

dirt so as not to scratch the metal. And what did he care what it was, so long as it fetched a good price?

He couldn't believe it; they were going to be rich.

Dirt showered his face again, and his fury at Pedro's incompetence erupted. "Stop moving around— I can hardly work."

"It's not me—it's the ground." Pedro's voice faded as if he'd retreated to the tunnel entrance, then grew louder as he poked his head up near Miguel's boots. "This doesn't feel good. I'm getting out."

Miguel barely registered Pedro's whine as he worked feverishly to uncover the third symbol. The shape of a sword emerged from the damp, crusted dirt, and his hand froze. He stared at the glyph in blind fascination, struck with awe, and all the hairs at the back of his neck lifted.

Eye of God, hand of God, sword of God.

The words ran through his mind, a cold whisper that set up a peculiar tension in the pit of his stomach. In a reflex that had all but deserted him, he muttered a brief prayer and crossed himself.

A cool wind blew against his legs, making his stomach clench and his bladder spasm with the urgent need to urinate.

Vaguely, he registered that the cold breeze had been caused by the tarpaulin flap being lifted as that weasel, Pedro, scurried from the tunnel.

A split second later, the almost imperceptible

shaking turned into a sickening roll, and the two stone blocks that were wedged over Miguel began to move. With a grating noise that was lost in the roar of the earthquake as the leading edge of the shock wave hit the valley, one block ground down the face of the other, crushing Miguel's back and chest, and completely severing the lower part of his body.

Seventeen

"The first body found at the entrance to the temple was severed in two by the earthquake two weeks ago. Now the ruin has claimed a second life—a member of the Peruvian archaeological team that arrived to investigate the ruins revealed by the quake has been found dead in his tent. As yet, the cause of death is unknown, but with several other members of the team suffering the symptoms of a mysterious illness that local people claim is the result of an ancient curse protecting the temple, the remaining archaeologists are spooked. Apparently a number of personnel have already walked off the dig, including a large Peruvian contingent.

"With the second death, the Peruvian government is investigating the possibility of closing the site altogether and—"

Quin turned off the radio as she drove her Jeep over the new steel bridge that now spanned the Agueda, her amazement that the old rope bridge had finally been replaced superceded by the tension that had driven her for the past forty-eight hours.

The quake had been a five point two on the Richter scale—and a ten on the panic scale when she'd finally gotten the news in Honduras—twelve days *after* the event—and found out that the epicenter had been less than fifteen miles from the valley.

Communications had been restored, but apart from a brief telephone conversation with Olivia assuring her that they were fine, all she'd had to go on were the sketchy news broadcasts she'd caught on various radio stations as she'd driven overland from Lima.

Frustratingly, the news reports hadn't concentrated on the mission or the village, only on the fact that the quake had revealed a "lost city."

Pulling onto the shoulder of the road, Quin killed the engine, her gaze sweeping the mission. She'd been away from the valley for nearly ten years. As finances had eased—thanks to Jay's investment skills—the aunts had taken to visiting her when she had vacations. She'd heard plenty about the valley, but this time, even though she knew Olivia and Hannah were fine, verbal reassurance hadn't been enough.

Relief poured through her when she saw that the buildings appeared to have suffered minimal damage, if any at all, but her tension reasserted itself as her gaze drifted past the mission and further down the curve of the valley.

From the information she'd gleaned from the radio while she'd driven from Lima to Vacaro, the find was slated as the most important since Machu Picchu and the most enigmatic since the Sphinx. Enigmatic because the entrance was on comparatively low land, not built high, as Cuzco and Machu Picchu were. The size of the uncovered gateway to the temple alone had excited major interest, and, in addition, there was evidence that a part of the temple, at least, had been built by a civilization that far predated the Incas.

As singular as it was, in no way did the find please Quin. She felt fiercely protective of Olivia and Hannah—of the entire valley—and now Valle del Sol was open and exposed, not only to archaeologists and the inevitable stream of looters, but to the world. Despite the fact that she was an archaeologist and uncovering the past was her business, a stubborn part of her rejected the incursion.

As she surveyed the ruin, at first all she could see was mud. The slip, which had been caused by the earthquake, was huge. Thousands of tons of mud and debris had moved, plunging all the way to the valley floor, tearing away the face of an entire hillside to reveal the remnants of ancient terraces and tumbled buildings.

Automatically, Quin traced the symmetry of the terracing, gauging distances and angles, the evidence of colonnades at what must be the temple gate, the blurred lines of avenues and squares, the large sunken area where the tavern had been....

She blinked and froze, gooseflesh rising as if someone had just walked over her grave, and for a moment she wondered if she *was* crazy, not different, not psychic—just plain, staring crazy.

With slow, deliberate movements, Quin hooked her sunglasses off her nose, rubbed her eyes and looked again. She felt strange, both hot and cold, and a little shaky, as if she was coming down with a fever, and abruptly reality shimmered and dissolved beneath the burning heat of the sun as the torn bones of an ancient city laid bare were replaced by another image entirely. Pristine buildings flowed along steep contours, the harsh granite softened by sun-bleached plaster and lush plantings spilling over terraced walls. Shady squares provided cool resting places as people scurried out of the sun along narrow paved streets filled with barefooted children and men bent double beneath baskets laden with colorful produce. Knots of soldiers strolled the avenues and squatted beneath shade trees, weapons glinting where they caught the sun. And over all, smoke from braziers hung in air that rippled like water in the noonday haze.

For a disorienting moment that stretched and

clung, the image remained, as sharply real as the broken spring that protruded through the cracked vinyl of the Jeep's driver's seat, the grainy, pockmarked texture of the steering wheel beneath her fingers.

Blinking, she fitted her sunglasses back on the bridge of her nose and started the Jeep. "You *are* going crazy, Quin."

The vivid dream she'd experienced when she was thirteen—and almost succeeded in forgetting—had just come back and bitten her on the ass in full Technicolor.

It had been years since she'd thought of that dream, years since she'd stopped trying to work out what was real and what was fantasy; it had been years since she'd healed. In leaving Valle del Sol, she'd left that whole part of her life behind, but the moment she'd reentered the valley, it was as if she'd driven into an invisible force field and something had gone haywire.

Her fingers tightened on the steering wheel.

No more running, no more pretending that what she'd experienced didn't exist, because a part of it, at least, did. Jay was real, and the temple was real.

Curse or not, she was going into that temple to find some answers.

Minutes later she pulled to a halt beside a knot of vehicles grouped to the side of a small canvas town that stretched to the foot of the mission orchard.

When she'd left ten years ago, the orchard had consisted of a scattering of scrawny, diseased trees clinging to the edge of the compound—just enough to provide the mission itself with fruit. Now, rows of well-kept trees, protected from the wind by trimmed shelterbelts, flowed over several acres, and she could see the corrugated iron roof of what looked like a packing shed in the distance.

A lot of things had changed.

A flurry of movement, the flash of sun off glass, drew her eye back to the canvas encampment.

Elias Cain was posed in front of a camera, hair perfect, classic dust-colored drill shirt neatly pressed, his voice as smooth as dark honey for the sound mike.

On the other hand, some things stayed exactly the same.

"Sonovabitch."

Cain was here before her.

Pulling the key from the ignition, she swung out of the Jeep and slammed the door.

Elias Cain.

She'd walked off a site in Honduras just days ago, a site that Cain had run through with all the finesse of a hurricane, milking the media that followed him like a pack of bloodhounds—then abandoning the lot for fresh pickings. The fact that the fresh pickings were in Valle del Sol—*her* valley—didn't please Quin one little bit.

As she strode between the tents, studying the layout of the encampment, she pocketed the keys, fished out the photo ID tag she'd used in Honduras and clipped it on to the lapel of her shirt. The sorting tents were easy to identify—they were little more than tarpaulins stretched overtop of trestle tables. It was the large tent with the closed flap and Keep Out sign that interested her the most.

As she strolled, she noted patches of dead grass where tents had been, illustrating just how many personnel had already vacated the site. Evidently the illness or curse that had sent most of the Peruvian team running hadn't been enough to scare off Cain or the media.

A student cleaning pottery shards with a soft brush sent her a curious look, but the second his gaze settled on the ID tag, he relaxed and went back to his work. All of the other students and personnel that formed Cain's archaeological hit team were too focused on the man himself, and his smooth delivery in front of the camera, to notice a stranger in their midst.

Cain's voice, pitched for an audience, was now clearly audible. "...the seal is only the first of many wonders, and it points the way to an archaeological find that could possibly rival that of Tutankhamen's tomb. And..." he paused for dramatic effect, "if local legend is correct, we could be on the verge of finding an ancient treasure that rivals the Holy

Grail—a treasure that not one, but two cultures held sacred. If the protective seals are anything to go by—"

Jaw clamped, Quin stepped inside the tent, dismissing Cain and his sideshow, which was designed to create hype and publicity and keep his major sponsor, a multinational pharmaceutical company, happy with the number of times their logo appeared on newscasts. Evidently, this time, he'd hit gold.

Lifting the sunglasses off her nose, she slid them into her breast pocket and allowed her eyes to adjust to the soupy green light.

The tent was filled with wooden packing boxes and large plastic bags of packing material. Work tables were set up either side of the tent. On each table, artifacts were neatly placed in labeled boxes, ready to be shipped.

Cain couldn't have been here long. The temple itself had only been uncovered when the quake struck.

Someone had found a seal….

Restlessly, her gaze swept the tables, then caught on a shape that was wrapped in cloth and stored in a separate box. Without hesitation, she reached for the bundle, and for a split second she felt again the dizzying sense of displacement she'd experienced when she'd handled the stone artifact Olivia had found all those years ago.

Shaking off the uncanny feeling, she lifted the object out, surprised by the weight of it.

As the final fold of cloth fell away, for an endless moment she floundered, caught between two worlds, one ancient—obscured by mists and shadows and indecipherable puzzles—the other brash and commercial—too easy and too fast to comprehend the dissolving echoes of the past.

The seal was gold.

A heaviness grew in her head, accompanied by a pressurized, smothering sensation as if she'd just been rolled under a dark wave. For a disorienting moment her heart pounded and she struggled to breathe. The absurd thought hung in her mind that for the first time in her life she was actually going to faint, and it *had* to be on Cain's turf.

The heavy gold plate slid from her fingers, and the sharp clatter of the artifact hitting the table broke the eerie effect. Sucking in a breath, Quin shook off the claustrophobia that had materialized, unwanted, out of thin air.

Cold seeped into the pit of her stomach as she studied the seal where it lay, unwilling to risk touching the artifact again. The first row of symbols were universal, a warning and a protection in one: the eye, the hand and the sword. As for the rest… The glyphs were smaller, more intricate, and completely unfamiliar, but the doorplate as a whole was easy to understand.

Only the most important messages were delivered in gold. And this one was a keep out sign. A double whammy when taken in context with the Incan serpent Olivia had found. Two cultures didn't want whatever was beneath the ground dug up.

The tent flap was thrown back, letting in a cooling breeze, and the familiar sharp features of Cain's right-hand man appeared.

Hathaway straightened, his narrow face darkening. "What are *you* doing in here? Didn't you see the sign? This is a restricted area."

"Hathaway. It never rains but it pours." Deliberately, Quin picked up a shard of pottery and examined it. The fractured edges were fresh, which figured. Speed was of the essence with Cain. The bastards weren't preserving, they were mining—dredging the ground for significant artifacts, while the real treasure, the fragile imprint of the past, was crushed beneath Cain's expensive boot.

Hathaway's gaze fastened on the gold seal where it lay, glowing dully on the table. *"You handled the seal."* His jaw compressed so hard a pulse ticked in his cheek. "If you damaged it—"

She replaced the pottery shard in its box. "What, Hathaway? You'll sue? That doorplate, along with every other artifact you've uncovered, belongs to the Peruvian government, not you."

Quin watched as he retrieved the gold plate with

a soft cotton cloth, careful not to touch it with his fingers and risk contaminating it with skin oils and salts, as he returned the seal to its box.

His gaze darted over the table to see if she'd handled anything else. "How do you know it's a doorplate?"

"Anyone with half a degree in archaeology would—and besides, in my spare time I watch CNN."

"Bitch."

She lifted a brow. "Sticks and stones... You can call me any name you like, Hathaway, but it won't change your basic problem—you're just not that bright."

The low, smooth register of Cain's voice sounded just outside the tent as he spoke to the student working at the cleaning table. A split second later he dipped his head and entered the tent. *"Mallory."*

It wasn't a compliment. She and Cain had butted heads on more than one dig. Quin hadn't been able to stand his shoddy methods and attention-grabbing tactics, and Cain hadn't liked her having an opinion about anything at all. Even if they hadn't clashed professionally, it was a sure bet they would never have gotten on. There was a basic gulf in values between them that meant she and Cain would never co-exist comfortably.

"Cain, as I live and breathe. Why didn't I know you'd be here?"

"I'm here with permission—you're not. Get out."

Quin resisted the urge to say, "Make me." Cain would, despite the fact that she was female. If he had ever possessed a scruple, it had long since been lost in the stampede to find fame and fortune in front of the television cameras. If she wanted to oust him from the valley, she would have to play the game on a field she could win—a professional one—and, as always, with Cain and Hathaway, the battle would be fraught with mental and political maneuvering.

Cain straightened as if reaching for more height and jerked his thumb at the tent flap. "I want you out of this valley—*now.*"

Quin lifted a brow. She was taller than both Cain and Hathaway, and neither of them liked it. Too bad. "You'll have trouble kicking me out of my own backyard. As it happens, this is where I live. Looks like, this time, Cain, you're just going to have to suck it up."

"And like it."

The voice was low and succinct and as dry as the Atacama Desert, sending a small shiver up her spine.

A shadow flickered over the canvas, and Quin's heart jumped a beat as Jay ducked and entered the tent.

Cain stiffened. "Didn't you read the sign, Lomax? This is a restricted area."

"I can read. The question is, can you listen?" Jay's gaze caught on Quin's, night-dark and utterly cold; then his attention shifted back to Cain. "The only reason you're here is because some bureaucrat in the government screwed up. Like I said before, one wrong move and you're gone."

"You're bluffing. You don't have that kind of power."

Jay opened the tent flap wide. "Take a look, Cain. Jungle, hills, mountains—and one treacherous bitch of a river. A government permit and TV cameras don't mean much here. When you run out of diesel, or your generator breaks down, don't expect a helping hand. And by the way, you're camped on a flood plain. If you don't move to higher ground, you'll lose everything in the next downpour."

Cain's face reddened. "You know what, Lomax? You look familiar. I don't know where I've seen you, but I've seen you somewhere. I might just do some research."

"Be my guest. If you find anything interesting, let me know."

Jay jerked his head, indicating that Quin should precede him out of the tent.

As they strode through the camp, Quin was acutely aware of him beside her, his gait smooth and unimpeded. "You've lost your limp." And gained a whole lot of something that made her chest tight and her stomach turn somersaults.

Physically, Jay had always been imposing, but now she felt on the back foot mentally, and that hardly ever happened. In her profession, she met a lot of bright guys, most of them academic nerds who lived for the power of information, but none possessed the edge and sheer masculine confidence that were as much a part of Jay as his lean, muscular height. With Cain she'd witnessed something she thought she would never live to see: Cain's ass being thoroughly kicked.

"And you've lost your shyness."

"I don't remember being shy."

"Maybe 'discretion' is a better word. Olivia expected you up at the house an hour ago."

"I was on schedule until I saw Cain."

"So you thought you'd beard him in his den."

"I don't think of Cain as a lion. His belly's too low to the ground for that."

He opened the driver's door of her Jeep and gestured she get in. "Don't underestimate him. He's smooth, but he's dangerous."

And you would be the one to know.

Even in a comatose state, he'd been able to reach out and mentally grab her by the scruff of the neck, but now there was no sign that he'd ever suffered a stroke and partial paralysis, no sign he'd ever lost any part of himself but his patience. "Don't worry, I know what he's like. I just wanted to put him on notice."

Jay closed the door, walked around the bonnet and climbed into the passenger seat. "Same old Quin. Live by the sword."

Humor surfaced despite the roiling in her stomach because Cain, the desecrating bastard, was actually here, in *her* valley.

She turned the key in the ignition, reversed and turned onto the winding drive that led to the mission. "When it comes to Cain, that's the only way."

He grinned, teeth white against the hard line of his jaw, and Quin almost drove into the ditch.

Clamping her jaw, she stared rigidly at the road and drove.

Here we go again.

Ten years, and she still had it as bad as snakebite.

Eighteen

From the library windows, Quin watched the sun slide below the western hills while the gentle strains of Beethoven's "Adagio Cantabile" wafted from the lounge—another of the changes at the mission. Olivia and Hannah had a CD player.

In the last of the fading light, the earthquake damage to the mission was more evident. The shadows emphasized hairline cracks in the exterior walls and "bald patches" on the roof, where tiles had been dislodged. But apart from the visible damage, and a few broken windows that had already been repaired, the mission had escaped relatively unscathed and looked better than ever.

In the years Quin had been away, the exterior walls had been resurfaced and newly limed, the fences and outbuildings had been put into good repair, and a new apartment had been built for Jay, linking the garage and outbuildings in a U-shape that enclosed the courtyard on three sides. Instead of the hunting ground for free-ranging chickens that the courtyard had once been, the area was now neatly paved and overhung by shady trees, with a fountain tinkling in the center.

Quin turned when Olivia entered the room with a tea tray. "Does Cain know who you are?"

Olivia didn't look happy. "Not yet, but give him time. My books are still in circulation. I'm almost certain I saw that weasel, Hathaway, reading one yesterday."

"You could move. You can afford it."

Olivia's jaw set. "I'm not going to be pushed out of my home. All we have to do is sit tight. Cain doesn't usually stay any place longer than a month or two."

Quin glanced at the corner of Cain's encampment, which was visible from the window. "He could be longer on this one, if the legend he's pushing has any credence."

Olivia made a rude sound. "He's setting himself up for a fall. Apparently he's been interviewing the villagers and old Elena has given him some spiel about a jewel called The Eye of the Sun God." She lifted her shoulders. "Maybe there's something there, and maybe there isn't, but the odds are against it, even if the temple did have a gold seal. Whatever was kept there must have been very important—too important to leave. If the temple was abandoned, for whatever reason, in all likelihood the place was stripped centuries ago. Cain will bull his way in to find nothing but stale air and dust."

Quin strolled across the thick Turkish rug that now softened the library floor. "If a natural disaster happened, like an earthquake, or the slip that buried the city, all of the temple possessions could still be there, which would explain why the gold seal was still intact."

Olivia's glance was sharp. "In my opinion that's an unlikely scenario. The slip could have happened at any time."

Quin was inclined to agree. Greed was a factor in any age, and the ancient ones weren't exempt. If there had been treasure of any kind inside the temple, the people of the temple's time would have known about it. Chances were it would have been ransacked at the first opportunity.

But her stomach, and the memory of the dream, said something else. In the dream she'd been on her way to collect something important—to remove it for safekeeping—and she'd never made it.

Quin studied the artifact Hannah had sitting on a pile of notes, acting as a paperweight. The afternoon light caught the fragment of stone, making the serpent seem even more deeply incised. She indicated the reams of notepaper covered in Olivia's neat hand. "You've been working."

"And I've made progress. I even made it inside the maze a few times, until I got caught. Now Cain's upped the security."

Quin weighed the chunk of blue granite in her palm, studying the way the embedded quartzite sparkled in the light. "This is definitely Incan, but the doorplate isn't."

Olivia went still. "You've *seen* the seal?"

"And handled it." Jay's dark voice cut through the gentle strains of the adagio as he strolled through the door and deposited a bundle of mail on the desk. "She broke into Cain's tent."

A grim smile twitched at Olivia's mouth. "I'll bet he's messing his pretty pants about that. He hasn't released any information about the seal, because he's afraid someone will work it out before he does."

Tension tightened all along Quin's spine as she watched Jay help himself to tea, then take up the position at the window she'd just vacated.

Since he'd intervened with Cain and hitched a ride with her back to the mission that afternoon, Quin hadn't seen Jay at all. Apparently he spent his day managing the orchard and running an engineering workshop, which employed several men from the village. In his spare time he took care of any maintenance the mission required. According to Olivia, the place was now run with military precision, and she had nothing to do but complain, get under Hannah's feet, make trouble and cook.

Olivia taking over the kitchen wasn't an ideal arrangement, because cooking wasn't her favorite pastime, but she had insisted. Jay had taken on the responsibility of making the mission solvent, and now that it was a productive enterprise that provided employment for a good deal of the village, she'd argued that the least she could do was provide them all with one hot meal a day.

Quin replaced the artifact and accepted the mug of tea Olivia handed her. "The excavation needs someone with depth and integrity. That doesn't exactly describe Elias Cain. He's already pushed the local guys aside. I didn't see any of the Peruvian team guarding the tent, but then, that's his style. He uses his fame and the cameras to intimidate."

Jay turned from his vantage point at the window. "Not to mention the illness, which seems selective. Most of the Peruvian team went down."

Olivia made herself comfortable in the old-fashioned leather chair that was positioned behind the desk. "And when Garcia died, all but a handful pulled out."

Setting her mug down on the desk, Quin pulled a blank piece of paper toward her and deftly began drawing glyphs. "That's why you should be running it. Cain wouldn't stand a chance."

"That's a nice theory, but if I came out of the closet, it's highly unlikely the Peruvian government would let a woman who harbored a child illegally get anywhere near the site."

Quin set the piece of paper with the glyphs down in front of Olivia. "It's an old crime, if it was ever a crime at all."

Olivia slipped on a pair of spectacles and leaned forward. "We'll see. Chances are the salsa's going to hit the fan soon, anyway. I might have been out of the loop for nearly thirty years, but sooner or later, someone's going to recognize me."

She frowned as she examined the glyphs. "An eye, a hand and a sword. They're easy enough—as clear as a 'Keep Out' sign, and they look almost Egyptian. As for the rest…" She slid the glasses more firmly in place. "Not Incan or anything distinctively meso-American, *or* Egyptian." She shook her head, finger tracing the smaller glyphs. "They're completely different in form, size and composition—they look more like a mathematical equation."

"Or a language."

"Exactly." Abstractedly, Olivia searched the bookshelves, reached for a book, flipped pages, then ran her finger slowly down lines of scripts. "Aramaic is the closest thing to it, but even that doesn't quite…"

She set the book down on the desk and reached for another, opening to a page that was already marked. "The whole city is a mystery, but there's a connection here somewhere…. The fact that the Incas got into the act and built over the original structures shouldn't cloud the issue. We've seen it happen often enough before. The new culture supplants the old, and the new temple gets built on the site of the old one—sometimes beside it, sometimes right on top of it—*and* using the old materials. It comes down to practicalities. Why shift stone when you don't have to? Why clear a new site when the groundwork's already done and construction materials are at hand? In this case we have a city that is patently *not* Incan. And the maze—" She shook her head as she opened a drawer, pulled out a large sheet of paper and spread it on the desk. "The maze was used by the Minoans."

"Did you say a maze?" Quin stared at the sketch Olivia had started, and the sense of déjà vu she'd felt when she picked up the gold seal hit again, although this time not as strong and minus the claustrophobia. She'd seen a map of the maze before.

Riveted by the certainty, she reached for a pencil, pulled the map toward her and began to draw, filling in the blanks using information that had no basis in science, ephemeral glimpses of another life, another time, that made her chest tighten and her throat close with grief. When she had finished the rough outline, she stared at what she'd drawn.

The temple complex was huge. Cain had found only the western corner.

Jay watched as the sketch of the ruin grew more detailed and complex beneath Quin's deft hand. Her eyes were slightly unfocused—dreamy—as she worked, the tension that emanated from her palpable, and all the hairs at his nape lifted as not just a temple but an entire city slowly came into focus.

Her hand slowed, stopped, the pencil poised.

He indicated the blank section of the sketch that had stopped her. "The filler tank for the aqueduct goes there."

Quin lifted her gaze to Jay's. In the dim light of the library, the disturbing sense of the present and the past merging intensified. For a split second Jay's face wavered, became subtly different—his eyes a shade narrower, cheekbones even sparer. "How did you know I was drawing the well?"

"Simple engineering. Common sense."

Quin was certain she'd heard him say those same words before, even though she knew she never had. Then, as abruptly as if a switch had been flicked, the déjà vu was gone.

Olivia indicated a large chamber she'd drawn in the center of the maze. "What's that?"

What the maze was designed to protect.

"I don't know. Maybe the center of the temple itself." She stared at the drawing, then transferred her gaze to the line of glyphs. They were small, precise—easily handwritten. "Another enigma."

"And Cain's in charge of solving it." Olivia's expression was grim.

Quin's jaw tightened. "I don't know how he wangled his way in here."

"Money and influence," Jay said curtly. "The Peruvian government doesn't have the funding to excavate. Apparently Cain's come in with a seven-figure budget."

The fact that Cain had begun exploring the maze itself made her stomach churn. "Just how far has he gotten?"

"According to Cain, all the way. He's been exploring the temple and the maze for the past ten days. He's found some household utensils, all of them broken, as if the place was ransacked, and the crumbled remains of furniture and clothing, but so far, apart from the seal, none of the gold he's looking for—and no human remains. Like Olivia said, looks like someone beat him to the punch about three thousand years ago."

Nineteen

Quin eased off her hiking boots and sat down at the table that was set beneath a towering magnolia in the courtyard—and which, lately, had become her office. Rummaging in her rucksack, she pulled out her diary, set it beside her laptop, then simply sat while the computer booted up, absorbing the cool after the baking heat of the day.

Reaching into her pocket, she extracted a fragment of granite and examined the partial glyph carved into one edge of the stone. What was left of the symbol was shallow and blurred, almost erased by time and the constant abrasion of water and silt, but even so, the lines and curves had a power that held her.

As her fingertips moved over the symbol, she felt like a sleeper waking, once again alive to senses that had been dulled by years of academia and lost in the sharp hustle of Washington, with its clipped vowels, old buildings and even older money.

She'd spent the past week skirting the closed-off ruin, working a grid pattern in all the areas Cain wasn't interested in, trying to physically map the city and find one of the alternate entrances to the temple. So far she'd found what had always been there: thick undergrowth, trees and rocks.

To make the search more difficult, in the wake of the earthquake, cut rock was everywhere, as if a giant hand had played a game of dice with the city. When the side of the hill had originally slid millennia ago and buried the temple city, it must have sheared off almost every intact building that had been above ground. With this second massive slide, the devastation was revealed. Debris was scattered all the way to the Agueda. Unfortunately, the confused jumble of mud and rocks didn't help solve many puzzles. Quin was more interested in where the rocks had been before the landslide, rather than where they'd ended up.

Her simple enjoyment of being back in the valley aside, one thing was certain: she wasn't achieving much hiking around the hills. The landscape had altered so much with earthquakes, slips and thick undergrowth that trying to visualize the location of the ancient buildings and temple gates was proving impossible. So far, the hypothetical city she'd drawn was just that: a theory. What she needed was to get inside the ruin.

Placing the glyph beside the computer, she opened a file and began transferring data from her diary, logging the location covered, along with any significant terrain data or finds. Unhappily, her major find for the day—the glyph—had been found by sheer chance as she'd waded across the Agueda on her way home.

As she entered the details, a familiar form emerged from the shadows.

"*Luis*. What are you doing here?" The last she'd heard of him, he'd moved to Lima and was working for a construction crew. He had always drifted in and out of the mission—although this time, according to Hannah, he'd been gone for a good eighteen months.

"I heard there was some work going, so I headed back. Olivia told me to wait for the boss." He ran liquid dark eyes over Quin. "Looking good, girl. You got yourself a man yet?"

Quin lifted a brow, and Luis held up his hands in surrender. "Hey, enough said. What use have you ever had for a man? Still…" He flexed his arm, showing respectable biceps. "It's good to have some muscle around, eh? Just like the good ol' days."

As he sidled closer, a four-wheel drive came to a halt on the other side of the courtyard and Jay climbed out.

A whiff of cologne teased her nostrils as Luis leaned closer still, ostensibly to examine the geological map she was studying. Quin gave him a direct look. "Don't even go there, Luis."

He looked chagrined. "Hey, a guy's gotta try, but don't worry." He made a production of examining his hands. "I've always liked my fingers."

"It's not your fingers that are at risk."

Luis backed off, the grin diminished but not vanquished. "Ay, ay, what am I thinking? Trying to seduce the oldest virgin in Peru."

The oldest virgin in Peru? She had to be the oldest virgin in creation.

Jay's head jerked up. For a disconcerting moment his gaze fastened on hers, direct and unsettling; then he continued on toward the mission's office, with Luis falling obediently in behind.

Quin stared at the long line of Jay's back as he walked up the veranda steps. When he'd looked at her, the air had been charged. She transferred her attention to the computer screen.

He couldn't have picked up her thought.

That mind-reading stuff had happened years back, and only twice: once when she'd dreamed of healing him, and again when they'd had the break-in at the mission. It had been an aberration, just one more kicker to the Chambers curse, and it had seemed to be linked to the healing, something she didn't do anymore.

* * *

At midnight Quin slipped out of bed and dressed in black jeans and a T-shirt. Shouldering a small day-pack containing water, a flashlight, spare batteries and her notebook, and carrying her boots, she padded down the stairs, careful to avoid the steps that creaked. When she reached the kitchen, she laced on the boots, stepped outside and quietly closed the door behind her.

The moonlight was strong, its cold beam turning the Agueda to liquid silver, and making the shadows that surrounded the exposed ruin look black and impenetrable.

Walking with care, she picked her way around the outbuildings, avoiding the gate, which also creaked, and climbing over the fence instead. She intended to circumnavigate the ruin and the armed thugs Cain paid to pull sentry duty, and approach the ruin from the high ground to the north. With any luck, she would be able to slip through the temple gate unnoticed.

The moonlight made the going easier, but as she picked her way over a jumble of boulders, then waded knee-deep across the shallow part of the river, she could have wished for clouds and humidity. In the clear, thin air, every sound carried.

The old track to the grove was thickly overgrown, making the going difficult, but she'd walked it so often that she still remembered where the gnarled roots of trees snaked across the ground, and where the hillside was pitted with dents and holes.

Nervous excitement added an edge to the tension that gripped her as she skirted a dip that was little more than an inky pool of shadow in the moonlit landscape. She felt as if she was picking her way across a graveyard. Seeing the landscape from the perspective of an archaeologist put the sinkholes in a whole different context. Maybe they were a natural phenomenon, formed when the limestone beneath had eroded—but it was also possible they were indications of collapsed structures beneath the ground.

When she finally reached the high ground above the ruin, she paused and took in the view. Some of the exposed city that lay below had been cleaned up and laid bare, and the string lines marking out dwellings and avenues gleamed like cobwebs in the moonlight.

Picking her way through the thick growth of trees and ferns, she slowly made her way down to the slip, skirting the raw edge until she judged she was directly above the location of the temple gate. Taking a breath, she stepped out of the concealment of the forest, expecting at any moment to hear a staccato demand to halt. She'd dressed in black to make herself more difficult to see, but that had been a mistake. Against the bleached clay pan of the slip, her black clothing stood out like the proverbial sore thumb.

Minutes later, she eased down a terraced wall and

took cover in the shadow of an outcropping of rock. Her spine tightened as she pressed against stone that still retained the residual warmth of the sun. For an unnerving moment she was sure someone had seen her, but as long seconds ticked by and no demand was issued, she shook off the creepy feeling.

Taking a deep breath, she stepped out into the open. Simultaneously, a man emerged from the shadows that swamped the temple door. He was less than fifty meters away—so close she could make out his profile and the glint of something metallic in his hand. Heart pounding, she dropped to the ground. As the man stepped over a string line, his back was turned fully to her. Grabbing at the chance to escape the glaring exposure of the moonlight, Quin pushed to her feet and ducked behind the rock, wincing as a pebble rolled down the slope. As the man vaulted down a level and disappeared from sight, something about the graceful way he moved made the back of her neck prickle. She couldn't be certain, but for a split second she had thought it was Ramirez—although she had no idea what he could possibly be doing poking around the ruin. If he wanted to steal artifacts, he would have better luck raiding the tent down at Cain's encampment.

Long minutes passed while she waited, watching and listening as her heart rate and breathing dropped to something approximating normal. One of the guards strolled by the gate, then descended several levels and perched on a step that formed part of the main avenue, his back to Quin. The guard further down the slope was more difficult to spot, but he was less of a threat. He seemed content to patrol the lower reaches of the cordoned-off area.

Frowning at the laxity of security at night, when during the day security was so tight that even authorized personnel couldn't enter or leave the site without being searched, Quin adjusted her pack and once more started toward the temple door. If the night-watchmen were slack, that was Cain's problem and her advantage.

Abruptly, a hand snaked out of the darkness and clamped over her mouth. Off balance and effectively muffled, Quin found herself pulled tight against a warm, firm body.

Jay's gaze connected with hers, and his hand over her mouth loosened a little, but he didn't immediately release her. As the seconds stretched out she became increasingly aware of the masculine arm banded around her waist and the heat that radiated from Jay, even through the extra layer of the daypack. She turned her head enough that she could make eye contact again, her temple brushing his jaw.

He lifted a finger to his mouth and pointed in the direction of the temple gate just as another figure detached itself from the shadows and followed the man who had reminded her of Ramirez.

Cold invaded the pit of Quin's stomach at how close she'd come to a head-on confrontation. She would have managed to evade the temple guards, but she had been about to walk into a bear trap.

A tap on her shoulder and a hand sign signaled that he wanted to move back. Slowly, he removed his hand from her mouth.

Treading with care on the stone-hard surface, Quin followed Jay until he literally disappeared, dropping silently into a natural dip into the ground. A hand came out to help her as she slithered down the side of a gouge that angled toward the edge of the forest. When they reached the cover of the trees, Jay turned and lifted a compact pair of binoculars to his eyes. Seconds later, he handed the glasses to her.

"Night vision?"

He shook his head. "Too much light with the full moon. These are infrared. They operate on thermals. Anything with a heat source, like a human body, will stand out."

Quin panned with the glasses. She had seen four men, two on active guard duty and two exiting the temple gate. According to the infrared glasses, there were eight.

An image of the man who had reminded her of Ramirez replayed itself in her mind. With a small shudder, she handed the sleek piece of equipment back to Jay. "Are they all Cain's men?"

"Good question." He pushed a branch aside, waited until Quin had stepped through, then flicked on a flashlight. The narrow beam illuminated a thick tunnel of undergrowth, which almost completely blocked out the moonlight.

Extracting her own light from her pack, Quin followed Jay deeper into the jungle, stepping along a path that was worn enough to indicate he'd been this way more than once. "You've been watching Cain."

"Ever since he arrived. I also keep a guard on the mission. Jorge saw you leave and woke me. The only trouble was, I lost you when you went up the hill."

If he'd followed her, then he had been silent, because she'd checked her back trail more than once and hadn't heard or seen a thing.

The track grew steep, winding down into a gully that was choked with vines. It was a way she'd never used before because the terrain was so difficult, a puzzle of rocks and sinkholes, and too thickly overgrown to push through easily. Minutes later, they followed a stream bed until it culminated in a wall of rock. The silvery trickle of water formed a small pool, the surface as shiny and still as black glass, before the water simply disappeared beneath the ground.

Above them, the bluff rose, silvery gray and impressive in the moonlight, creepers and lianas clinging to its face like dark garlands.

As Quin picked her way over tumbled rocks, she automatically assessed the stone on the ground, gauging size and any regularity that might suggest it had been hand-cut and dressed. Her gaze lifted briefly, swept the rock face and caught on a moss-encrusted line almost hidden by the fall of a creeper. She stumbled and corrected, her heart missing a beat as she stared at the arrow-straight groove. It was no more than a few inches long, and so subtle it was a miracle she'd seen it at all. Chances were, if she'd searched this part of the valley during the day with the sun overhead she would have missed it. "There's something here."

The height of the cut in the rock was above her head, which meant that in all probability it continued down to the ground. Her heart pounded as Jay shoved back a heavy fall of creeper to reveal a shadowy opening, and abruptly she was sure: after days of searching, she'd finally located one of the doors.

Jay shone his light into the opening. "It's not a cave."

Ducking beneath his arm, Quin stepped into the tunnel, watching her step, because the floor was littered with debris where part of the door and wall had collapsed. Now that she was inside the tunnel, slabs of cut stone were everywhere, lying amidst drifts of leaves and smooth deposits of silt where the small stream had overflowed and spilled into the opening. Like the groove in the stone she'd seen outside, the jagged edge of the broken door was blurred by lichen, indicating that the breach wasn't recent. This particular door had been lying open and exposed for years.

Jay concentrated the beam ahead, and the stale, acrid odor that permeated the tunnel registered.

A shiver swept her as she identified bat guano. In her job, bats, snakes and creepy crawlies were an occasional hazard, but that didn't mean she had to like them. "Don't tell me this is where vampire bats hang out."

"Too big. They'll be fruit bats—basically harmless—but there could be snakes and a few spiders."

Repressing another shiver, Quin adjusted the straps on her pack and followed Jay further into the tunnel.

The debris on the floor gradually decreased, until they were walking on a smooth, level surface, although the floor itself was thick with leaf litter and compost from years of being open to the wind and weather. "We're going downhill."

"And it's as straight as a runway." Jay flipped open a compass, the directional reading glowing fluorescent green. "We're headed directly toward the temple, although we must be at least a kilometer from the main entrance."

Ahead, the beams of their flashlights bounced off a wall, and Quin's heart sank. The tunnel ended in a pile of rubble.

Jay climbed the rocks until he was close to the ceiling. Debris cascaded down in a shower of pebbles and stone dust. "Looks like this is it, unless we start moving rocks, but the chances are this is a separate building from the temple, anyway."

Quin played her light over the walls. Her gaze caught on a glyph, partially obscured by the rock fall. A wisp of "memory" tantalized.

Like street signs, the glyphs were only placed where direction was required.

"No," she said flatly, staring at the wall of debris. "There's more. This was a door."

Twenty

Quin examined the blurred symbol, excitement overriding caution as she scrambled over loose scree and leaned close. The formation of the glyphs was similar to that of the gold seal—definitely not Incan or meso-American. She stared at the lines and curves, abruptly hungry for knowledge—her mind impatient to leapfrog the years of study that would be required to research a people who not only no longer existed but who weren't even *known* to have existed.

Tracing the shape with her finger, she let her mind go loose, but the glyph could have been carved from plastic for all the response it elicited. She was left with nothing more than the odd wisp of "memory" and the initial feeling she'd had when she'd first walked into the underground tunnel—more an impression than actual knowledge. "I don't think this is a separate building. It's connected to the temple."

"If this is part of the temple complex, that would make it at least four times larger than Cain estimated."

"But Cain's mind is still stuck in Incan and meso-American cultures. The people who built these core structures weren't Incan. They were something else—literally. Something so far back, they were probably a myth to the Incas."

She placed her palm on the smooth granite, absorbing the chill and the quiet, the ancient stillness of a structure that had remained intact not just for centuries, but millennia, since before Christ had walked the earth, and long, long before the Spanish Conquistadors had cut their bloody swath through South America.

Excitement stirred, gripping her so powerfully that all the skin down her back tingled. So far there hadn't been one bend in the tunnel; it had been dead straight, built for speed, not to confuse and conceal. "Whoever built the maze around the temple did it to protect the inner structure. A secret escape route fits in perfectly with that logic. We've got to find a way through this."

Jay watched Quin's excitement, vibrating just below the surface, the way she practically melted into the glyph she was studying.

Shifting the beam of the flashlight, he examined the intact portion of the tunnel. Moisture seeped between stone blocks and pooled to one side of the tunnel before draining somewhere beyond the collapsed wall, which indicated that, flat as the elevation seemed, the tunnel continued to slope downward.

Going down on his haunches, he examined the gritty fragments and powdery dust that littered the floor. Like the rubble that blocked the tunnel, the stone chips were fresh, the edges sharp and lighter in color than the weathered surface of the stone. "It'll be dangerous. The damage here is recent, probably from the last quake."

Quin climbed down from her perch. "No more dangerous than what Cain's doing."

"A lot more dangerous. Cain's got bracing equipment."

"We can't just leave this." Her gaze locked with his. "Or maybe we should tell Cain, so he can come here and dig—"

"Keep your voice down." Jay straightened and found himself standing toe-to-toe with Quin. "If the tunnel's as old as you say, then it's unstable. The wrong pitch could set off a collapse."

"It's stood this long, it'll last another week."

"It could take months to get through the blockage."

"Then it'll take months."

Jay's jaw tightened. He could see why Olivia and Hannah had spent years tearing their hair out over Quin. When she hadn't been running around like a wild child, she'd been handing out orders. It had been a moot point who had actually run the mission before he'd taken over, and even then, the legend had lived on. Quin had liked to have her own way, and she'd usually gotten it. "If I tell you this place is out of bounds you're not going to listen."

"Neither will Olivia."

He frowned. For days his mind had been fastened on Quin; he'd forgotten how fixated Olivia was on investigating the ruin. "That's a point. If Olivia finds out this is here, she'll set up camp."

He watched as Quin climbed over rubble and began examining it, stone by stone.

When it came down to it, as important as this find was, he didn't care if the temple stood or fell: all he wanted was Quin safe, but short of locking her up, there was no way of keeping her out of here.

His gaze swept the tunnel again, his mind automatically calculating angles and loads—the viability of the building material—and his gut tightened. The place wasn't safe. It was a fact that man-made structures always crumbled. It was just a matter of time— and this one had endured a lot longer than most.

To compound the problem, water was flowing through the wall, which was a bad sign. If there had ever been a drainage system, like the network of aqueducts Cain had found, it had long since failed. The water would have etched through the granite, soaking in over time, the acid dissolving salts and minerals, and breaking down granular structures. The rock now resembled nothing so much as a rotten tooth on the verge of collapse. The whole temple network would be in the same kind of shape—not an accident waiting to happen, but an accident in progress.

As he studied the seeping wall, automatically cataloguing the residue of salts and minerals encrusting the leak, his mind did a familiar sideways shift into…blankness. He couldn't remember how he'd gotten the geological and engineering knowledge that was always there at his fingertips; it was simply there.

"All right," he said bleakly. "But you don't come here without me, and when we're in the tunnel, you follow my orders."

Or what? hung in the air, but Quin found the sense not to utter the words.

Grimly, Jay jerked his head. It was past time they left. The moon wouldn't stay up forever, and if they had to walk in pitch darkness, they wouldn't make it back to the mission until after sunrise; then Cain would know they'd circumvented his security. Not that Cain's security was great. In fact, it was piss-poor—but that didn't mean he couldn't lift his game.

Jay might not be able to remember how he'd obtained his engineering expertise, but he knew people, and, on a level he couldn't explain, he *knew* Cain. The man was a bottom-feeder. It didn't seem likely that he was connected with any of the radical groups like Shining Path, but Jay wouldn't trust him as far as he could throw him. The two men who usually pulled night shift were armed with Skorpions, and Jay would like to know how Cain had managed to come up with Czech automatic weapons that were more commonly used by guerilla forces.

As Quin walked past him, plait swinging down her spine, that long-legged swagger doing bad things to his libido, he held his temper in check.

He was a whole lot harder than Olivia had ever been, but even so, Quin had gotten what she wanted—and more.

Now, if she had her way, he would be in her company practically twenty-four seven.

They reached the mission just before moonset, the night silent except for the hoot of an owl, the buildings looming with a ghostly luminescence.

Quin climbed the fence and shrugged out of her daypack. With Jay helping, she would get much further, faster, than on her own, and with his engineering skills, it was entirely possible they would succeed and actually gain entry to the temple.

They reached the split in the covered walkway that ran between the original mission house and Jay's apartment.

"Wait."

Quin caught a flash of the intention in Jay's gaze

a second before his hand tangled in her plait at the base of her neck, sending a hot bolt of adrenaline through her.

His head dipped, his breath warm on her cheek. She had a moment to register the scent of soap and clean male skin, the sharper scent of sweat, and then his mouth was on hers. The kiss was short, matter-of-fact—the no-frills variety—but even so, after ten years of anticipation, it sent a hot thrill up her spine that beat to death any other lip contact she could ever recall.

His head lifted. Her gaze followed the line of his jaw, those sharp, mouthwatering cheekbones and dark eyes, and she fought the instinctive desire to rise up on her toes, wrap her arms around his neck and cling. "That's *it?*"

She might be the last surviving twenty-eight-year-old virgin on the planet, but that didn't mean she didn't know what it felt like to be thoroughly kissed.

A hand landed on the wall behind her, effectively caging her, and she was once again reminded that the only real fact they had about Jay's past was that it had been obliterated by three bullets, every one of them designed to kill.

"What did you expect? You threatened to cut off a certain part of Luis's anatomy if he so much as touched you."

This time she met his gaze, and her heart thudded at the way he was watching her. Ten years ago she would have given her eyeteeth to have him look at her like that—but after ten years she should have been immune. The problem was, she was used to city men—men who played by a convoluted set of rules based around their careers and social positions, men she had never particularly wanted. Jay was utterly different—direct and completely male—and the gauntlet she'd just thrown down had been the equivalent of throwing a chunk of raw meat in front of a hungry lion. "Luis is Luis. He nails anything that moves."

"That would explain the explosion in the village population, then."

She took a breath and let it out slowly, unbearably aware of his hand at her nape, the hold male and possessive. Abruptly, she lost her temper. If she had an Achilles heel, Jay was it. She was tired of telling herself that he didn't matter—that he hadn't overshadowed every almost-relationship she'd ever had. "I've waited ten years."

"And you think I haven't?"

His blunt statement was somehow shocking, even though she'd always known the tension between them went both ways.

The silence stretched, thick enough to cut. She felt the faint tug as he jerked the band from her plait, the faint stirring on her scalp as his fingers sifted through her hair.

Jay's gaze locked on hers, and suddenly the night was hot and airless. "Then let's try that kiss again."

She felt herself moved back a half step, the plastered wall cool at her back; then his mouth came down on hers, firm and frankly hungry as his tongue slid into her mouth.

Quin angled her mouth and stretched as she wound both arms around his neck, and he groaned and shifted, sliding one thigh between hers. His palms slid beneath her T-shirt to settle against the naked skin at the small of her back, and her belly clenched. She wanted more, and, abruptly, he obliged, as his palms shifted, peeling up her T-shirt until his hands found her breasts.

His mouth lifted from hers, and she sucked in a lungful of air as his teeth closed on the sensitive join of neck and shoulder. The raw tension peaked, shimmering into liquid heat.

An odd sense of disorientation shivered through her, as if her sense of balance had temporarily gone and nothing was stable or fixed, not even the ground.

Jay lifted his head, the movement reluctant, as if he wanted to sink back down and go for a repeat performance. "The earth did just move," he murmured, his gaze unreadable in the moonlight, "but it wasn't the kiss—it's another quake. Looks like Valle del Sol's on the move again."

Twenty-One

Quin and Jay breached the barrier of rock in the tunnel just before lunch. They'd systematically excavated near the ceiling, on the simple logic that up high, the rock pile narrowed, so there was less to dig through.

Jay disappeared through the hole. "Don't come after me until I call you."

Interminable minutes later, he appeared and held out his hand, and Quin scrambled through.

This part of the tunnel, she discovered, was exactly the same as the entrance, straight and featureless, and sloping ever so slightly downhill. As they walked, splashing through puddles and casting their flashlight beams over walls that were seeping and encrusted with mineral deposits, the tunnel gradually broadened and flattened out, and the trickling stream that had developed dropped beneath a deep fissure in the floor.

Jay stepped over the yawning split and held out his hand. "Don't think about it. Just do it."

Quin accepted his grip, a tingling jolt traveling up her arm at the contact, and stepped across. He let her go almost immediately, but the awareness that brief touch had engendered remained.

They rounded a corner, the first bend they'd encountered, and were stopped by another wall of rubble.

Jay played his light over the jagged seam where shattered granite met the smoothly cut ceiling and swore softly.

Quin stared at the rock fall, counted to ten and resolutely began shifting stones.

Half an hour later, they were still shifting rubble without any discernible change to the wall.

"Take a break, you're tired."

Quin gripped a chunk of granite and hauled, her back aching. Abruptly, the rock gave and she staggered back into Jay's chest.

Leather-gloved hands gripped her arms, steadying her. "I said take a break. What's your hurry?"

She dropped the rock, temper flashing. She was tired and filthy, her boots and the bottom half of her jeans soaked from wading through water, her tank top glued to her skin with a mixture of sweat and stone dust. She had no way of explaining her hurry without sounding like a madwoman. All she knew was that she had to get into the temple, and she had to find whatever had gotten left behind before Cain got his filthy hands on it. "You said it yourself, this place could come down any time."

"Then maybe I should haul your ass out of here right now."

Quin regarded him narrowly. He was tough enough to do it, but she wouldn't go quietly. "Don't even try it."

"Or what?"

Her teeth snapped together. Good question. They'd been warily circling each other since that intimate little episode last night, but there hadn't been time for anything personal. The aftershock itself, registering four point five on the Richter scale, had broken windows and brought down roof tiles. It had also collapsed a section of the tunnel that Cain had excavated but not braced, and claimed a third life: one of the security personnel who had apparently decided to take a nap inside the maze.

"This." Quin's hand landed in the center of his chest. She shoved him back a step and kept shoving until his back hit the wall. She could feel his heart slamming against her palm, smell the scent of his skin. His gaze locked with hers.

She stripped off her gloves, then reached up and pulled his head down. He came without restraint, mouth sinking onto hers, the kiss even hotter and hungrier than it had been last night.

When he finally lifted his head, she let out a breath. "You should have kissed me like that years ago."

"And wrecked your life?" He peeled off his gloves and let them drop to the floor. "The last thing either of us needed was a relationship."

She studied the pulse at his throat, cupped the hard line of his jaw. "And now?"

"Now," he said, sliding the band from her hair, "we see where it takes us."

His mouth feathered her neck, and her eyes drifted closed, a shiver running through her as he peeled her tank top over her head and unclipped her bra. "This is no place to make love."

"It's the only place."

She caught the edge of his grin and found her mouth twitching in response, despite the intense emotion. With Cain at one end of the valley, Olivia and Hannah at the other, and who knew how many news crews, sightseers and looters roaming the hills in between, he was right. In Valle del Sol, there was no privacy.

Jay brought her hands to the fastening of his jeans. "Do the honors, I'm busy."

His mouth settled on hers as she unfastened and unzipped, and he groaned, abandoning the niceties and yanking at her zipper.

"Damn, I hate jeans."

She braced herself against his shoulders as he peeled down her jeans and panties, then slipped them off with her boots. "Too bad. Get used to them."

"Are you telling me you don't own a dress?"

"The closest I've got is my graduation gown."

His teeth gleamed as he toed off his own boots and stepped out of his jeans. "I must be a masochist," he muttered, but she was too busy taking in the real estate as he made a crude bed out of their clothing to argue that point.

He held out his hand and pulled her down with him. "I won't argue—as long as you don't wear pants and boots to bed."

Her legs tangled with his, and her heart caught in her throat as he moved her beneath him, the weight of him heavy and male and shatteringly intimate. This was new—she was more used to fighting than acquiescing. "No pants. I can't promise about the boots."

His hands framed her face. "I won't hurt you."

His gaze fastened on hers, soft as warm chocolate, and, as suddenly as if a switch had been thrown, she understood. "You *know* I'm a virgin."

For a moment his gaze was unreadable. "I heard."

His mouth touched hers, and he slid into her, the movement slow and complete, the fit perfect. Then there was no time for thinking, just the rise and fall of their breathing, the heat and the rhythm building like slow, hot honey, until the intensity coiled tight, then broke. For a shimmering moment the murky dimness of the tunnel was pushed back, and the hard chill of the stone beneath, the oppressive weight of the earth above—even time itself—dissolved.

For an indeterminate period Quin floated, hazily exploring the intimate fit of their bodies, the pure tactile pleasure of skin on skin, the almost imperceptible touch of his mind, and she *knew* him—knew that he was stubborn and ruthless and uncompromising, knew that beneath all the strength and steel there was a core of softness, knew that on this level—the man/woman level—she didn't have to fight.

She lifted her head from his shoulder and risked breaking the calm. "Have you ever explored the fact that you're telepathic?"

A lazy hand trailed down her back. He gave her an "Are you crazy?" look, and she had to remind herself that he was close to being another species: male, loaded down with testosterone and a whole other chromosome that she didn't possess.

"Something does happen between us," he admitted, gliding to his feet and pulling her with him.

Quin began searching for her clothes. "It's called mental telepathy."

"I can see that it's got its uses."

Uh-huh. It had gotten her into bed—even if the bed had literally been hard as rock.

After a makeshift attempt at a sponge bath with tissues from her pack, she stepped into her underwear and pulled on her tank top and pants, grimacing at their dampness and trying to ignore the filth. "You can fight it all you want, but to a greater or lesser degree, you're psychic."

His hands closed on her waist, and she found herself pulled into a loose embrace. His forehead touched hers. "Define psychic for me, and then I'll decide whether I'm happy or unhappy. Right now, I'm trying not to think about it."

Twenty-Two

A second body was discovered in the ruin late in the afternoon, bringing the number of lives the Lost City of the Sun had claimed to four.

As soon as the body had been discovered by one of Cain's students, Jay had moved to take over the ruin—confiscating the automatic weapons, and ejecting Cain and his people from the site. There had been initial resistance, but when Cain and his security team had measured their chances against the nine-millimeter Glock in Jay's hand, the Remington rifles clasped by three ex-military personnel from the mission's engineering workshop and the sniper positioned in the hills, they'd backed down.

Cain hadn't been happy. His men had automatic weapons, but Jay had a trained and well-armed combat force. While the Skorpions might look impressive, they were a piece of shit in anything but close quarters combat, and Cain's men knew it. They had been paid well, but not *that* well.

Jay lifted off the tarpaulin that protected the body from the flies. "There's congealed blood all down his front, which means he didn't die in the tunnel—he was killed elsewhere and placed here, probably until the body could be moved out of the valley. Whoever the killer is, this time he didn't bother trusting to poison."

Quin stared at the body, holding her nose against the sickening stench. Aside from multiple contusions dappling his face and chest, the entire base of the man's skull was caved in, making his face look oddly misshapen.

Jay rose to his feet as Luis and Jorge arrived with the stretcher. "He's been dead at least twenty-four hours. By the bloating and rigor, I'd say even longer."

Luis directed Jorge to take the man's feet. As they shifted the corpse, Luis's expression darkened. "I know him. Pedro Chavez. He's been shacked up with Juana down at the village." He swore softly in Spanish, bent and smoothly retrieved an item from the body; a moment later he straightened, a gun in his hand, his expression incredulous. "You can't blame this one on the curse or Shining Path. Pedro is related to Ramirez; I hear he works for him sometimes. Looks like, this time, he got a little too greedy."

Quin recognized the distinctive scratch on the

Browning's handgrip, and an image of the man she'd seen leaving the ruin the previous night popped into her mind: the strong profile and the graceful way he'd vaulted down a level, the glint of metal in his hand. *Ramirez.* "What on earth is *he* doing here?"

Jay dropped the tarp back over the body. "He wants the same thing all the other vultures want. Money." He uttered a curt order in Spanish, and his men began dispersing the small crowd of reporters and sightseers that had gathered.

Ramon, the sniper, appeared at the top of the slip, rifle held in one hand, pushing a tall, thin man in front of him with the other. "Look what I found hiding in the jungle."

Jay studied the intruder as the man delivered an explanation as to why he'd been crouching in a hide constructed from woven branches, just above the entrance to the temple. He was English, a bird-watcher on a hiking holiday, and while he was in Peru, he'd decided to combine bird-watching with taking a look at the newly discovered ruin. The man's face and arms were burned bright pink, which bore out that part of his story. Whoever he was and whatever he was doing, he hadn't had time to acclimatize to the sun. He was also dressed for hiking, wearing boots, tough, khaki drill trousers and a sand-colored drill shirt, but the colors were too much like DPM—disruptive pattern material—for Jay. It was possible he was another reporter, but Jay didn't think so—if a story was all he wanted, he would have been down here with the rest of the vultures, getting a close-up of the latest body. "Who did you say you were?"

The man's gaze darted beyond Jay. "Sanderson. Hogarth Sanderson."

The voice was clipped and English: South London. Jay moved, deliberately blocking Sanderson's view of Quin. He didn't believe the man's explanation; it was too smooth, too practiced. He also didn't like the way Sanderson watched Quin. He issued a curt order in Spanish.

Sanderson's face turned even pinker. "Hey! What are you doing?"

Ramon took his pack and began searching it. He came up with a camera. "No weapons."

With a nod, Jay indicated that Ramon should replace the items and return the pack. There was no point in confiscating the film, when every part of the valley had been photographed and televised for the past three weeks, but even so, he was tempted. As bland and harmless as Sanderson seemed, he was a liar.

He met Sanderson's light gray gaze, his own cold. "Leave."

As Ramon escorted Sanderson away from the ruin, a smoothly coiffed television reporter, with a salon tan and just the right shade of bronze lipstick to go with her military-style shirt and trousers, ducked beneath Jorge's arm, resisting the order to vacate the ruin. Her expression was unruffled as she took in the tarpaulin-covered body. "What's happening?"

Jay's expression was shuttered. "The site's closed."

Her cameraman crowded in close beside her, sensing more interesting footage.

She lifted a mike. "By whose authority?"

Jake shifted the television camera out of his face and confiscated the mike. "Mine."

Sydney, Australia

Gray Lombard studied the CNN footage of the latest death at Valle del Sol. He'd caught the edited version on the morning news. That had been frustratingly brief, but interesting enough that he'd gone directly to the source and pulled in a favor from an ex-SAS contact who now worked as a foreign correspondent, and obtained a copy of the direct satellite feed.

The footage was choppy and unedited, and showed a lot more than the ten-second spot that had finally been aired. He watched as the camera tracked a tall dark man, and listened to the curt series of orders issued in a mixture of English and Spanish. The camera zoomed in on the man's face. A second later a hand covered the camera, blotting out the feed, and the tape ended.

"That's it," he said curtly to the dark-haired man sitting at his side. "It's Jake."

* * *

By nightfall, Jay's men had cleared the ruin and closed it off to the public. They didn't have official support, and Jay wasn't holding his breath waiting for it, either. With the series of earthquakes that had occurred all the way along the cordillera, disrupting power and water supplies, the military and the police were up to their necks with disaster relief and controlling looting. Another dead *huaquero* at Valle del Sol wasn't enough to make them come running.

By nightfall most of Cain's canvas encampment had disappeared. A few tents and several students who were stuck with no transport still remained, along with two television crews, who had stubbornly resisted leaving.

When Jay and Quin reached the mission, the lights were on in the clinic, and Luis was standing guard over Cain, who was occupying one of the clinic beds.

Luis grinned. "Look who we found hiding in his tent. Didn't wanna go home, did you, Cain?"

Cain's face was pale, and he was sweating.

Hannah rose from the edge of the bed. "He's sick," she said calmly. "Only it's not a virus, or food poisoning, or any of that hooey about an ancient curse." She indicated the ECG monitor Cain was presently hooked up to. "At first I thought it might be either Ross River or Dengue Fever, because some of the symptoms were consistent—but it's neither."

She pointed to the screen. "See that? At the bottom here the wave is long and shallowed out with each beat, when it should kick up in a sharp vee. That's textbook for an overdose of Digoxin."

Jay studied the heart rhythm wave. "A standard heart drug."

"Uh-huh. Derived from digitalis. Give it in high doses and people suffer from tiredness, nausea, diarrhea, depression, hallucinations—you name it. Dehydration makes the effects worse, because Digoxin alters the salts."

"Which would explain why the Peruvian team went down so fast. They were doing the heavy work."

"And taking water from the communal water supply. Most of Cain's crew had bottled water."

Jay's gaze shifted from the ECG monitor to Cain. "And if a person is already on heart meds, like Garcia was, they die fast. The first dose would have knocked him over."

Cain sat up, ripping off the wire to the heart monitor. "Don't look at me. I didn't kill Garcia, and I don't know anything about poisoning the water."

Quin's expression was cold. "What about killing Pedro Chavez."

Cain uttered a crude phrase.

Jay caught him by the shirtfront, stopping him from leaving. "Cain's no organizational genius. Despite the degree, he couldn't put a taco together without assistance. It's his partner who makes the decisions and sets up the deals."

Cain's face reddened. "All I know is that no one's been paid but the security team," he said shortly. "Hathaway was trying to get our sponsorship renewed, but after the Honduran government lodged a lawsuit, our backers wouldn't play ball. The foundation went belly-up a couple of weeks back."

"So you're broke—"

"Bankrupt," Cain interceded viciously.

"—and out in the cold. What lawsuit, exactly?"

"I don't have to tell—"

Jay tightened his hold. Cain's face turned beet red.

"I've got no time," Jay said curtly. "Hathaway's gone AWOL, and that makes me nervous. If I have to hurt you to get the facts, I will."

Raw fear flickered on Cain's face, and Jay eased his hold.

Cain sucked in a breath, his color turning from puce to gray. "The Honduran government claimed that certain artifacts had gone missing."

Quin's voice was flat. "The Copatyl sun totem, and the jade owl that was in with the burial goods. Not the most important finds, but two of the jewels in the crown. Who's he selling to?"

"I don't know, and if I did, I wouldn't tell *you*—"

"He doesn't know," Jay cut in, "because Hathaway's always taken care of the finances. Cain's just the window dressing."

Cain swore. "All right. It is Hathaway you're looking for. Hathaway and Ramirez." He bent forward, retching. When he was finished, his face was ashen, and spittle glistened on his chin.

Jay tossed him a towel and nodded at Luis. "Keep him restrained. Lock him in the cellar if you have to."

It was an hour shy of midnight by the time the news crews finally decided there was no more to be gained by hanging around an almost deserted valley, staking out a ruin that had been shut down.

As dramatic as the earlier broadcast had been, featuring yet another body and with guns clearly in evidence—not to mention the theories about Maoist insurgent forces taking over the temple ruin—the story was now dead. The Maoist forces, according to a local source, weren't Maoist at all, but a lone member of a local gang—a *huaquero*—looting the ruin, and the only artifact found on him had been a labeled shard of pottery pilfered from Cain's tent.

With no sign of incipient guerilla warfare, and with the theory of an ancient curse brought to life by a killer plague in tatters following the discovery that Garcia's death could now be attributed to a drug that was routinely prescribed to millions of heart patients every year, the news crews had lost their mandate.

Quin let the library curtain drop as a set of vehicle lights disappeared over the bridge. "That's the last one." She sank back into the wing-back chair that was positioned near the window and picked up the notes she'd been working on. The desk was presently occupied by Jay and the mission accounts. It was a sad fact that, despite murder, plagues and earthquakes, taxes were still due. "So that's why Cain's people were leaving." She shook her head. "They haven't been paid."

Jay dropped his pen and sat back in his chair. "Once the temple had been opened up, Hathaway didn't want them around. Especially not the Peruvian team. He wanted the whole place to himself so he could have a clear run at whatever he thinks is in there."

Smothering a yawn, Quin gave up on studying glyphs that were beginning to merge on the page. She was beginning to get a feel for them. The inner excitement that came when she was close was fizzing just below the surface. She had found a common thread in the symbols, something to do with time or numerals of some sort, but she hadn't quite figured the context. Her mind was teetering on the brink of grasping…something…but so far nothing had gelled. What she really needed was sleep.

As she strolled past the desk, a hand caught hers. "Where do you think you're going?"

"To bed."

Jay rose to his feet. "Then you're heading in the wrong direction."

Twenty-Three

Hammering on Jay's front door woke Quin.

Reluctantly, she lifted her head from the pillow. The luminous dial on the bedside clock said it was four in the morning. She had had less than two hours' sleep.

A hand on her shoulder kept her in place. "Stay there, I'll get it."

With quick grace, Jay pulled on the jeans he'd dropped on the floor, then collected the gun he'd left on the bedside table. The sound of the magazine slotting into place as he left the room brought her fully awake.

When Quin heard Hannah's voice, she pushed back the covers and dressed.

By the time she made it downstairs, Hannah was seated in the kitchen in her nightgown and robe, a glass of something alcoholic in her hand. Jay was on the phone.

Jay's glance fastened on hers. "Olivia's been kidnapped."

Hannah's hands shook as she took a sip of her drink. "Hathaway found out who she is. He saw her photo on the back cover of one of her books. He's taken her into the ruin."

Jay roused Luis, who was sleeping in the accommodation block. Minutes later, Luis climbed into the Bedford and headed for the village to get help.

Jay tossed a fleece-lined jacket at Quin. "Dress warmly. If we're underground for any length of time, the cold's going to affect us."

She pulled on the jacket, not bothering to ask exactly how Jay knew so much about working underground. She watched as he loaded two daypacks with sandwiches she'd made, water, flashlights and spare batteries, then slipped the large black handgun in, along with a spare magazine.

The air was cool and thin, the stars hard and bright in the night sky, as Quin put an arm around Hannah and helped her to the house, while Jay loaded their gear into the Range Rover.

Concern turned to fear as, for the first time in her

life, Hannah leaned on Quin. She felt light, little more than skin and bone.

Hannah reached into the pocket of her robe and came out with a piece of paper. "If you're going into that hellhole after Olivia, you'd better take this."

Quin examined the sheet.

"It's a map of the maze," Hannah said. "Cain had it in his pocket. We had to give him a change of clothing before Jorge drove him to the police station at Vacaro. Olivia found it when she did the laundry."

The map only covered part of the maze, but it was precisely drawn. Quin's chest squeezed tight. "Olivia should have taken this when she went with Hathaway."

Jay's expression was grim. "She left it for us. If Hathaway needs Olivia, chances are Cain's made sure he doesn't have a map, and Olivia doesn't intend to take Hathaway anywhere he wants to go. That was her way of making sure she can't."

"Just get Olivia back," Hannah said rawly.

Jay held the door of the Range Rover open and waited while Quin climbed into the front passenger seat. "Don't worry about Olivia, she's as tough as rawhide. We'll have her back before dawn." He turned the key in the ignition and headed toward the workshop.

Before the whole place came down like a rotten stack of cards.

Ramirez was a killer, and so was Hathaway. It was an unholy alliance, and Jay didn't know which one was worse. They had kidnapped Olivia in the belief that her extensive archaeological knowledge would lead them to the artifact—but Olivia had deliberately blinded herself. She would lead them by the nose precisely nowhere, stalling for time until either she was rescued, or Hathaway and Ramirez lost their patience and killed her.

Jake brought the Range Rover to a halt next to a windowless concrete block shed. The shed was small and squat, a bunker for storing dangerous goods. The weakest part of the building was the door, which was solid steel. But, strong or not, the building had been breached; the thick steel door was hanging off its hinges—the steel hasp that had fastened it cut through.

Jay examined the hasp, the telltale discoloration and warping of the metal. Whoever had broken in had used a gas axe, probably stolen from his workshop.

Pulling the door wide, he stepped into the room, switched on the light and scanned the shelves. Normally, chemicals and inflammables were stored in here, but lately, with the bridge construction, they had also stored explosives.

And the shelf that had held the C4 was empty.

When they reached the temple gate, Luis was already there with a crew from the village.

"Hathaway's closed the gate," Luis said curtly.

"We're working on it, but the stone's thick, and it looks like he's collapsed part of the tunnel inside."

Jay examined the solid partition of stone and jerked his head at Ramon. "Keep working on it. We'll go in another way." He sketched a map of the second entrance and handed it to Ramon, along with a string of orders. Hathaway and Ramirez would be armed, and it was likely he had also set a trap at the door, so once the door was safely breached, no one was to move into the ruin unarmed.

Quin climbed back into the Range Rover, fear literally making her blood run cold. "What if it's already too late?'

Jay turned the key in the ignition. "Don't worry. Hathaway might not know this game, but Ramirez does. Even if Olivia can't lead them to the artifact, they won't kill her. Whether they find anything or not, they'll still want to get out of this with their skins, and for that they need a live hostage. It might sound cold, but in their situation, it doesn't make sense to kill Olivia."

The hidden entrance to the temple loomed, the brush covering it dark and tangled in the fading moonlight. Jay studied the ground, looking for evidence that anyone other than he and Quin had been there. "Wait here. I'll check it out first."

"No. I'm coming with you. We don't have time for that kind of caution."

Jay's jaw tightened. He wasn't superstitious, but this whole place gave him a cold itch up his spine. He was no archaeologist, but he was experienced at pot-holing and cave diving and—

For a molten instant memory flashed: a man in a dripping wet suit, black hair cropped military short, a wide, white grin.

Knowledge tantalized, then slipped away, like a stone dropping through murky water, and Jay shook his head, his frustration mounting. Every now and then he glimpsed a piece of the past; then the chink in the blankness closed up, leaving him trying to fit yet another disjointed fragment into the puzzle that was his past.

"What is it? What's wrong?"

"Nothing."

He eyed Quin, tall and lean, her face delicate in the moonlight, eyes with that mysterious, provoking slant. *Everything.*

He didn't want her anywhere near the place, but she was fit and experienced at this kind of work, and she was right, they didn't have time for caution—not when Olivia's life was at stake.

Pulling back the curtain of trailing vines, he swept the interior of the cave with the flashlight, then stood back as the few bats that had taken up residence whirred out of the opening. When the cave was clear, they picked their way past the first rock fall and paused at the second. An hour later, they'd removed enough rubble to crawl through to the other side of the tunnel.

Skimming the walls and floor with their flashlights, they walked, only pausing when a faint tremor shook the ground.

Quin watched the stone dust floating in the beam she cast. "That's a two." Ordinarily nothing to worry about beyond the feeling of displacement that happened when solid ground shimmered like water.

"Watch out." Jay's arm snaked around her waist, and she found herself shoved forward in an awkward sprawl, palms stinging, knees bruised, as part of the ceiling peeled off and crashed down behind them.

A choking wave of dust filled the tunnel. Coughing and blinking, Quin attempted to push herself to her knees and found that she couldn't move. Panic expanded in her throat as she craned around and discovered that the heavy weight pinning her was Jay.

Adrenaline pumped, giving her the impetus to shimmy forward a bare inch, work one leg free, then haul the other out from beneath Jay's still form.

Feverishly, she grabbed her flashlight, which had rolled off to the side, and turned the beam on Jay. He was lying facedown and was clear of the rock fall—just—but he was unconscious, his stillness frightening. Blood trickling from a cut on the side of his head, along with a goose egg swelling, explained why he was out cold. Just to be sure, Quin placed two fingers at his carotid and instantly picked up a pulse. Relief left her feeling limp. A stray rock must have caught him as he'd flung them both forward, clear of the collapse.

After quickly checking for other injuries, Quin turned Jay onto his back. Relief that the injury didn't seem that serious was tempered by a new fear as she gently probed his skull. Jay had experienced a head injury once; a second injury was the last thing he needed and potentially more serious than it might otherwise have been.

After shrugging out of her pack, she searched through it for a handkerchief. As she folded the linen into a pad and pressed it to the wound, Jay's eyes flipped open.

His fingers took over holding the handkerchief. "We have to stop meeting like this."

Quin lifted a brow. "How do you feel?"

"Fine, except I've got one unholy bitch of a headache."

"Well," she muttered, "so much for that fear. Your vocabulary's still intact."

A large hand closed around her wrist, and she found herself slowly pulled down onto his chest. "And that's not all. Takes a lot to shut me up."

But it had happened once before.

The knowledge of just how close he'd come to dying all those years ago hung between them.

Strange and unresolved as their relationship was, she couldn't lose him again.

His arms closed around her, and they lay, still and quiet, his warmth seeping through thick layers of clothing, dispelling the chill of the tunnel. Despite the fact that they were stuck underground, buried beneath who knew how many tons of soil and rock, she felt oddly content.

"We've got two choices," Jay said quietly, his voice little more than a rumble in her ear. "We can either dig our way out or keep going. Either way, there's a risk we won't make it."

"If we dig our way out, you'll just go straight back in."

He didn't argue. "I can't leave Olivia."

"Neither can I." Quin eased to her feet, brushed dust and dirt from her hair and clothing, and watched critically as Jay rose, too. He might seem nearly invincible, but he had his Achilles heel, and she felt fiercely protective.

They cleared minor blockages as they went, then stepped through into an area where most of the tunnel had collapsed, leaving just enough space for them to walk.

Jay paused. "The stone just changed."

All the hairs at the back of her neck lifted as he indicated the difference in the size of the blocks, then ran the beam of his flashlight over the visible join that went the length of one wall, across the ceiling and down the other wall. "Whoever built the entrance tunnel didn't build this part. The construction material is the same, but the way the stone is dressed and fitted is different." He aimed the beam over her head. "Even the ceiling height has changed. Whatever this part of the temple is, it's on a much bigger scale than the rest."

A few meters later, the broad walkway ended in a wall.

"There's got to be a door." Jay ran his fingers along the join, then pushed at the smooth sheet of granite, but it was solid.

Quin stripped off her gloves, stuffed them into her jacket pocket, then studied the door and the glyphs that were carved into the adjacent walls. Knowledge tantalized but failed to coalesce into anything helpful. "The builders might be different, but the glyphs are the same."

"Let me try something."

He began systematically pressing the snugly fitted stones around the glyph, moving in the direction of the suspected door. When nothing happened, he studied the glyph, then pressed the center. The stone moved smoothly inward and another, lower down, slid out with a grating sound to protrude several inches from the wall. "That's it, the door's unlocked."

"How did you know to do that?"

"Common sense. The door had to have a mechanism somewhere close." Jay pushed against the door. This time it swung inward with ease, rotating on a rod that was fitted slightly off center.

Covering her nose and mouth against the dust that rose in a cloud as the door scraped over the remains of the plaster that had once covered the walls, Quin followed Jay into the chamber.

Her first impression, after the long tunnel, was one of space. Dust motes as fine as talcum powder spiraled upward, glowing incandescent in the beams of their flashlights as air that had lain still for century upon century stirred.

The chamber was empty except for a short stone pillar in the center, which culminated in a four-sided point—an obelisk. Quin swung her light upward, tracing the sloping line of the ceiling. The breath stopped in her throat when the beam, almost swallowed by darkness, picked out the unmistakable apex of a pyramid.

"Bingo," Jay said quietly.

Quin swung the beam down and around, critically examining the proportions of the pyramid. Something wasn't quite right. "It's smaller than I thought it would be."

Jay lifted a brow. "I'm not even going to ask the question." He flipped his compass open. "Magnetic north doesn't work—the needle's going crazy."

His gaze moved about the room. Lines carved

into the floor radiated out at odd intervals from the central marker, continuing up the walls and ending in symbols that looked remarkably like astronomical markings of some kind. The entire chamber looked like some kind of map of the solar system— a three-dimensional interstellar survey. The walls were covered in a code that looked remarkably like binary computer language—and the degree of detail of the star map that covered the ceiling was astounding, even including the Earth's position in the solar system, with its elliptical orbit around the sun factored in.

In another series of diagrams, Jay recognized what looked like, incredibly, configurations for other solar systems. "That's Alpha Centauri." He shook his head. "The entire room seems to be some kind of astronomical resource."

Quin studied the pillar in the center of the room; it was made of some plain, impervious material and was smooth to the touch. At first glance it looked like high-quality white marble or alabaster, but the surface wasn't cold. On the contrary, it warmed to her touch, more like plastic than stone, although that was hardly possible.

Focusing her beam on the pillar, Quin examined it for glyphs and lines that might indicate a secret compartment. If there was something she'd left behind in that previous life, then the only place it could be—assuming there wasn't a secret compartment in one of the walls—was the pillar.

Another tremor shook the structure, this one sharp enough to disturb her concentration.

Jake's hand curled around her arm. "As fascinating as this place is, it's time to go."

A dull explosion rocked the cavern, throwing her forward. Reflexively, she grasped at the slick surface of the obelisk but, like the floor beneath her feet, nothing about the pillar was stable. It shifted beneath her grasp, sending her tumbling.

Seconds later, Jay helped her to her feet.

The beam of his light flashed in her eyes as his thumb swept over a tender spot just above her temple, where she must have knocked herself when she'd fallen.

"Ouch!" Quin winced away, both from Jay's thumb and the glare of the light; then, as her gaze caught on the glowing, reflective shape of the obelisk, she wondered if the blow had somehow affected her perceptions.

The entire top section had moved—rotating a fraction of an inch, so that the pyramid's base was no long square with the pillar.

As a place of concealment it was ingenious, because the join was so finely executed that it was invisible when the top was in place.

Jay rotated the top of the obelisk until it came

free, then carefully set it down on the floor. Light coruscated off what appeared to be a diamond the size of her fist, formed into a perfect many-faceted globe. "Is this what you're looking for?"

Quin touched a fingertip to the jewel and waited to feel…something.

Aside from experiencing a surface coolness and an aesthetic appreciation for what was a surpassingly beautiful gem, she felt nothing. Like this chamber, the jewel wasn't what she'd expected. The temple seemed to be a repository for scientific knowledge, rather than the spiritual heart of a monotheistic civilization that had clung stubbornly to its beliefs when most of the world had fallen into paganism.

The distinct sound of footsteps jerked her head up. The low rumble of a male voice registered.

Jay put a finger to his mouth. He slipped the jewel in his pocket and fitted the top of the pillar back in place. A split second later, another explosion rocked the chamber. This time the shock wave knocked them both off their feet, the concussion deafening as the sealed door dissolved.

The tremors they'd taken for earthquakes were C4 induced. Hathaway was blasting his way through the maze.

Twenty-Four

Hathaway stepped through the opening, pushing Olivia ahead of him, one of the Skorpions his security team had used held carelessly in one hand, the stock folded back over the weapon so he could use it like a handgun. "Lomax. And what do you know—*Mallory.* Don't you have some other place to be?"

Quin met Olivia's gaze. "Not lately."

Jay chambered a round in the Glock as Ramirez and another man he recognized as Cortez, one of Cain's security guards, stepped into the room. Reaching down, he helped Quin to her feet and moved back a step, not taking his gaze off the trio of men and keeping the pillar between them. The cover was minimal, but it was better than nothing.

Hathaway's gaze rested hungrily on the pillar, and slowly—so as not to alarm Ramirez, in particular, who looked like he'd developed a taste for the drugs he'd been hawking all down the Peruvian coast—Jay reached into his pocket and extracted the jewel. "Is this what you're looking for? Let Olivia go and you can have it."

Hathaway's gaze fixed on the jewel. "No deals."

Ramirez grinned, his expression definitely off center. Cortez simply held the Skorpion in a two-handed grip, aimed squarely at Jay's chest.

If Jay had been in their position, he wouldn't have let Olivia go, either. It was a simple equation: you didn't give anything up unless there was something to gain, and the fact was, Hathaway controlled the odds. He had more men, more firepower and no conscience. If he wanted the jewel, all he had to do was start shooting.

Memories of bargaining for another hostage, in another time and place, surfaced, along with other more insubstantial memories that slid away before Jay could grasp them, but the certainty remained that he had done hostage-rescue work before.

A fine tremor shook through the chamber, this one not C4 induced. Stone dust shimmered down, and Jay threw the jewel in Hathaway's direction, further distracting him and his men, giving him the split second he needed to grab Quin and dive for the cover of the door they'd used to enter the chamber.

In the scheme of things, the jewel meant nothing

to Jay—it was life that counted, Quin's and Olivia's lives in particular.

As much as he wanted to save Olivia, there was no way he could reach her right now—Hathaway had too much firepower at his disposal—but he had a strategy.

Rounds thudded into the heavy stone door as Jay pushed it to and hit the mechanism, sealing it closed, Hathaway and his men on the other side—with Olivia.

Quin got to her feet, brushing dust from her eyes and hair. As Jay closed the door, she had seen something that made her blink with disbelief. The force of the explosion had swept the coating of dust from the floor, and with all the light, she had been able to see that the floor was an intricate mosaic, remarkably like a map of the maze—and something more. She frowned as the overall shape of the mosaic niggled in her brain. It had looked like a glyph—and a familiar one. That in itself had to mean something.

Jay pressed the center of the glyph on the adjacent wall and, with a grating sound, pushed a much smaller door open—this one leading to yet another corridor.

Jay's hand gripped hers as he pulled her down the corridor. Quin's throat locked up. As dangerous as it was to stay, she didn't want to go. "They've still got Olivia."

"And we can't risk going back that way. I guarantee you that Hathaway's just booby-trapped that door, and he'll be setting explosive charges in all the tunnels surrounding the chamber."

Quin's expression was fierce. "We can't leave her."

"This time we have to. Hathaway's gotten what he's come for, now he'll simply be trying to get out. Olivia will be safe until they're clear of the ruin. And when Hathaway comes out the other side, he'll run into Ramon."

But Jay wanted to catch Hathaway before then. As good as Ramon and Jorge were, they were no match for the explosives Hathaway and Ramirez were carrying, and Olivia had been limping. Years ago she had broken the ankle on a dig. If she used it too much, it swelled and became painful. If Hathaway decided she was slowing him down, he could dispose of her before he left the temple.

"There was a map of the maze on the floor of that room."

Jay squeezed her hand. "Have you got a photographic memory?"

"Nope." *Just a strange one.*

"Then forget it. With all the holes Hathaway's blasted in the place, we won't have a problem getting out."

If the structure remains intact.

Quin had no idea how old the temple actually was. It had weathered centuries of earthquakes, but it hadn't been designed to withstand the shock waves from blasting. With Hathaway playing fast and loose with C4, it wasn't a matter of whether the structure would collapse, only a matter of when.

Their biggest enemy now wasn't Hathaway or Ramirez but time.

As they walked, Quin began to feel warmth and a heady lightness—a fine tingling flow, as if she were walking into a shimmering current, and abruptly she recognized what the sensation was. They were close to the source of the mysterious energy that filtered up through the ground into the secret grove. If she didn't miss her guess, they were directly beneath the grove.

The corridor met several others and broadened into something approaching an anteroom, with a central set of doors on the opposite wall. The doors were massive, with a carved golden sun adorning the center. "This is it."

Stepping forward, she placed her hand on the center of the sun. Taking a deep breath, she pressed on the doors and pushed them wide.

As the doors opened, Quin was engulfed by a smooth flood of power, her senses overwhelmed by the sheer dissolving beauty of it. Ancient mechanisms ground one against the other, and light from a complex set of polished gold mirrors set high on the pyramidal ceiling flooded the inner chamber with sunlight that was momentarily blinding after hours of walking in near-darkness.

A golden dais, the only physical feature in a room devoid of everything but light and the beauty of its walls, sat directly beneath the apex of the pyramid. Apart from that, the room was bare of everything but a fine coating of dust.

As she stepped further into the room, Quin's gaze moved over decorated walls that soared cleanly. The gold paintings were elaborate, each stemming from a central figure radiating light, his/her hands showering golden seeds. On the first wall, the shimmering motes of gold turned into the moon and the stars, on the second, rolling hills, which were lapped by rivers and seas. The third wall contained an ornate filigree of flowers and trees, birds, animals and sea creatures, and the final wall was filled with rank upon rank of people: men, women, children and babies, each face individual, each figure perfectly executed, the detail of their clothing exquisite.

Quin stared at first one wall, then another, her throat tight at the sheer beauty that had survived not just centuries, but millennia, because there was no doubt in her mind that this part of the temple went further back than any of them could guess. In no way was any part of this Incan, Nazca or Moche—or any of the other tribes. The work was too elegant, too fine—more Grecian than Egyptian, although there were elements common to each. In short, she was stumped. The pyramids shouted a link with Egypt, but the sophistication of the glyphs, the technical brilliance of the engineering and the sheer flowing beauty of the paintings were millennia ahead of anything produced along the Nile.

She felt Jay's warmth all down her back.

"What is this?"

Quin's heart swelled tight in her chest. "Genesis."

No wonder the temple had fallen.

Carefully preserved and protected as it had been, it had been too beautiful and too direct, its ideology displayed for all to see in the simplest of forms: pictures. It had been a threat in a world turned primitive and brutal, where there was a convenience-store god for everything, including death and destruction.

Jay walked toward the center of the room, drawn by an odd effect in the air, like water rippling. He stepped up onto the dais and unaccountably lost his balance. He stumbled and corrected. The dizziness increased, and, abruptly, he lost awareness of the room and of Quin, but not of himself. He could feel his heartbeat, his breath, every nerve ending in his body. The surface of his skin had become ultrasensitive. He could feel the flow of the energy he'd unaccountably seen.

Heat flooded him, starting at his head and moving into his chest, burning at the points of all his old wounds. His head prickled with a fire that was both hot and cold. Pain shafted briefly in his skull, followed by a faint popping sensation, and he was aware that the vision in his left eye had just been corrected.

Dimly Jay was aware of Quin calling his name, felt her fingers on his forearm.

Quin steadied Jay, and then the room dissolved. Heat poured into her, the radiation in her chest, both hot and cold, as if her heart was on fire. Her head spun, and she could no longer see walls and exquisite gold paintings, but beings radiating light. One of them bent, touched the side of the dais and beckoned.

Quin investigated the area, a wisp of memory from the dream surfacing as she pressed on a glyph. A drawer slid out, revealing a simple blue box made of lapis lazuli, a ring nestled in the center. The being bent close, placing his hand over the ring, and instantly the shimmer in the air diminished. When he was finished, he looked directly at Quin, pointed to the box and jerked his thumb at the door. The message was clear: take the box and get out—fast.

A distant explosion broke the peace and beauty. Jay's hand wrapped around her arm as she closed the lid of the box, pulling her clear of the dais. His dark gaze connected with hers. "Are you all right?"

"Never better." And that was the truth. She felt warm, energized, as if she hadn't missed almost two nights' sleep.

As Jay pulled her toward the doors, Quin stopped him in his tracks. "Wait. This goes in your pack."

Impatience radiated from him as he turned his back and allowed her to stow the box.

As she fastened the flap, Jay shook his head. "It can't be."

"What?"

"This place. The floor. It looks like DNA coding."

Quin glanced at the intricate mosaic then, as they passed through the doors, she couldn't resist a last lingering glance around the room, but the shining being had already left. "Where have you seen DNA coding?"

Jay pulled one of the massive doors shut. "In a crime lab."

Quin flicked on her flashlight as Jay closed the second door. "Why am I not surprised? You're getting your memory back."

"In bits and pieces."

She surveyed the passages that converged at the main chamber. Since she still hadn't cracked the language of the glyphs, they would have to make an educated choice about which one to take.

Jay pointed. "I don't believe it. I can see a light."

Quin grinned, she could see the light, too, and it didn't emanate from them or from a mirror. "Don't ask, just follow."

Minutes later they walked into a section of the maze that had sustained massive damage.

Jay swept his light over the rocks. "It's a blast pattern. I can still smell the chemical. This is Hathaway's path."

Which meant they were now following him.

For several minutes they simply walked in a straight line, following the highway of destruction until they reached a three way convergence, with rubble flowing in all directions.

"Looks like our boy got confused here." Jay's hand closed around her arm as she took a step forward. "Keep to the sides. The walls give the structure stability, but Hathaway's removed so many, it's a miracle the whole lot hasn't collapsed."

They rounded a corner and found themselves staring at a dead end.

Quin indicated a faint glow illuminating a section of wall just meters from where they were standing. "I think we're exactly where we're supposed to be at this point." When they reached the place where the light had been, they discovered that the wall was intact but had sustained damage at the base.

Jay stared at the place where the glow had been and shook his head. Setting his pack down, he pulled on leather gloves and systematically began to remove rocks. Quin pulled on her own gloves and began scraping away the smaller rubble. After only a few minutes, Jay stopped. "I'm through to the other side."

Jay reached into his pack, extracted a fresh set of

batteries, inserted them into his flashlight, then consulted his watch. "We've been in here for four hours. Which means it took him between two and three hours to blast his way through to the small pyramid. It won't take him that much time to get out. Unless Olivia has managed to lead him in the wrong direction, we're almost out of time."

A muffled sound jerked Quin's head up.

Jay put a finger to his mouth and flicked off both their lights as the sound metamorphosed into voices.

"...you've led us in a damned circle—"

"Following *your* blast trail."

Olivia's voice was clear and sharp, as precise as a razor, and she was cutting Hathaway to pieces with it. Quin's heart pounded in her chest. Hathaway was only meters away, on the other side of the wall.

The voices finally faded, absorbed by the twists and turns of the maze, and the insulation of layers of granite.

"Way to go, Olivia," Jay murmured, flicking on his light and rummaging in his pack. "Keep the bastard busy."

He pulled out a roll of duct tape, then began taping his flashlight until only a narrow strip of illumination escaped.

Quin continued to work, removing rocks from the small hole and placing them to one side, careful not to make the hole too big in case she weakened the wall to the point of collapse.

Removing her gloves, she sat down, her back against the wall, and shoved stray strands of hair away from her face. "What now?"

Placing the flashlight on the ground, Jay slid the Glock out of the waistband at the small of his back. Quin watched as he checked that the magazine was secure in its housing, then pulled the slide back and chambered a round. "I'm going hunting."

His mouth touched briefly on hers. "Wait for me here. I won't be long."

Gun first and cramping his shoulders, Jay snaked through the hole and straightened on the other side, not bothering with his flashlight, because there was enough ambient light from Hathaway's group for him to make out the dim shape of the tunnel. The fact that there was light at all meant they had stopped either to eat or to figure out where they were, which worked perfectly with his plans. If Hathaway had continued moving, Jay would have had to have gone back and collected Quin, because there was no way he would leave her alone in the maze. This way, he could retrieve Olivia without bringing Quin anywhere near Hathaway or Ramirez.

As he rounded a corner, he recognized the shadowy figure of Cortez at one end of the tunnel.

Withdrawing back into darkness, he slipped the

Glock back into place at the small of his back and slid a knife out of its ankle sheath. He didn't want to use the gun unless he was pushed. By his calculations, Hathaway had already blasted away any safety margin the honeycombed structure of the maze had to offer, so silence was preferable. As he approached Cortez, who had his back to him, Jay heard a trickling sound. Cortez was urinating against the tunnel wall.

As Cortez fastened his pants, Jay stepped quickly into him, clamped a hand over his mouth and brought the haft of the knife down sharply on the side of his neck—the blow precisely placed to shock the carotid and jugular veins. Cortez dropped like a stone. Jay picked up the man's flashlight and turned it off.

The light grew brighter as Jay approached the juncture Hathaway and Ramirez had chosen as a stopping-off point. Ramirez was eating, and Hathaway had a map spread on the floor. Olivia was hunched as far from both men as the light would allow.

Bending, Jay picked up a stone chip and lobbed it.

Olivia's head jerked up, her gaze locking with his. Jay made a beckoning motion with his fingers. She nodded and slowly got to her feet, and he slipped further back down the tunnel, the Glock now in his hand.

"Where do you think you're going?"

Olivia stopped in her tracks, her back to Hathaway. "I need some privacy."

"You mean you need to take a piss—like Cortez. And speaking of Cortez," he snarled, "what's taking him so long?"

Ramirez muttered something low and crude, and Hathaway laughed.

"Leave the light," he ordered. "Can't have you running off and leaving us, now can we?"

With stiff movements, Olivia laid her flashlight on the floor, lifted her gaze to Jay and walked steadily toward him.

Twenty-Five

A faint glow through the hole in the wall alerted Quin that someone was on the other side.

Slowly, she straightened, using the wall for both support and guidance, because the darkness was close to absolute. She'd been sitting in pitch darkness while she waited, conserving her batteries.

A faint rustling made her heart pound. Feeling around with her hands, she picked up one of the rocks she'd selected and piled beside the opening, and flattened herself against the wall. If anything came through that hole that didn't look like either Olivia or Jay, the solution was simple: she would drop the rock.

Two small, birdlike hands appeared, illuminated by the faint glow, and, letting out a breath, Quin set the rock down and helped pull Olivia through.

* * *

After they'd filled in the hole and placed a marker, just in case they needed to use it again, they retreated to the last glyph Quin had noted.

Jay set his pack down beside Olivia. "A present for you."

Olivia's eyes glinted. "Cortez's flashlight."

"He doesn't need it anymore."

Quin looked at the light with silent fascination, and Jay caught her gaze. "It's all right, he's still breathing."

Olivia flicked the light on, testing the batteries. "But if he'd made a noise, he wouldn't be."

"Something like that. Now sit down while I do something about that ankle."

Olivia complied, but grumpily. "You're getting worse than Hannah. There's nothing wrong with my ankle."

"You're limping."

"I'm over seventy, I always limp."

"Not like that, you don't." Jay slipped off Olivia's boot and bound her ankle tightly with an elastic bandage. "If it gets any worse, I'll carry you."

Quin eased out of her pack and began handing out wrapped packages. There was nothing gourmet about peanut butter sandwiches, they were simply fuel, and they needed the calories. As they munched their way through the sandwiches and sipped water, she pulled out the diary she'd kept her field notes in, slipped out a folded piece of paper and handed it to Olivia. "I brought the map you snitched out of Cain's pants."

Olivia set her half-eaten sandwich down, spread out the map and examined it. "I knew you would. Unfortunately, it won't do us much good in this part of the maze. He never got this far." She tapped her finger on a blank space to one side of the mapped area. "This is where I think we are—although I could be wrong. I've been walking in circles so long, it's possible I've lost my sense of direction."

Jay studied the map. "Don't worry about the direction." He slid the compass out of his pocket and flipped it open. The dial glowed neon bright in the semidark, the needle accurate once again.

As Jay and Olivia discussed distances and directions, Quin took another bite of her sandwich, blinking sleepily. By her calculations, she'd had all of four hours' sleep in almost two days. If she could stay awake to get out of here, *that* would be the miracle. Smothering a yawn, she leaned back against the wall and let herself drift. Vaguely, she listened to the low, soothing tone of Jay's voice.

"If walking west takes us away from Hathaway and his blast area," Jay said quietly, "then that's got to be the safest option."

Smothering another yawn, Quin shifted her head slightly to ease the ache in her neck. "We can use the secret gate. The one that comes out above the cloth merchant's house."

There was a small silence; then Quin realized what she'd just said. Abruptly, her lids flipped open, and she found herself staring directly into Jay's dark, assessing gaze. The last thing she remembered, he'd been sitting on the other side of Olivia with his compass out.

The silence stretched. Olivia folded the map and stowed it in her jacket pocket. "Don't ask," she said.

Jay's fingers laced with Quin's. "I never do."

As he drew her to her feet, she was tempted to lean, tempted to wrap her arms around his waist and melt right into him.

"And you can keep holding hands if you want," Olivia said acerbically. "I know you two are sleeping together. By now, I'd say the whole valley knows."

Reluctantly, Quin relinquished her hold on Jay and shrugged into her pack. Her cheeks burned with unexpected color. Suddenly she felt like a teenager again. "You don't mind?"

"Why would I mind? I just wanted you to get your degree first. I thought you'd be back sooner to get him, but no, you had to go all extreme and get the doctorate, as well."

The way was blocked.

Olivia leaned against the blank stone wall, resting

her ankle, while they stared at the smooth surface. "Another dead end."

"Story of my life," Jay murmured.

Quin examined the glyph. A wisp of knowledge pulled at her, gone before she could grasp it. "It can't be. This leads somewhere."

Jay swung the beam to the ceiling, picking out the outline of yet another glyph—this one with a crack clear through the center. "Clever. Most people don't think to look up."

As Jay reached up and touched the center section, Quin studied the simple, symmetrical outline and abruptly the context fell into place. The key was numerical—a simple sequence. After a certain point in the maze, every dead-end glyph had contained the same symbol at its center—a null—while this one contained a character she hadn't yet come across.

A grinding, grating sound broke her train of thought. Abruptly, a section of the floor collapsed, and Quin pitched forward into a yawning black hole.

She scrabbled wildly for the edge of what appeared to be a primitive trap door. Her fingers scraped on stone, momentarily slowing her fall; then the edge of the hole crumbled and darkness came up to meet her.

Hathaway stared at the three-way split in the maze and the mark he'd scratched into the wall. A vein throbbed at his temple. They'd walked another circle, and there was no sign of Olivia, which meant that somehow the wily old bitch had escaped. She'd found a way out.

And someone had knocked Cortez out cold. Olivia didn't have either the stomach or the expertise for that, which meant someone else had entered the equation. Hathaway's teeth clamped. No prizes for guessing who that might be: Lomax.

He swore softly. They were out of food, nearly out of water, and their batteries were running low, and now Lomax was creeping around in the dark. It was quite a predicament.

Calmly, Hathaway lifted his gun and shot Ramirez twice in the back, the concussion of the shots deafening as the soft-nosed nine millimeter rounds punched through Ramirez and shoved his chunky body forward into the wall.

He teetered upright for a second, by Hathaway's calculation now minus his heart, most of his left lung and a good deal of his liver; then the weight of the pack that Ramirez had slung over one shoulder pulled him backward, and he crumpled and slid to the floor.

Well, that solved the supply shortage.

Powdery stone dust shivered down as Hathaway examined the wide-eyed blankness of Ramirez's face.

"Don't look so surprised," he murmured as he bent to release the catches on Ramirez's pack, holding his nose against the stench of burst entrails. "No-body liked you."

As Hathaway extracted the gold artifacts Ramirez had been carrying, a further shower of dust jerked his head up. He had a moment to reflect that maybe firing the gun hadn't been the best idea he'd ever had. Cursing beneath his breath, he heaved the gold at the far wall and threw himself after it. A split second later, an explosive crack was followed by a grinding rumble.

Twenty-Six

For a dizzying moment Quin lay on her back on the unyielding floor of the sublevel she'd just fallen into, unsure whether she was conscious or dreaming. A tunnel swam before her—not the impenetrably dark hole she'd fallen into, but a neat, clean corridor lit by the golden glow of a primitive torch burned low. Directly opposite where she lay, a symbol was incised into the wall.

They had finally worked out the puzzle of the maze. No wonder it had been so difficult to get anywhere. They'd all been stumbling around on one level, but the maze was three-dimensional—operating on who knew how many levels, and it was formed in the shape of a glyph: the glyph that symbolized the name of the Sun God.

A sound drew her attention. Carefully she moved

her head, wary of the stinging ache, and to her surprise saw Jay, biceps flexing as he worked the mechanism that closed the trap door she'd just fallen through, sealing it shut. In that case, she must have been knocked out, because she didn't remember him following her.

Her heart thudded in her chest as he turned and she saw him face-on. The glow from the torch spilled over coppery tanned skin and cheekbones that were a little sparer than she remembered. His black hair was long and caught back, making him look even wilder. He held his hand out to her, a fierce demand in his gaze as he spoke in a language that was both liquid and abrupt, and sharpened by urgency. She didn't understand a word, but, as alien as the language and the intonation were, she understood the basic meaning.

"Get up. We've got to keep moving."

She reached out to clasp his tanned, scarred hand, the wrist thick and muscular from wielding the sword that hung at his hip, and the vision wavered as her head spun and she found herself clutching another broad, callused hand and staring into eyes that were just as dark, just as demanding.

"That's better," Jay murmured. "For a minute I thought I was going to have to carry you out of here."

He shone the light into her eyes, making her wince. "Ouch," she muttered. "Do you have to do that?"

He held her wrist, checking her pulse. "Would you rather I just told you to get up?"

She blinked, for a moment having trouble separating this Jay from the one she'd just "seen." The physical similarity, while uncanny enough that they could be twins, was just that—a similarity—but their practical warriors' minds and that acerbic brevity of speech—as if they were both used to snapping out orders—was *exactly* the same.

"That," she said, pushing the flashlight away while she eased to her feet, using both the wall and his shoulder to steady herself, "would work for me."

Olivia's voice sounded, thin and echoing from above, and seconds later, her legs appeared over the edge of the trapdoor opening.

While Jay helped Olivia down, Quin probed the tender spot at the back of her skull, where her head had come into sharp contact with the stone floor. Her gaze caught on the glyph on the wall, and the skin all down her back went goosey.

A brief examination of the corridor revealed her flashlight, tumbled among the crumbled and mummified debris of what must once have been a wooden ladder. Retrieving the light, she examined the simple outline of the glyph, and her stomach clenched. It was the same one she'd just seen in the vision. "This is the way out."

Jay turned, and the light caught on high taut

cheekbones, the straight blade of his nose, that dark, direct look that always sent a shiver down her spine—and the name that had eluded her for so many years surfaced, as ancient and mysterious as that other Jay in the vision: *Achaeus*.

Hathaway coughed and wheezed, blinking stinging dust from his eyes, as he crawled through the pitch black on his hands and knees, feeling for his flashlight. He had saved the gold; he hadn't stopped to think about what would happen to the light.

His fingers came in contact with still-warm flesh—Ramirez's arm—and relief flooded him. He'd never thought he would be so glad to find a corpse. If Ramirez hadn't been buried, chances were neither had his flashlight.

He patted the ground, working systematically, cursing when the sharp edge of a piece of granite took a chunk out of his palm.

"Bloody granite." He hated the stuff; it was like razors when it broke.

He kept feeling for the light, working a grid pattern in his head. He would find it; he had to find it. He would use Ramirez's body as his reference point and work from there.

He felt his way back to Ramirez's leg. His flesh felt a little cooler now, as if rigor was setting in, and panic spasmed through Hathaway. How much time had passed while he'd searched? He would probably never know, because he couldn't see his damn watch.

"Stop," he muttered to himself, and the faint echo was reassuring. If there was an echo, even though he couldn't see jack, it meant there was empty space out there, and air—not tons and tons of granite locking him beneath this stinking mound of dirt. "Think, *think.*"

He couldn't remember what he'd done with his flashlight; he must have put it down while he was getting the gold out of Ramirez's pack. But Ramirez had also had a light, and he'd been carrying it when he'd been shot, therefore…

Hathaway crawled over Ramirez's legs, ignoring the sickening stink, and began patting the ground. His palm landed on something wet and squishy, and as he recoiled, his fingers brushed an object and closed on the curved shape of the flashlight. Ignoring the sticky wetness of his fingers, Hathaway depressed the button. A beam of light lanced the darkness, bouncing off a towering wall of rubble only feet away.

Before the collapse, there had been a tunnel ahead with three splits; now there was nothing but solid rock. The walls and the ceiling had collapsed, sealing him into this part of the maze.

But there would be a way out—there had to be—and he would find it.

Systematically, Hathaway reorganized his pack

to include the gold Ramirez had been carrying, then hefted it onto his back, groaning at the extra weight.

Picking up the light, he began to walk.

Quin's flashlight stabbed ahead into a tunnel that was dead straight and built on a slight incline; they were climbing.

It was the faint stirring on her cheek, the sensation almost imperceptible, that first alerted her. She turned to Jay, who was carrying Olivia. "I can feel a breeze."

"That's it," Olivia said shortly. "We're almost out. You can let me down, I intend to leave this hole the same way I came in, on two feet."

As the beam of light illuminated a damaged section of the tunnel, an unexpected streak of color caught Quin's eye.

Bending, she picked up a red ribbon amidst mounds of rubble where a section of the roof had collapsed. The red was dull, the fibers so fragile the fabric crumbled as she held it, but for a moment the color seemed brilliant, the silk new.

For a disorienting moment her mind shifted, touched on a memory that slid away almost before she could grasp it.

Fingers combing through dust-coated, tangled hair, searching for the ribbon and not finding it. A throbbing lump on the side of her head. Hard arms coming around her. That dark voice soothing. His mouth on hers.

Tears clouded her vision. Her fingers closed on the remnants of the ribbon, and abruptly the memory was as clear as if it was a part of this life and not the last. *They had made it.*

"What is it?"

She wanted to say, "We made it," but that would seem even crazier than everything that had already happened.

Hathaway rounded a corner, stumbled over the half-buried body of Ramirez and feverishly began hauling off rocks and digging him out of the rubble, hoping to find the second flashlight—and anything else that might help him survive.

He'd scoured the maze for some evidence of how Lomax and Olivia had managed to escape and come to the conclusion that the way out must be in the passage that was now blocked by the collapse.

He'd walked in circles for the past hour, and now his batteries were low. If his flashlight failed, he would be walking in the dark. He might not get out before the whole place came crashing down, and he *had* to get out. He had fifty million reasons for leaving here alive. With that kind of money, he could buy a new identity, a new life.

"Come on, come on," he muttered. "You've got to have something useful on you."

The pockets came up empty except for a flick

knife. The pack contained a bottle of water, extra magazines for Ramirez's handgun and a loaf of some strong-smelling bread. His jaw clenched so tight that his teeth began to throb. "No batteries."

He kept the water and the food, and left the rest. He was already armed, and if anything down here moved, he would shoot to kill. Not that anything was likely to move in the dim light that was all his flashlight would throw out. Nothing lived down here: no rats or mice, no insects—nothing. The place was a tomb.

He kept walking, studying the glyphs, committing the collapsed piles of rubble to memory. When he came upon Ramirez's body for the third time, he kicked viciously at the corpse. Simultaneously, the frail beam died, so that the last image that was burned onto his retinas was Ramirez's dust-coated face.

Hathaway froze, staring at utter blackness. Panic clutched at his bowel. He hadn't noticed the silence before, but now it pressed in, crushing him, as absolute and smothering as the darkness.

Twenty-Seven

Quin focused the beam of her torch on a glyph. "This is it."

She pressed the center of the glyph, then stepped back so Jay could push against what looked like a wall. Stone grated on stone as the apparent dead end opened outward, yielding a few inches before progress was halted. Daylight spilled through the narrow aperture, the glare blinding after the endless night of the maze.

Jay leaned on the door, straining as he forced it wide enough that they could squeeze out into an overgrown tangle of shrubs and vines.

Quin helped Olivia through, supporting her as they picked their way through a spongy mass of undergrowth, their feet sinking ankle-deep in mud.

Jay went first, pushing back branches and vines to

clear the way until the undergrowth thinned and they found themselves at the edge of the massive slip.

Baked soil and clay shifted like marbles beneath their feet as they worked their way down to the first line of terraces, and Quin shielded her eyes from the sun as the vista of the ruined city opened up beneath her.

Jay vaulted down, then helped both Olivia and Quin. He didn't let Quin go immediately. "So where is this cloth merchant's house?"

Distracted by his closeness, Quin closed her eyes and tried to call up an image. She could remember the paved courtyard, the lines of drying cloth, as clearly as if she'd crept through the merchant's back-yard just days ago. Turning slightly in his grip, she opened her eyes. The line of the terrace was correct, but little remained of the structure beyond the blurred outline where the house had once been. "There."

She stared at the outline and wondered what had happened to the people who had lived there, and all the other families who had grown crops and built houses—raised children....

"Don't," Jay said curtly.

Startled, Quin caught the touch of his mind, feather-soft as he withdrew. She couldn't help the past. It was gone, and it was the now that was impor-tant. And if the "now" was a bit confusing, then at least with Jay she didn't have to explain a thing; he could read her mind.

* * *

A shout went up as they worked their way down the hill to the temple entrance, where Luis was still working with a team of men from the village to open up the entrance that Hathaway had closed.

Luis whooped and wrapped Olivia in a hug, lifting her off the ground. "Hannah's running the search-and-rescue operation from the house. There's another team working at the other entrance, but it keeps caving in. How did you get out?"

Jay spread the map out on the ground, anchoring it with rocks, and pointed out the entry points to Luis and Jorge. "Watch all three entrances, just in case Hathaway, Ramirez or Cortez makes it out under his own steam before the police team arrives."

"Don't worry." Luis drew a gun from the small of his back. "If either of them so much as makes a peep... Bam!"

Quin stared at the familiar shape of the Browning and suppressed a groan. The gouge in the hand-grip looked even bigger, and part of the firing mechanism actually looked rusted. "I think I need to sit down."

Jay held out his hand. Reluctantly, Luis handed over the gun.

"Take this instead." Jay exchanged the gleaming black Glock for the Browning. "It's more likely to work."

"Did you see that?" Luis murmured to Jorge as he watched wide-eyed while Jay ejected the magazine from the Browning and slid both the weapon and the ammunition clip into his backpack. "I *told* you he likes me. He just gave me his gun."

Quin rolled her eyes. *Tell me the Browning's going to disappear forever.*

Down a deep well.

Jorge offered to drive Olivia back to the house, but Quin and Jay preferred to walk. After the grim darkness of the maze, they craved sunshine.

As they walked down the terraced slope to the river flat, a helicopter skimmed over the rim of the valley.

The machine hovered briefly, the turbulence from the rotors shivering over the water and bending the reeds that sprouted in thick clumps at the river's edge as it settled clear of the slip on a grassy piece of turf.

Two men and a woman climbed out, ducking beneath the still spinning blades as the whine of the engine died back to an idle, then cut out altogether.

The men were tall and dark—one with hair cut close to his skull, the other with long hair pulled back in a ponytail. If Quin had seen them in a crowded street, she would have known who they were instantly, the resemblance was so strong. Jay's family.

Jay's gaze swept the people walking toward him, then settled on the helicopter.

It was a Black Hawk, dark and sleek and mainly used by the military. He knew that in the way he knew other technical information—like the back of his hand—and as abruptly as if a door had just been kicked open, he knew *what* he'd been, and where: a hostage rescue expert for the SAS—the Special Air Service. He'd operated predominantly out of Australia in the Pan Pacific, Asian and South American theaters, although he'd put in time with the British 22 Regiment, working Ireland, Afghanistan, even Chechnya.

The recollection after years of blankness was subtly shocking, kicking open the door to other, older memories. In the first few seconds the people walking toward him had been strangers, but suddenly he could remember the man with the long hair as a hell-on-wheels teenager, the pretty woman as a cute toddler, the quieter, short-haired man—

He'd seen him before—*remembered him before*— wearing a wet suit and grinning, but now something that had always been missing connected and fused in his mind, and the emotions that went with the memories were swamping. Hannah had always said that the reason he couldn't remember was probably psychosomatic—an emotional blockage. What had happened to him had been so traumatic, his mind had simply shut down every memory that related to that event.

A large, tanned hand closed on his, the handshake firm, the gaze that went with it intense.

"Hi, Jake." The voice was low and laced with a Down Under drawl. "My name's Gray Lombard."

Jay studied dark eyes so like his own that it was like looking into a mirror, and felt his world shift and slide. "I know who you are." And abruptly, the blankness in his mind dissolved.

An hour later, after Hannah had dispatched Olivia to bed, and Jay's family and the helicopter pilot had been settled in the guest quarters, Quin levered off muddy boots, peeled off her socks and walked through the kitchen in bare feet.

The police had arrived and taken over the search-and-rescue effort, along with an agent from Interpol, who was inordinately interested in both Hathaway and Cain. Apparently the Honduran government had pressed charges, and Hathaway was also wanted in several other countries, under a number of different aliases, for fraud and embezzlement.

Ramirez's body had been recovered just minutes ago, along with what was left of his vital organs— all packed in separate plastic bags for identification. He had been tough and wily, terrorizing a large chunk of the *cordillera* and evading the law for years, but he'd made the basic mistake of turning his back on

Hathaway, which only went to show it was the middlemen who got you in the end.

Quin paused at the door to the library. She was bone tired, barely capable of keeping her eyes open, let alone moving. If she could climb the stairs to her room without falling asleep, that would be an achievement—but something about Hannah's very stillness stopped her. As calm as Hannah was, she was seldom still, and she never just sat.

The afternoon sunlight glowed off an envelope in Hannah's hands. "This came for you—from England."

Quin's heart thumped as she crossed the narrow, sunny room, took the cream vellum envelope and perched on the edge of the couch facing Hannah. The top left-hand corner contained a discreet logo, which stated that it had originated from a law firm called Aristotle and Sons in London.

Carefully, she slit the heavy envelope and unfolded the single sheet inside. The message was brief and to the point. The writer, Phineas Aristotle, had been informed by a private investigator who had been retained by his client, Lady Mallory, that Quin was alive and well and presently residing in Valle del Sol, Peru. He requested the pleasure of a meeting at her earliest convenience, concerning the estate of her deceased father, the late Earl of Maldon, Lord Jonathon Edwin Rudyard Mallory.

"It's a letter from my father's solicitors."

Hannah's hands jerked in her lap.

Quin handed the letter to Hannah. "It's all right, we don't have to worry any longer—he's dead."

Olivia appeared at the door. "Thank God."

Hannah put the letter down as Olivia hobbled over to sit beside her on the sofa. "You're supposed to be in bed."

Olivia peered at the letter. "Suddenly, I'm feeling a lot better. If Mallory's solicitor wants to talk about the estate, he must have left Quin something. Who would have guessed that John Mallory would have developed a conscience before he died?"

Hannah's voice was dry. "I doubt the conscience belongs to him. I'd wager this originates from the poor girl he married after Rebecca."

Olivia looked startled. "How do you know anything about her?"

Hannah's expression was calm. "I didn't trust John Mallory an inch. I kept tabs on him through a colleague in London. I knew the family of the girl he married—the Wimbledon Bradshaw-Smiths. Nice people."

Quin felt a tug on her plait, followed by the familiar frisson that ran down her spine whenever Jay was near. The fact that she hadn't felt the frisson before the tug demonstrated how tired she was. Even her radar was down.

The couch depressed as Jay sat beside her; then

she found herself scooped onto his lap. A small silence reigned as he settled her firmly against him. As a statement about how things stood between them, it was profound.

A long finger stirred a strand of hair, which was stuck to her cheek. "So you're a lady?"

"Apparently." Quin brushed the strand behind her ear and grimaced when she realized she had just smeared more mud over her face. Not that that would make much difference; if she was as coated as Jay, it probably wasn't possible to get any dirtier. The title "Lady" had always seemed as illusory and distant as England itself, with no more substance than the fairy tales the aunts had read her when she was little, but it was real. "The eldest daughter of the Earl of Maldon."

"That's a fairly large skeleton to fall out of the cupboard."

"Nowhere near as large as yours." Jay, it turned out, was a Lombard, the eldest son of one of the wealthiest and most powerful families in the Southern Hemisphere, and when he'd been kidnapped, he had been engaged and on the point of marrying. When Jake's memory had flooded back, he'd had to cope with both his inability to save Rafaella's life, and his grief over her death. Ten years might have passed, but that hadn't made the emotions any easier to deal with.

"But then, a skeleton, is just that," he said flatly. "Dead and gone."

"Like John Mallory," Olivia chipped in with satisfaction.

Twenty-Eight

Australia, two months later

Quin's grip on the telephone receiver tightened, her expression growing stony as she listened. "Ever heard the saying, 'A little bit of knowledge is a dangerous thing'? Live by it, buddy." Calmly, she set the phone down and removed the phone jack from the wall.

Someone had talked, and they had been found. Not that the leak was surprising. Ever since she and Jay had arrived in Australia, they'd been news. It wasn't every day that the heir to a substantial portion of the Lombard empire and the daughter of the missing Duchess of Maldon returned from the dead. But, after years of lying low, providing the media with her inside leg measurement and brassiere size didn't come easy.

"Who was that?" Jay strolled into the lounge, chest

bare and hair still wet from the dip he'd just taken in the ocean that fronted his family's beach house at Noosa.

"Some crackpot industrialist wanting the inside story on the diamond."

And before that it had been a magazine columnist, a film director, someone hosting a television game show and, according to the answering machine, every news reporter born since Adam was a baby.

Ever since Hathaway and Cortez had been brought out of the ruin in cuffs, the press had gone wild over the jewel that had been extracted from Hathaway's pack, excited by its antiquity and the legend attached to it, entranced by its size and rarity. As the saying went, "There is only *one*..."

Except, in this case, there were two.

Not that the press or anyone but Jay, herself and Olivia would ever find out *that* piece of information. Quin had been as surprised as Olivia at the presence of the second jewel. Spectacular as it was, it had come out of left field. She had no "memory" of it, and she was almost certain that in ancient life no one else had had the slightest clue it was there. Like the real Eye it was a mystery, and likely to remain so.

The real Eye was tucked away at the southern end of Valle del Sol, closer to the village, in a small lime-stone cave whose entrance was hidden beneath the surface of the Agueda. The cave, which Quin had found as a child, was clean and spare—nowhere near as beautiful as the pyramid—but infinitely safer.

Jay and Olivia had refused to have anything to do with deciding where the jewel went, claiming it was Quin's responsibility—as it had been in that strange, vivid last life. In the end, she'd decided that as precious and important as the jewel was, it didn't belong to a government, a museum, or to any one person, it belonged in the valley where it had been for millennia, and where it could continue to do what it had done since time immemorial: quietly radiate its healing power.

Jay perched on the corner of her desk and picked up the newspaper she'd discarded before the phone had gone crazy. "By the way, according to the Peruvian government it's not a diamond," he said absently. "One too many carbon atoms in the structure. And it's not quartz, either—no silicon present."

Quin shuffled the sheets of notes she'd compiled while Jay was swimming and slipped them into a folder. She was supposed to be taking a break from all the ancient sleuthing, but Achaeus was one topic she hadn't been able to drop. At first she had been sure he'd been Greek. He'd had iron weapons, when there were none in South America in the time period in question—around 1200 B.C. The earliest records she could find for Greeks possessing iron were indeterminate but did date as far back as 1400 B.C. Then again, as Achaeus had been a seafarer and a mercenary, he could have obtained his iron armor and weapons from Egypt—and the sun motif suggested that he had probably done just that. The clincher for pinpointing Achaeus's origins had been the name of his city, Ilium.

The name had stuck with her when most of the details of the dream had faded, because Achaeus had been certain she'd hailed from Ilium.

During the course of her degree and doctorate, she'd completed several papers on the ancient civilizations of Asia Minor, read *The Iliad,* and learned that Achaeus's city *had* existed: Ilium was an ancient name for Troy.

The time factor was a little fuzzy, and there was guesswork involved, but she was almost positive that before his ship had foundered on the eastern coast of the Americas, Achaeus had been one of a group of dispossessed Trojans, and the war he'd spoken of had been the destruction of Troy.

Slipping the file into her laptop case, she regarded Jay's profile, fielding a now familiar mental double take; when she looked at Jay from certain angles, he *was* Achaeus. "If it's not a diamond," she said absently, picking up on the thread of the conversation, "then what is it?"

"The experts are still trying to figure that one out. Apparently the gem's on loan to some research group that's connected with NASA, because they've decided there's a potential for use in space flight. On top of that, some genius mathematician played around with the atomic structure and thinks it might be some form of inert cold fusion." He went back to his newspaper. "But they'll never make that theory fly."

Her mouth quirked. *That* was vintage Jay: stone-cold practical. "How can you be so certain?"

"Simple politics. The bureaucracy surrounding the stone is monumental, and now they're limiting access because they've decided the radiation could be harmful, and the various agencies conducting research on the stone don't want to be sued by their employees for radiation poisoning. It'll take them years to decide anything. With any luck, they'll leave it alone altogether."

She glanced at the article Jay had just read and the smooth, corporate mug shot that fronted it up. "Not if Hathaway has anything to do with it."

According to the front-page report, Hathaway had been extradited to the States and was presently on remand, awaiting trial. Infamous thief and murderer or not, getting the man to shut up was another thing entirely. After making a fuss about police brutality, wrongful arrest and possible radiation poisoning from the jewel, he'd finally gotten some attention, although it wasn't the attention he'd wanted. He was now in an isolation unit in a maximum security prison until medical professionals could get more data on exactly what it was that he'd carried in his pack for the best part of twenty-four hours.

Jay pulled her into a loose embrace. As she clasped her arms around his neck, she felt the faint tug as the fastening on her plait went, then the slow stirrings as he began the process of unraveling the strands.

Jay's head dipped, his forehead rested briefly on hers. "Hathaway can squawk all he likes, but his credibility's shot. If the press learn about that pyramid, it won't be from me. We're already high-profile enough."

Quin shuddered. The publicity, if it was discovered that one of the pyramids had been built by a people who had a sophisticated knowledge of space, combined with the fact that the jewel was an unidentified substance, didn't bear thinking about. There were no prizes for imagining the questions the press would be most likely to ask. "And did you actually see any little green men down there?" or, "Where did you say the spaceship was parked?" And the clincher, "Won't the aliens be angry that you removed their homing device?"

Uh-uh. No way.

Hathaway's blasting had eventually succeeded in collapsing the entire temple structure and wiping out the most conclusive evidence that a uniquely evolved ancient culture had ever existed. The police team had barely made it out in time. Moments after Hathaway and Cortez had been cuffed and choppered out, and Ramirez's body had been removed from the crime scene, the whole place had pancaked, and Quin wasn't sure that was such a bad thing.

Jay withdrew his fingers from her hair. "I checked with Olivia and Hannah this morning. Apparently the Peruvian government's got a team in there drilling, taking core samples. If they come up with anything out of that pile of rubble, as far as I'm concerned, the ball's in their court. I'm not saying a word. But…while we're on the subject of rocks…"

He drew a small velvet case from his pocket.

Gingerly, Quin flipped the lid and drew a deep breath.

It was a ring for its time, with a broad band of gold and three diamonds, deeply seated, because she would want to wear it every day and not just for special occasions. The center diamond was inordinately large and shimmered with a pure, molten fire that made her blink. "How much did this cost?"

"A king's ransom…and then some." His hands framed her face, dragging her attention from the ring back to him. "Just say 'yes.'"

She stared at the ring, her throat locked. She'd never had such an exquisite piece of jewelry. She'd never been so loved. "Do you know how lucky I am?"

He took charge of the ring and slid it onto her finger. "We'll discuss it after the wedding."

The kiss that followed melted her bones and practically brought her to her knees, which reminded her… "Aren't you supposed to do this on your knees?"

She caught the edge of a grin just before he stole another kiss. "I've been on my knees for years. And by the way, you'd better pack. We're leaving for London tonight."

The offices of Aristotle and Sons occupied a Georgian townhouse in Bellevue Square in Kensington, less than a mile from Buckingham Palace.

After they had been cleared by security, Jay and Quin were escorted up an exquisitely paneled staircase, lined with portraits—presumably of the previous Aristotles and Sons—to Phineas Aristotle's office. The man himself was dressed in funeral gray, relieved by the discreet red stripe of his Eton tie, his appearance as neat and precise as his letter had been.

After introductions were made and they were all seated, Aristotle got to the point: the information he had to impart was simple—Quin's share of the Mallory estate.

Aristotle consulted the paperwork on the desk. "Umm, let's see, your—*Lady Victoria's*—mother's jewelry and a few personal effects, of course, several works of art, cash and bonds, and a one-third share in a shopping complex in Oxford Street."

Quin's eyes burned at the mention of her mother's personal effects. She had only a handful of things: a photo, a wristwatch and an old passport. Rebecca had left everything else behind in the rush to escape John Mallory.

Jay squeezed her hand, and she forced herself to focus. She didn't need the money. Her earning power, now that she was a sought-after expert in ancient antiquities, was substantial, and Jay was hardly struggling; the Lombard asset base was mind-bogglingly colossal. Neither she nor Jay needed the money, but damned if she would leave any of it behind after the way the Mallory family had behaved. Olivia and Hannah could use it.

"I'll take it. Hopefully, there'll be enough to replace the townhouse Olivia and Hannah had to sell to pay for my education."

"More than enough." Aristotle cleared his throat. "And change. One of the works of art is a Van Gogh, presently on loan to the London Museum, and when I said a share in a shopping complex, perhaps I wasn't clear. I meant the *entire* mall, the office block on top *and* the land beneath. Mallory Towers is one of the newest, most modern mall complexes in London, and it occupies more than an acre of London's central business district."

Quin watched Aristotle's precise movements as he shuffled papers. After years of blank nothingness from her family, their generosity now was baffling. "How did they find me?"

And more to the point, why had they bothered? It

can't have been all the hype about the jewel, or any fear of the Lombard Group, because the solicitor's letter she'd received had been dated before she had personally become newsworthy.

Aristotle looked uncomfortable. "Lord Mallory followed Olivia and Hannah to Peru. It wasn't difficult to trace the travel records, because neither Olivia nor Hannah assumed false identities. When he found out Rebecca had died, and that her child was female, he simply left them to it."

Quin's fingers tightened in Jay's. "It doesn't matter. He's gone."

Aristotle cleared his throat. "Lord Mallory didn't have a conscience, but his second wife does. She was always concerned about the mystery of the disappearance of Rebecca's aunts, and the fact that, eminent as they both were, neither had resurfaced in England. Six months ago, upon Lord Mallory's death, Lady Mallory instructed me to investigate the disappearances. When we found out that Rebecca had given birth to a live child, she retained a private investigation expert—Hogarth Sanderson, of Sanderson and Sanderson—and made legal provision for Quin to be included in Lord Mallory's will."

Jay said something low and succinct. "So that's what Sanderson was up to."

He eyed Aristotle, who had started to sweat—as well he might. Jay had done some checking, and Aristotle and Sons had been the Mallory family lawyers since the firm had started doing business more than eighty years ago. Aristotle would have been aware of all of John Mallory's dealings—good and bad. It was also more than probable that he had known of Quin's existence, but had done nothing about the knowledge beyond advise his client of the legal implications. Aristotle was protected by his oath, but even so… Jay's jaw tightened. "What, exactly, do you mean by legal provision?"

"Lady Mallory petitioned the court on your fiancée's behalf, claiming an equal share in the estate that was bequeathed to the children. Of course, the title and manor don't come into the equation, but—"

Jay leaned forward, his patience abruptly gone. "When did Mallory find out he had a *live* daughter?"

Aristotle stared at the paperwork in front of him, as if he had to consult notes to remember. "Twenty-eight years ago."

About the time Quin had been born.

Jay held on to his temper by a thread. Aristotle shrank back in his seat, his gaze abruptly glassy, and Jay's jaw unclenched. Message received.

Despite the fact that he was the senior partner, Phineas Aristotle wasn't overly bright, but he had a healthy respect for money and power. One word from Jay and his business could die overnight.

Quin wriggled her fingers where they were caught

in Jay's bone-crushing grip. His gaze snapped to hers, and amusement surfaced, breaking the tension.

Jay looked as if he would like nothing better than to lock his fingers around Aristotle's plump throat and drag him across the desk. Her fiancé might be wearing a designer suit, but the basic man hadn't changed. Put a sword in his hand and he was happy.

The fingers holding hers relaxed, and she caught the faint twitch of answering amusement at the corner of his mouth.

Aristotle just didn't get that he was dealing with one pissed-off Trojan.

Epilogue

The wedding was simple—as simple as it could be, that was, given that it was a Lombard wedding and the bride was a member of the British peerage.

Somehow the media got wind of the location, and a TV crew turned up and circled noisily in a helicopter.

However, given that it *was* a Lombard wedding, the security was tight. Every guard was handpicked and vetted—their lives coming under the kind of scrutiny that would make a vicar blanch. Not that the security personnel were saints; on the contrary, only two qualities were mandatory. The first, that they were absolutely loyal to the Lombard family, the second that—regardless of gender—each and every one of them was a ruthless, uncompromising son of a bitch.

The annoyance of the helicopter and the press aside, Quin made it to the church *exactly* on time, along with Olivia and Hannah, who were giving her away, and Jay's sister, Roma, who had agreed to be her maid of honor. A van containing an assortment of Lombard pageboys and flower girls pulled up behind the limousine, and the children, varying in age from three years to eight, climbed out, clutching small wicker baskets of rose petals and arguing who was going first.

The limousine door swung open, and for the first time in her life, Quin waited to be helped from a vehicle.

It had taken fully an hour to get her into The Dress, which was made of pure white silk and organza, the confection hand-stitched and embroidered, and elaborately encrusted with pearls. Olivia had wanted her to have a high neck, but Quin had dug in her heels on that one. Since she'd been tiny, she'd hated anything that buttoned up anywhere near her chin, and if she was actually going to wear a dress, she was determined to make the most of it.

She chose a medieval style gown, with a square neckline that dipped low enough to make the most of her compact bust, and allowed her to wear an exquisite diamond-and-pearl pendant that had belonged to her mother.

She had high heels and big hair, and makeup that had made her blink and look at herself twice in the mirror—and for the first time in her life she had nails. In her opinion, they ought to be classified as dangerous weapons, and she couldn't imagine how women got anything at all done with them, but she had to admit they were gorgeous.

The driver offered his hand. Ignoring the murmurs from the crowd, the brash demands of reporters and the flash of cameras, Quin allowed herself to be gently maneuvered out of the limousine.

The bodyguards closed in, giving her a few moments of almost-privacy while Hannah and Olivia adjusted the train of the gown and twitched her veil into place, and while Roma took the children in hand.

Olivia, severely elegant in lavender silk with a tiny silk moire hat and veil, glanced at her wristwatch. "It's time."

They'd all decided that, in the case of this wedding, lateness wasn't an option. If Quin didn't start up the aisle at eleven o'clock exactly—regardless of the leeway the bride traditionally enjoyed—Jay would come looking for her, and the formality of Olivia and Hannah giving her away would give way to good old-fashioned possession.

As the lilting notes of Vivaldi's "Four Seasons" faded to be replaced by the strains of the wedding march, Quin mounted the steps to the church doors. In direct contrast to the noise and confusion of the crowd outside, the church was an oasis of calm, the air filled with the scent of roses, the dimness relieved by the diffused sunlight that streamed through the jewel-paned lead lights that soared over the altar.

Jay was waiting, handsome in a morning suit, with Gray beside him as best man, and his brother Blade and a cousin, Cullen Logan, standing up as groomsmen.

To even up the wedding party, once Olivia and Hannah had gone through the formality of giving Quin away, they then turned into maids of honor. It wasn't traditional, but, hey, it was Quin's wedding.

The vows were said, and the wedding party was finally able to leave center stage and retire to the registry. For a brief time in a day that had started at six o'clock with an early breakfast and briefing session, followed by back-to-back hairdresser's and beautician's appointments, Quin was able to catch her breath.

She signed her name, then handed the pen to Jay. As she lifted her head, a familiar shimmer of light in the corner of the room caught her eye.

In the cool dimness of the registry office, with its mahogany-veneered walls and tall bookshelves packed with dark, leather-bound volumes, they were unusually bright, their facial features—the folds of robes and exquisitely detailed garments—clear and distinct. Quin glanced at Jay's bent head, at the vicar who was busily overseeing the paperwork, and at Hannah and Olivia, who were chatting with Jake's brothers as if nothing out of the ordinary was happening.

Bemused, her gaze swung back to the glowing figures. Nobody else appeared to have noticed that the wedding party had just expanded.

A familiar figure lifted his hand in silent benediction, and abruptly the room filled with gold light.

A wave of emotion swamped Quin. The last time she'd seen him was in the Pyramid at Valle del Sol, warning her to get out—fast.

She didn't know who they were, but she knew *what* they were. Angels.

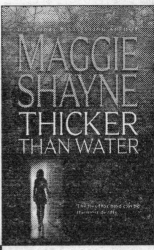